I looked at the shawl. It didn't look that old. Anyway, would anyone sell something that had been in the family for so long? I was being spun a tale. Still, I liked the feel of the shawl. "I'll take it," I said, and cringed. I'd just made the worst mistake a buyer can make. The woman knew I wanted it, so the price would go up accordingly.

"Of course ye do, lassie," she said. "It's been waiting for ye all these years. Ye are the one."

I'm afraid I gawked at her. The one what?

"'Tis so," she said. "The shawl is yours. It always has been. Can't ye tell?" She reached out and took it from me, holding it up under my chin. She nodded. "Aye."

At that moment, feeling almost as if I were in a trance, I think I would have paid any amount for it. But the price she named was reasonable indeed, and I paid it without hesitation, silently blessing the woman for her lack of avarice.

"It's a Farquharson," she said. "Did ye ken that?"

"No," I told her, "I'm not familiar with that clan," and started toward the door.

"Och, ye soon will be," she said.

I held the shawl tight against me as I headed back toward the main street. I couldn't imagine what she meant . . .

A Wee Murder in My Shop

Fran Stewart

BERKLEY PRIME CRIME, NEW YORK

THE BERKLEY PUBLISHING GROUP
Published by the Penguin Group
Penguin Group (USA) LLC
375 Hudson Street, New York, New York 10014

USA • Canada • UK • Ireland • Australia • New Zealand • India • South Africa • China

penguin.com

A Penguin Random House Company

A WEE MURDER IN MY SHOP

A Berkley Prime Crime Book / published by arrangement with the author

Berkley Prime Crime Books are published by The Berkley Publishing Group.
BERKLEY® PRIME CRIME and the PRIME CRIME logo are trademarks of
Penguin Group (USA) LLC.

For information, address: The Berkley Publishing Group,
a division of Penguin Group (USA) LLC,
375 Hudson Street, New York, New York 10014.

ISBN: 978-0-425-27031-8

PUBLISHING HISTORY
Berkley Prime Crime mass-market edition / March 2015

PRINTED IN THE UNITED STATES OF AMERICA

10 9 8 7 6 5 4 3 2

Cover illustration by Jesse Reisch.
Cover design by Diana Kolsky.
Interior text design by Kelly Lipovich.

Acknowledgments

I would be remiss if I didn't thank these special people who've helped me on this ScotShop journey: my agent, John Talbot, who found me to begin with, and whose quiet encouragement spurred me to a better story; researcher par excellence, Erica Dagny Jensen, whose expertise about Middle English kept me from making numerous egregious mistakes; Nanette Littlestone (who edits my Biscuit McKee Mysteries), for reading this manuscript and catching a number of errors early on; Andy Andreasen, who answered my numerous questions about old safes. If Peggy's safe isn't up to scrutiny, it's my fault, not Andy's; my NLAPW and Sapelo Island compatriot Mozelle Funderburk, who is the only person I've ever known who's fallen off the frame around a dinosaur exhibit; Darlene Carter, my dear friend and Master Mind buddy, who listened to me whine without ever judging me; my friends Peggy Dixon and Karaline "Petie" Ogg, who loaned me their first names; and the original "Tessa," who, via her mom, Jan Grimshaw, got into this series; C. Scott Rogers, who (five decades ago) taught me the value of silence; my heart-connected editor, Michelle Vega, whose diligent attention to what was important—and what wasn't—gave me one of the greatest gifts an author can receive: a chance to place absolute trust in my editor; Andy Ball, whose copyediting expertise polished my words like hidden jewels—his attention to detail blew my (virtual) socks off; and the entire managing editorial staff at Berkley Prime Crime, who took my manuscript and turned it into something beautiful.

1

The Benefits of Yoga

Yoga is supposed to relax you, isn't it? But the yoga manuals never say anything about what kind of breath to take when yoga class ended early because the teacher's water broke and you crept into your boyfriend's house at ten p.m. as a special surprise and found Andrea, your as-of-this-very-minute *former* best friend ever since fourth grade in bed with your as-of-this-very-minute *former* almost fiancé.

"I thought you were at yoga class," Mason said, and, yoga composure be damned, I hauled off and slugged him. Then I took a strangled breath—the kind yoga practitioners always make fun of—and threw my key at his formerly well-loved head. I stomped down the stairs, slammed the front door, opened it, and slammed it again. Then I ran to Karaline's house. Karaline Logg. My friend. My real friend. A better friend than Andrea Stone, damn her hide. So what if Karaline had to get up at three thirty? This was an emergency.

"Kill him," she told me after I'd sobbed and sworn and gurgled and howled numerous times and in no particular order. "Think of it as a thirtieth birthday present to yourself, and it'll make you feel better."

I growled and punched her couch cushion. "Hell isn't hot enough for Mason Kilmarty."

"That's *cold* enough, Peggy." We'd both read Dante. His version of hell was frozen over, colder than a Vermont winter.

She swiped her hand as if to erase all thought of Mason. "You still planning on going tomorrow?"

"Yeah."

"So, by the time you get back from Scotland, he'll be sorry as a hound dog in a skunk hole." She'd never liked Mason, or Andrea either. "He'll try to get you to take him back."

I made a face. "I wouldn't take him back if he crawled."

Karaline yawned. Her grandfather clock chimed quite a few times. "Go home," she told me, "before I turn into a pumpkin."

By that time I felt better, even though Karaline would have to get up in a few hours to start making maple pancake batter for the tourists. "Like I said," she reminded me as I left, "just kill him and be done with it."

2

A Shawl of My Own

I made it through the morning somehow, and I didn't even speed too much as I drove to Burlington to catch my flight to New York. The layover at JFK was long, but I always had my e-books. This time, though, they weren't as much comfort as usual. The night flight to London was the normal hassle with all the increased airport regulations, yet I felt unusually restless, unable to snooze on the plane the way I generally did. I started to doze, but visions of Andrea—why did she have to have such a gorgeous body? *Stop it, Peggy.* I kept telling myself that, but then, just as I was about to doze off again, I thought about Karaline's solution to the problem. Tempting. Maybe I'd get arrested by that new cop in town, the one with the exquisite eyes. Officer Harper. Then I could explain the reasons—justifiable homicide, isn't that what it's called?—and he'd let me go, after a suitable interlude of . . . *Stop it, Peggy.*

A woman sitting across the narrow aisle wore a red-and-green Kilgour tartan skirt. Kilgour was close enough to Kilmarty—Mason Kilmarty—to set me off again. I pulled out my cell phone and reprogrammed all his numbers to read JUNK on my caller ID. I considered something a bit more graphic but decided I didn't need to lower myself.

Then I worked on my calendar, blocking off one whole day the Sunday after next to balance my checkbook. I was four months behind on it. Somehow or other the statements just kept piling up. I was pretty sure I had enough money in there, but it would be a good idea if I knew for certain. I blocked off that Saturday night for the surprise party Karaline was giving Drew and me—the party I wasn't supposed to know about. Eventually I dozed.

At Heathrow, I practically staggered onto my flight to Edinburgh, and by the time I eventually stepped off the bus in Pitlochry, my eyes were as droopy as a basset hound's. I took a deep yoga breath to wake myself up, and in came that special air of Scotland. Not that it was particularly special next to the bus; it was just the thought of what awaited me here in this town I loved. I waited for a large family to clear out of my way, then looked around. Linklater Sinclair always met me at the station. There he was, kilt ruffling around his sturdy legs as he stepped forward to take my bag.

"Mr. Sinclair," I said. "Thank you for meeting me."

"As if I wouldna?" he said, scrunching his gray eyebrows together in what I had learned over the past six years was his way of covering a sweetness I'd seldom seen in a man before. I think he was old enough to be my father, maybe even old enough to be my grandfather. I'd never had the nerve to ask him his age.

He wore his kilt, in the muted blues and greens of the Sinclair hunting tartan, as if it had been made for him, as I supposed it had. It suited him somehow. Well worn, with a slightly shabby texture to it, he wore it with an ease and a grace that I often wished American men would—could—adopt. But no. Life was different in Scotland. Slower. I did wonder briefly, not for the first time, what Officer Harper would look like in a kilt.

Too bad our Hamelin town cops wore dark blue pants. Kilts would have been more in tune with the tourist aspect of the town. I put that thought out of my head, though, as I smiled at the sparkling blue eyes of my dear Scot friend.

He looked me over, ran his free hand through his silvery white hair, handed me into the left front seat, and stuffed my bag in the trunk—the boot. I'd been to Scotland on numerous buying trips, and I had never mustered up the courage to drive. If I were on the road all by myself and driving slowly enough, I was sure I could remember which side to drive on. But approaching a traffic circle—they called it a roundabout—I knew I'd always go the wrong direction. And if an oncoming car appeared on a narrow road, I knew I'd dive to the right without thinking. If it weren't for Linklater Sinclair, I'd have been dead twelve times over. Thank goodness I'd found him and his wife on my first visit to Perthshire.

"Will ye be wanting to go straight to town first," he asked in a tone that clearly said I'd better not, "or do ye need to freshen yourself? Mrs. Sinclair will want to see ye, and there's always time for tea."

As much as I wished to get into the shops, a quick inventory of my head warned me how fuzzy it was. A bracing cup of tea would do it, I thought. *Good grief, I never say "a bracing cup of tea" when I'm in the States. Must be something in the atmosphere.* "I'd love a cup," I told him, and I wasn't surprised when he nodded emphatically.

The Sinclairs had a quiet sort of respect for each other. In the six years I'd known them—I always stayed at their bed-and-breakfast when I was in Perthshire—neither one of them had ever said an unkind word about the other, and they tended to finish each other's sentences.

He pulled up in front of their small cottage, where a compact stone wall surrounded a neat garden of herbs and flowers. Climbing roses arched over the paned windows of the tidy stone structure. I knew from experience that the house was considerably deeper than it looked, and the roses surrounded the house on all four sides.

My room—they rented it to others when I wasn't there, but I couldn't help but think of it as my very own—was a cozy garret in back above the kitchen, reached by a narrow, twisting stairway. The climbing rose that grew up to my window had yellow blossoms. It wouldn't be blooming yet, but I'd seen the Sinclair roses at every season and loved them regardless of the time of year.

Mrs. Sinclair opened the front door and waved me inside. I didn't throw my arms around her sturdy body, even though that was what I wanted to do. Mr. Sinclair followed with my bag. The first time I stayed with them, I'd brought four suitcases—four! Ridiculous. Mr. Sinclair had gently refused to let me carry any of them inside. "Part of the service we offer, lassie," he told me. I'd wondered about his ability to carry them up those stairs but learned soon enough not to worry about him. He could walk circles around Mrs. Sinclair and me when the three of us hiked the dirt and gravel trail up the side of Ben y Vrackie, the friendly mountain that loomed a mile or so to the north of Pitlochry. It had been a couple of years, though, since I'd hiked it with them.

When I walked into the Sinclairs' front room, Bruce, their aging Scottish terrier, made eye contact and slowly lowered his head onto the edge of his round padded bed.

I looked at Mr. Sinclair and he shook his head. "The wee boy is feeling his age."

Bruce picked his head back up, hauled himself to his feet, stepped across the edge of the soft bed, and came over to sniff my feet.

I bent to scratch his wiry head. "You're just taking your time, aren't you? That's okay, boy."

Mr. Sinclair had been telling me for the past few years that I needed *a wee dog* of my own—a Scottie, naturally—but with Shorty, my cat, I wasn't sure a dog would work out. Anyway, I got plenty of doggie kisses from my brother's dog every time they dropped by. Still, I could imagine a Scottie in the ScotShop. Maybe with a little tartan jacket? I whipped out my phone and took a picture of Bruce as he lay back down.

I wasn't even a third of the way though my cup of tea when Mrs. Sinclair said, "So, what's bothering ye, dearie? Ye're not . . ."

". . . your usual bright self," her husband concluded for her. "We can tell there's something wrong."

As much as I hated to disturb the peace of their cottage with my lousy love life, I needed their sense of perspective. "It's Mason," I said.

"Mason Kilmarty?" Mrs. Sinclair rubbed her chin thoughtfully. "Wasna that the young man . . ."

". . . ye were stepping out with, no?" Mr. Sinclair's eyes wrinkled in worry.

"He's not my young man anymore." I tried to sound matter-of-fact, but the look on their faces told me I'd failed. Often enough they'd listened to me brag about how well suited Mason and I were to each other. In retrospect, I wondered if I'd been trying to convince myself. "We broke up night before last." They looked so concerned, I added quickly, "It's okay. I'm fine, really."

Mrs. Sinclair pursed her lips. "He found someone else?"

"The rat turd," Mr. Sinclair pronounced at the same time, and Bruce growled from his doggie bed.

I laughed in spite of myself. "That's about the size of it."

He set down his cup. "So now ye are free . . ."

". . . to find just the right one for ye." The Sinclairs passed a look back and forth between them, soft as an ancient velvet box designed to hold love letters. Finally, she stood, setting the teacups onto a tray. "Why do ye not head into town before the shops close," she said, but without a question in her voice. "Mr. Sinclair will drive ye."

"No," I said. "I'll walk. It's only half a mile."

"Aye, and he's going to drive ye there and bring ye back as weel."

I knew a losing battle when I saw one. "Well, that will be a help if I collect any packages."

"Of course ye will," she scoffed. "When did ye never have parcels to lug around?"

I thanked her and ran upstairs to change from my wrinkled travel clothes. I took a moment to lean out the window and sniff. I knew there weren't roses blooming now, but I could swear I smelled them, not exactly a rose smell but something sweet and springlike. I turned around and spotted a bouquet of early wildflowers on the dresser beside a heavy pewter candlestick. The yellowed candle matched the color of the wild daisies. I'd walked right by without seeing them. My head was fuzzy indeed. I'd need to go to bed early.

Mr. Sinclair dropped me off at one end of the Atholl Road, Pitlochry's main shopping street. "I'll come back whenever ye're ready with your parcels, my dear," he told me as I lugged myself out of the car. I was more tired than I'd thought. "If ye need to warm up"—he pointed down the street to where his sister had a lovely little tearoom I'd visited often—"ring me, and I'll come to fetch ye." He patted the worn cloth seat beside him with what looked to me like deep affection.

He'd always told me the same thing, every time I'd been in his car. He didn't often drive me into town, only if the weather was blustery or if rain was in the offing. Same words. Same intonation, his light tenor voice sounding like a rather settled golden retriever. He even looked like a retriever, an old one. His white hair swept to one side from a part that hopped around the left side of his head. His habit of running a hand—sometimes both of them at once—through his hair any time of day made tidiness impossible.

I stepped out of the car and leaned down to look at him again. "I won't be long."

He arched his bushy black eyebrows, which were an odd

contrast to his silvery hair. "In that case, I'll wait at least two hours before I come back."

I laughed. "No, I mean it."

Despite my indignation, or maybe because of it, he chuckled and headed back the way we'd come.

I waved and started along the main thoroughfare but stopped as I came to a side street bordered by a low wall of stacked stone. I couldn't remember ever having walked down that way. I headed toward a tall larch tree about half-way down the lane but was sidetracked by a gated arbor covered with an early blooming vine I didn't recognize. The flowers were a dark peach color with darker brown veins in the petals. Feathery leaves whorled around the sinuous stems like Christmas greenery around a bannister. I breathed in an almost citrusy scent with an underlying spicy hint of—of what? Cinnamon? I glanced through the arbor to see a little stone shop tucked in between two rowan trees. A discreet sign in the door said *Open*. I ducked through the gateway under the bower of fragrant blossoms.

Three women stood inside, huddled in conversation. They looked up at me, and one of them, wearing a blue-and-green plaid skirt, motioned me farther in. "Ye are well come to the Scot Shop," she said.

What a lovely old-fashioned phrase, I thought as I closed the door behind me, but all I said was, "To the what?"

"The Scot Shop. Did ye no see the sign beside the door?"

"No, I didn't notice it. I guess I was too busy looking at your flowers. Have you been here long?" They looked a bit confused until I added, "I've been to Pitlochry many times and never saw your store before today."

"Aye. Well. That's no bother. Ye've found us now."

"I'm intrigued with the name. I own a store called the Scot-Shop back in the States. I come here often on buying trips."

"Do ye now?"

One of the other women spoke up. "The Scot Shop? For

aye? Like this?" She waved her arm in a slow arc that took in the whole room.

"I live in a tourist town called Hamelin. It was founded by Scots years ago. Many of the men in town wear kilts."

The first woman nodded. "And would ye be wearing an arisaidh yourself?"

"Oh, yes, at least when I'm working at the store. That or just a long skirt, white blouse, and tartan scarf."

"That's lovely. Feel free to look around, dear. Let me know if ye have any questions."

I thanked her and moved to my right, but a sudden impulse turned me toward the back left corner of the shop, where I saw piles of felted fabric. It was darker there. I normally prefer a brightly lit store, but this was Scotland, after all, and I supposed the darkened corner was deliberately planned to invoke a sense of mystery. The items certainly did seem a bit mysterious. No price tags, for one thing. I touched as I went—I do love the feel of wool, particularly fabrics that are handwoven.

A pile of plaids called to me, and I stepped closer. There's a certain look to beautifully handwoven and hand-felted cloth that can't be reproduced by anything machine made. I reached for them, and then I turned back to the proprietor. "May I rummage a bit?"

"Of course ye may," she said with a nod of her grizzled head.

I set the top few pieces to one side and stopped when I reached a dark plaid with blocks of blue, wide stripes of green, and thin crosshatchings of red and what looked like yellow, although in this low light I couldn't be sure. Maybe it was white. I didn't recognize the pattern. I knew quite a few clan tartans by name, but this one was unfamiliar to me. That wasn't surprising, since nowadays there were dress tartans, hunting tartans, ancient tartans, and something called a modern tartan for every clan. I'd long ago given up trying to recall even the names of all the clans, much less their various plaids.

I lifted it, expecting a square or rectangle of material, but the felted fabric, surprisingly lightweight and supple, was shaped to drape around the shoulders. "A shawl," I said, more to myself than to anyone else, and clutched it to my chest. A wave of warmth, coziness, and comfort spread through me.

"Och, lassie, don't go picking up that aulde thing." The nasal voice came from the third woman, the one who hadn't spoken before. She turned to the plaid-skirted woman. "I surely don't know why ye keep it around."

The woman murmured something, but I paid little attention. The shawl felt so warm in my arms, so enveloping.

". . . from my great-grandmother."

I fingered the edge of the shawl. I couldn't imagine anyone having something that old. It didn't look like it could be—what would it have to be? A hundred years old? The woman in plaid looked like she was in her late seventies, so the shawl, if it had belonged to her great-grandmother, would have to be 120 years old maybe? It certainly looked in good shape for something so ancient. "Did you say your great-grandmother made it?"

"Och, no," the woman whispered. Her skirt matched the pattern of the shawl I held, and it swished as she swayed from side to side. "Her great-grandmother's great-grandmother was the one who saved it from the fire that took the village."

The other women nodded knowingly. There was always a story of some devastating fire that had swept through a village, claiming not only the houses but lives as well. That was why, I was sure, this town was built of stone.

"It was her great-grandmother's before her, and that woman's great-grandmother even before, and another nine great-grandmothers before that. It always passed to the eldest great-granddaughter, but now"—her voice quavered with what sounded like regret—"I'm the first to have no daughter of my own. 'Twill have to go to my sister's branch in Nefyn."

I couldn't imagine that many great-grandmothers. I often wished I could have known my great-grandmother. She sounded like such a hoot. My grandmother—my mother's mother—had told me often that her ma always claimed to be able to see ghosts. It was something of a family joke, but there was an undertone of chagrin that there could have been someone so crazy in the family. When my brother and I turned ten, though, I blew out my half of the birthday candles secretly wishing I could see a ghost someday.

My ancestors, the ones I knew of, went back almost to the 1700s, when Hamelin was founded, but the records before then were destroyed when half the town burned down. That was well close to three hundred years ago.

But how many hundreds of years was this woman talking about?

I looked at the shawl I still held. Ridiculous. It couldn't be that old. Anyway, would anyone sell something that had been in the family for so long? I was being spun a tale. Still, I liked the feel of the shawl. "I'll take it," I said, and cringed. I'd just made the worst mistake a buyer can make. The woman knew I wanted it, so the price would go up accordingly.

"Of course ye will, lassie," she said. "It's been waiting for ye all these years. Ye are the one."

I'm afraid I gawked at her. The one what?

"'Tis so," she said. "The shawl is yours. It always has been. Can't ye tell?" She reached out and took it from me, holding it up under my chin. She nodded. "Aye."

At that moment, feeling almost as if I were in a trance, I think I would have paid any amount for it. But the price she named was reasonable indeed, and I paid it without hesitation, silently blessing the woman for her lack of avarice.

"It's a Farquharson," she said. "Did ye ken that?"

"No," I told her, "I'm not familiar with that clan," and started toward the door.

"Och, ye soon will be," she said.

I held the shawl tight against me as I headed back toward the main street. I couldn't imagine what she meant.

For some reason, I wasn't much in the mood for shopping

that afternoon. I kept thinking about Ben y Vrackie, the mountain a mile or so north of town. I felt an urge, almost a yearning, to climb it. I hugged the shawl more tightly, relishing its softness. "Let us climb," an inner voice urged me. At least, that's what I imagined. Maybe it was a fragment of an old poem I'd read but couldn't recall. I laughed the thought away and returned to the cottage, surprising both the Sinclairs.

I placed the shawl over their hall tree. "Mrs. Sinclair? Would you like to take a walk up Ben y Vrackie?"

"Today?" Her eyebrows rose right into the wrinkles across her forehead.

"No. You're right. It's too late for that, but maybe tomorrow?"

For some reason, she looked at the shawl.

"That sounds lovely," she said, glancing at her husband, who raised his bushy eyebrows and shrugged.

"Of course." She sounded like she was answering an unspoken question. "'Twould be a lovely day for a walk, dearie. We'll leave here just after midday and take our tea with us." She headed into the kitchen.

"I don't want to be any bother," I protested.

"Nonsense, lassie." Mr. Sinclair looked toward where Mrs. Sinclair has disappeared into the back. "We've not been up on Ben y Vrackie for . . ."

". . . nae for a year or twa," she called.

I ate a quick dinner at the pub down the lane and turned in early. I'd set my clothes out on the chair beside the window with the shawl draped across them. Tomorrow, the mountain. Why did I feel so excited about climbing a big hill? With the moonlight streaming across the bed, I slept.

3

A Wee Ghostie in the Meadow

Breakfast was the usual porridge, sausage, and a coddled egg. Mrs. Sinclair set them in front of me with an admonition to "eat heartily. 'Tis hungry you'll be on the mountain this afternoon otherwise."

I passed the morning pleasantly enough wandering around town and ate lunch at a small pub. It was such a lovely day, I'd left the shawl in my room.

Finally, I couldn't stand the wait any longer, and headed back to the B and B.

Within moments Mrs. Sinclair appeared, tucking in the flap of a rucksack, two others slung over her arm. "Tea, nuts, and biscuits," she said, handing one pack to Mr. Sinclair and one to me.

I ran upstairs and grabbed the shawl. It was likely to be chilly on the side of the mountain. As I climbed into the back of their little car, I hoped I wouldn't regret that I hadn't taken the time to go to the bathroom. Karaline always accused me of TBS—tiny bladder syndrome—whenever we hiked at home.

Mr. Sinclair parked in a small graveled area at the beginning of a well-defined trail. He hefted the rucksack. Some well-meaning person had placed a blue porta potty—here it was called a Portaloo—at the mouth of the trail. I excused myself to make use of it. I couldn't recall it from the last time I'd hiked here, but was quite grateful for it this time.

Why, I thought, had I chosen to come here rather than to explore more of the Pitlochry shops? This trip was short to begin with, and here I was wasting several hours.

Mr. and Mrs. Sinclair had gone ahead. They sat on a large stone outcropping a few minutes up the trail, waiting patiently. "Thank you," I said, and we headed uphill.

The climb to the summit is supposed to take less than an hour, but I've never been much of a hiker. Oh, I like to take long walks, but I have a tendency to stop—often—to look at odd stones, bits of plant, and puddles of mud. Also, I must admit, I do get out of breath if I try to keep up a regular pace. So I'm afraid I slowed the Sinclairs down, but they were used to me. We'd taken this walk before. They adjusted their pace to mine, and Mrs. Sinclair stopped occasionally "to look at this lovely view," she said, but I knew it was so I could catch my breath.

I spotted a charming meadow a ways off the main trail and called to the Sinclairs.

Mrs. S cocked her head at her husband. "Did I not tell ye?"

He didn't answer, just disrupted his hair again with both hands.

We drank our tea from pottery mugs. Mrs. Sinclair disliked plastic and Styrofoam as much as I did. The grassy meadow flowed down the hill beside a gurgling brook that tumbled toward the loch below. Most of the mountainside was covered in heather, which tends to be prickly, but this one place sported grass, and a towering larch spread its deep green branches like a billowing cape. There were other trees on Ben y Vrackie, but none so large as this. How could I have missed it on my previous hikes?

After we munched a bit on filberts and walnuts, Mr. Sinclair stretched out on the turf beneath the tree and pulled his hat forward over his eyes. "A wee nap," he muttered—an unnecessary explanation.

"A lovely idea, my dear," Mrs. Sinclair said, and settled down beside him, her back up against the enormous larch. She smiled sweetly at him and then at me. "Rest yourself, Peggy," she said, and patted the ground beside her.

I felt restless, though, and shook my head. "I'm going to walk down by the brook." She waved gaily, and I turned my back on her.

The grass was spongy beneath my feet. I've always thought the smell of newly cut grass was the best smell in the world. This grass didn't look newly shorn at all, but the smell was there just the same. Heavenly, I thought.

I'd chosen to travel in a sturdy calf-length walking skirt. I felt very old-world when I wore it, because it wasn't the sort of thing Americans wore on airplanes or on hikes. I'd packed some jeans, of course, but the skirt felt better somehow. My hiking boots laced above my ankles. I'd learned the hard way that my tendency to slip on any uneven surface required me to buy good footwear. When I reached the stream, though, I slipped off the boots and my practical white socks. After a moment's hesitation, I dipped my toes into the cold water and quickly out again, tucking them beneath the soft folds of my skirt. I pulled the shawl off my left shoulder, where I'd been carrying it, and wrapped it around me, covering the back of my neck, for I'd begun to feel a chill. I glanced back up the hill. The Sinclairs were, fortunately, out of sight behind a slight rise in the meadowland. What lovely solitude.

Mason, damn him, floated into my mind. I was better off without him. If I were completely honest with myself, I hadn't really trusted him, ever since the day I'd found him rummaging through my purse, my checkbook in his hand. No, I was not going to let him ruin this day. The utter peacefulness of the meadow slowly sank into me the way butter melts into hot toast. I took a deep breath and then another.

I didn't hear anyone walk up behind me, but the voice hardly startled me at all, it felt so much a part of this place. He called my name.

"Peigi? Are ye now well then?" the voice said, soothingly, gently. Pay-ee-gee was how he pronounced it. I rather liked that, and I turned my head uphill to see who had spoken. My shoulder-length hair swung forward, and I brushed it back.

"Och no!" the voice said. "Peigi! What have they done to your hair?" The distress of the burly gentleman who stood there was almost palpable, but there was a wavering shimmer around him, like heat waves above hot pavement, and I could—almost—see the far edge of the meadow through his billowing belted plaid. Heavy black hair blew back from his face, although I didn't feel a wind. I began to think that perhaps I wasn't the Peggy he was expecting. I began to wonder, too, if my great-grandmother had been telling the truth about seeing ghosts.

"I knew ye were ill, my love, but they kept me from ye. Was it the Fever? Is that why they cut off your beautiful . . ." His voice faded a bit as he stepped nearer, and his left hand went to the hilt of his dirk. "Ye are no my Peigi," he said in an accusing tone that contrasted horribly with the gentleness of his earlier words.

I slid back on my butt, farther away from him. I was going to have grass stains on my skirt, damn it, and it was *his* fault. I pulled my shawl closer about me. This couldn't be happening.

"Ye are no my Peigi," he repeated.

"Well, no," I said. "I'm Peggy, that's true, but not *your* Peggy." Why was I conversing with this lunatic? I should be yelling for the Sinclairs, who were, unfortunately, out of sight. "What are you doing here anyway?"

"Doing here?" His indignation practically exploded. "What are ye doing on my land?"

"What do you mean your land? This is a public walking trail. I have every right to be here." It occurred to me that maybe I didn't, since we'd strayed off the trail to this meadow. Come to think of it, I'd never seen this particular meadow before, despite all the times I'd walked up this mountain. Maybe we were trespassing, but I wasn't about to admit that to this cantankerous guy. "Just ask the Sinclairs," I said. "They walk here all the time."

"The Sinclairs?" He planted his booted feet wide apart and crossed his arms in front of his massive chest. "And what would ye be having to do with that clan?"

"What are you talking about? They're my friends, and they're asleep under the larch up there." I pointed.

"What larch? The goats roam over this entire hillside, and there are no trees big enough to sleep under."

I gathered my skirt out of the way, picked up my boots, stuffed the socks in them, and stood in a huff. "You just come with me, sir," I said, "and you can see for yourself." Without waiting, I marched up the small rise and started across the grass toward the ancient tree. Mrs. Sinclair had apparently woken up. Or maybe she hadn't slept at all. She held a small paperback book. When she saw me, she waved merrily.

"See?" I said out of the corner of my mouth. "There they are and there's the tree. And," I added with some spite, "no goats anywhere."

I turned to look at him as he walked up beside me. The shock on his face stopped me in my tracks. "Where did yon tree come from? It wasna there yester morn."

I shifted my boots to my other hand and headed toward Mrs. Sinclair, who seemed to be rummaging in her knapsack. Her husband lay inert. "Peggy," she called when she saw me, "come have a wee sit before we head back down the trail." She patted the ground beside her, the way she had a little while ago, and held up a red tin. "I've biscuits for us to share. All three of us," she added, and prodded her husband, "if the mister will deign to wake up."

Three of us? I looked sideways at the man standing right beside me. "I'll be there in a moment, Mrs. Sinclair," I called. "I . . . I left my socks by the stream." I turned and fled, and the man came along with me.

At the side of the stream I whirled around. "She couldn't see you." My stage whisper was indignant, unbelieving, and, I must admit, a trifle terrified.

"And do ye think," he practically spat at me, "do ye think I am enjoying this?" He paced a few feet uphill, turned around and paced down. "I woke up . . . I didna know I had been sleeping, but it seemed I awoke . . . thinking my Peigi had somehow been transported from her sickbed, restored to health, and brought here to my lands." He spread his arms to encompass the hillside. "Instead, I find a brazen woman striding around with . . . with her ankles showing." He shuddered, but I noticed his eyes drift down the length of me. I missed his next few words. ". . . a tree where no tree stood ever since my grandda's father cleared this land for our crops and the goats." His hand strayed to his dirk again. "And these strange clothes ye wear. Where did ye come from? Are ye . . . a spirit?"

A bird flew across the meadow, and I saw the wings flap as it passed behind him. He seemed so much a part of this place, but his clothes, his attitudes were—*Oh dear, this can't be happening*—from a very long time ago.

I took a deep breath. "I don't think I'm the one who's the spirit here." He looked incredulous. "I think you're . . ." I took another breath. "I think you're a ghost."

"That canna be. I dinna believe in them, despite what the aulde grannies say."

"But I can see through you—sort of."

He held a hand up in front of his eyes. I could see a shimmer of light through it. He swallowed convulsively; his Adam's apple bobbed up and down. "And I can see ye, too, like. Through my—" He sat down abruptly. "I'm deid?"

I sank down onto the grass beside him. "It sure looks like it."

"Why am I here, then?"

"I don't know." I gripped the shawl more tightly.

He reached out and fingered the edge of it. "This is her shawl, ye know," he said. "See this wee line of white that disrupts the pattern along this one edge?"

I doubt I would have noticed it if he hadn't pointed it out. A thin white line was clearly visible, even though the felting had blended the colors and made the pattern soft and indistinct. I checked the other edges, but no white line was there.

"It was her love message to me," he said.

He had a bad case of five o'clock shadow, about two days' worth. I almost wanted to reach over and run my fingers along his jaw to see what it would feel like. I restrained myself.

"She told me that her love for me would last as long as this white line was visible. And that when I was awae from her, she would keep me by her side." The shawl dropped from his fingers. "Forever," he added.

I looked around the hillside, half expecting to see a long-skirted, long-haired, long-dead woman walking our way. "When . . ." I didn't know how else to ask it. "When are you from?"

He looked puzzled for a moment until understanding sank in. "This is the year of our Lord 1359."

"Thirteen!" I yelped. "Thirteen-fifty-nine? How the heck did you get to the twenty-first century?"

He gulped again. "Twenty-first, ye say?" His wavering cheeks went a bit pale. He cupped his face in his hands and leaned his elbows on his knees—and very fine knees they were, I had to admit. His kilt was hiked halfway up his thigh. But I didn't need to be thinking about that. We sat in silence for a minute, maybe two.

What on earth would my great-grandma have done in a situation like this? Was I going absolutely nuts? "Do you have a name, or do I just call you *ghost*?"

He bowed in a surprisingly courtly manner. "I have the privilege of carrying the name of Macbeath Donlevy

Freusach Finlay Macearachar Macpheidiran of Clan Farquharson. My family call me Macbeath."

"Mock-beh-ath? Macbeth? Like Shakespeare?"

"Shake spear? What is shake spear?"

"You've gotta be kidding. Everybody knows Shakespeare."

"I assure you I do not."

"Oh, yeah; he was the sixteen hundreds." I watched a
small spider in the grass while I thought.

He raised his head and looked down the hill toward the
loch. "What brought me here?" He laid his hand gently on
my shawl, where the corner of it touched the grass. The
spider had begun spinning a web beside his soft-booted foot.
I was glad he hadn't stepped on her. I like spiders. "'Twas
the shawl brought me here, I am sure of it."

I looked away from the spider into his disturbingly alive-
looking eyes. "So you're really a ghost?" The idea was
beginning to sink in.

He nodded slowly. "'Twould appear so, but I've not
known it till now."

"And you're here because of the shawl." I fished my socks
out of my boots and pulled them on while he thought.

He shook his head. "No. Not just that. I think I came
when Peigi called."

"But—but," I sputtered, "she's been dead for"—I did a
quick calculation—"almost seven hundred years."

He heaved a heart-wrenching sigh. "So, it would appear,
have I."

Without another word, he followed me uphill. When we
were almost within sight of the Sinclairs, just before we
reached the top of the rise, I turned to him. "Don't say
anything, anything at all, while we're with the Sinclairs." I
spread my hands in the age-old gesture of helplessness.
"They wouldn't understand."

He nodded solemnly. "Nor do I."

He trailed disconsolately behind me. I couldn't make up

my mind what to say. *I have a ghost named Macbeth.* No.
My shawl is haunted. Nope. *You won't believe what just
happened to me.* They certainly wouldn't.

He circled behind me and approached the tree. I took a
deep breath. "I hope you had a good nap, Mr. Sinclair." I sat
gingerly on Mrs. Sinclair's left and accepted a cookie. Biscuit. I had to remember to call it a biscuit. If I could remember *a bracing cup of tea*—one of which I could definitely
use right about now—I could certainly remember *biscuit.*
"The clouds are lovely today, aren't they?"

Mrs. Sinclair looked at me as if she thought I'd lost my
mind. Maybe I had.

I looked over my right shoulder. The ghost had his hands
up, pressing them against the tree's crenellated bark. He
looked up at the lowest branches, which were a good eight
feet above his head. I wondered if he could feel the bark or
if his hands would pass through it. He looked up, as if he
were trying to gauge the larch's height, and light glinted off
the handle of his dirk.

"Yes, they are lovely, but what are ye looking at, lassie?"
Mr. Sinclair's voice broke into my reverie. "It is no the
clouds," he added.

"The, uh, the tree?"

Mrs. Sinclair chuckled. "Is it us ye're asking, dearie?"
She swiveled her neck around to her left, surprisingly flex-
ible, I thought, for a woman her age, and looked up at the
larch. She studied the tree longer than I would have expected,
and when she turned back to me, her gaze felt laserlike, but
all she said was, "The tree, was it?"

"I wonder how old it is?" I stole a quick look at the ghost.
He had turned his head to look at Mrs. Sinclair and then at
me. I could feel his gaze, and I shivered.

"Pull your shawl more tightly round your shoulders, dearie. Ye look like ye're catching a chill." She handed me the
little tin of cookies. Biscuits. She smiled. "To tell the truth,
ye're acting like ye've seen a wee ghostie."

Mr. Sinclair laughed. "Not so wee, from the look on her face."

The wee ghostie under discussion circled around to my left and knelt in front of me. The light of the setting sun poured through his hair, turning the black to liquid charcoal.

"Can she see me?" he whispered. "I canna tell."

"I don't know," I said.

"Don't know what, lassie?"

Damn. I couldn't talk to him when other people were around. They'd think I was crazy. I put on a bright smile. "I don't know . . . uh, but I just felt a little faint. I'm fine now, though."

Mrs. Sinclair looked at Mr. Sinclair, and they both turned back to me. "Are ye now?" They spoke at the same time, echoing each other.

I looked at my watch, remembered I wasn't wearing one, and took the last cookie. Biscuit.

Mr. Sinclair stood and helped his wife to her feet. We packed our few belongings in the rucksacks and headed back to the trail. I turned to look at the peaceful meadow one more time.

"It was here we—my Peigi and I—were together for the last time." The ghost stood close to my right shoulder but did not touch me.

"When was that?" I asked.

Mr. Sinclair turned around. "When was what, lassie?"

This was going to be harder than I thought. "Just muttering to myself," I said. And to the resident ghost. I waited until the Sinclairs walked farther downhill. "I guess this is good-bye," I said. What was I supposed to do? Shake hands? Nuh-uh.

He inclined his head.

I walked a few yards and tuned back to wave. He was right behind me. "Go away! I don't want you following me."

"I believe I must. My Peigi's shawl . . . I canna seem to . . . " His words drifted away into a silence almost as confused as the look on his face.

Whatever was I going to tell Karaline?

At the bottom of the trail, I veered off toward the porta potty.

"We'll wait for you . . ."

". . . in the car," the Sinclairs said.

I opened the blue door. "Inside, you," I whispered with my teeth clenched.

We were fairly cramped. These things were designed for one person at a time. His head brushed the top. Damn, he was tall. I thought people had been short in the fourteenth century. As close as we were standing, I had to tilt my head back. I got an unexpectedly good look at his upper incisors. They were big, strong, and very white. *This would be a great place for him to turn into a vampire. Stop it, Peggy.*

"What is this place?" He sounded a bit awed. Maybe that was why his mouth had been hanging open.

"It's a porta potty." When he looked blank, I added, "A loo." Still blank. "A privy."

Understanding dawned. "A necessary?"

I nodded.

"Why did ye bring me in here? I dinna have to pass water."

"We're here because it's the only place I can speak to you in private. Now, you listen. We're about to get into a car—"

"A what?"

"Hush. A car. It's like a little house on wheels."

"Why would we get into—?"

"No, wait, it's more like a wagon that's all closed up."

"And how d'ye open it?"

"That's not the point!" It's hard to shout when you're whispering. "The point I'm trying to make is that you have to be absolutely quiet. You cannot ask a single question while we're in the car. Do you understand?"

"Why not?"

"Because I won't be able to answer you. Mr. and Mrs. Sinclair are already looking at me funny. I don't want them to think I've gone barmy."

"What is barmy?"

"Mad. Crazy." I threw up my hands. "Now, will you keep your mouth closed until we're alone again." It wasn't a question.

"Ye tell me I have been deid for more than six hundred years. In all that time I have not said a word, and now ye want me to keep my mouth closed?"

"Yes. That's right." I almost felt sorry for him. Almost.

A small spider dangled down between us, slowly spinning out her silk as she passed in front of his face. I backed out and held the door open. This was ridiculous. How was I going to . . .

It was worse than I could have imagined. I slipped into the backseat behind Mr. Sinclair, motioning surreptitiously for the ghost to follow me in. But of course I had to slide to the other side to make room for him. And the door was still open. "You stay here," I said to him, hoping the Sinclairs would think I was talking to them. "The door seems to have stuck." I got out, walked around the car, checked to be sure his dirk was out of the way, closed the door, walked back to the passenger's side, and got in.

Mr. Sinclair adjusted the rearview mirror so he could peer at me. Mrs. Sinclair had swiveled around in her seat.

"The picnic lunch was a lovely idea, Mrs. Sinclair. I enjoyed it thoroughly."

She made a sound, low in her throat, and turned around to face forward. "Drive us home, Mr. Sinclair. I think our lassie could use a wee lie-down before bed."

I heard a whispered comment at my side. "Where are the horses?"

4

A Wee Pub of My Own

I conducted an extremely sketchy history lesson in a whisper while the Sinclairs thought I was napping. Finally, I asked, "Did you ever meet Chaucer?"

"Chaucer?"

"You would have loved the Wife of Bath."

"The wife—"

"Never mind. That's an English major joke."

"A joke? Ye've stolen my Peigi's shawl, I am apparently dead, and ye *jest*?" Each syllable sounded like a dirge tone. "Ye are most unladylike."

I expelled a heavy breath. "You think so? It's a good thing you aren't coming with me to America. You'd be appalled."

He looked faintly puzzled. "And where would that be? I know of no town by that name. Is this where your Mr. Shakespeare lives?"

I was supposed to teach a comprehensive history lesson to someone who'd never heard of the Declaration of Independence? Who last took a breath around the time of Chaucer?

"And just to set the record straight, I did not steal this shawl. I paid for it."

"My Peigi would never sell that shawl."

"I didn't say I bought it from *her*. What are you doing wearing a belted plaid, anyway? They weren't in common use until the end of the fifteenth century."

"My plaid?" He patted the fabric draped across his chest. "I wear it all the time."

"Tell that to the historians."

"Ye make no sense, woman."

"Come on, I'm hungry. There's a pub down the road where I usually eat my evening meal."

He trailed along beside me. When we got close, he sighed. "At last," he said, "some place I recognize."

"You know this pub?"

"Weel, not this precise building. I dinna ken your word *pub*." He looked at the surrounding hills as if to orient himself. "There was an inn here—built of wood it was, not fine stone like this. It was here when I was . . . when I used to . . ." His voice faded away. "More than six hundred years? How can that be?"

"I wish I knew."

"Aye. Me, too. But I suppose it would take more than six hundred years to design a way to put a hundred tiny horses underneath a carriage."

He obviously hadn't understood the internal combustion engine. "Too bad I don't have my college history book here. You could read up on what's been happening in the world for all this time." Thanks to my dad, I had a hefty interest in a lot of subjects, history included. Not that I always remembered the details.

"Read? Aye. I can read. But—ye own a book?"

"A book? Of course. I've got dozens of them."

He stopped walking. "I didna ken ye were wealthy."

"Huh? What are you talking about?"

"Books. Ye said ye had dozens of them." He sounded a bit exasperated. "How is that possible if ye are not wealthy?"

Six or seven hundred years ago, the only books were in churches and monasteries, and possibly the homes of the nobility. No wonder he thought I was rich. Even one book would have been a priceless treasure.

I put my hands over my face and shook my head. "There was this guy named Gutenberg, about two hundred years after you." I gave up for the moment and opened the pub door. "Let's eat."

"I wish I could," he said as the light streamed onto the pavement. He didn't cast a shadow.

I ordered at the counter, chose a relatively quiet corner, and pulled a chair out for him before I sat down.

He hesitated and sat carefully. "I didna ken if I would be able to sit on anything except the earth," he said with such a simple yearning in his voice, my heart went out to him.

"Looks like you made it," I said, careful to keep my voice low. "Congratulations. But you sat in the car, remember?"

"Och, aye. I'd forgotten that. I was so worrit about where the horses were, I didna stop to think about sitting."

I laughed, but then we lapsed into silence, which was a good thing because the waitress brought the soup and tea I'd ordered. "Anything else I can get for ye?"

"No. Thank you."

She looked at the chair pulled out away from the table. "Are ye expecting someone?"

"No. No, I'm not."

Her forehead furrowed.

"I like to stretch my legs out," I said.

"Shall I take awa' the chair then?" She moved toward it and Macbeth scrambled to stand.

"No! No, it's fine just the way it is. Thank you."

She gnawed a bit at her lower lip. "If ye say so."

I nodded, and she left with only one backward glance.

I wasn't much of a companion. Whatever was I going to

do with a ghost? I couldn't spend the rest of my life toting him around, could I? Did my great-grandmother ever have to pull out a chair so a ghost could sit? Did she ever have to watch her conversations so people wouldn't think she was crazy?

Doggone it. The whole family *did* think my great-grandmother was crazy. Was this why? Did she know a ghost? Ghosts? Was I hallucinating or had I somehow inherited this ability? Was I going to be able to see other ghosts? I looked around the pub. Surely over the centuries people had died here. Would their ghosts be hanging out? Everybody looked alive to me, but then, so did the hunk—I mean the guy—at my table.

"Are ye worrit?" His soft voice called me back to the pub. "That scowl on your face reminds me of my aulde auntie who had a roily stomach."

Could I tell him? *You show up in my life and I'm wondering how to get rid of you.* "I'm just a little worried about something going on at home." That was true enough. My cheating former boyfriend, who I did not want to see ever again. "Still, I can't do anything for a couple more days. I have to shop tomorrow." *And stop thinking about Mason. Oh, good grief, Winn. Chill out.* "And then we have to leave. I've already paid for the ticket. . . ."

"Ticket? What would . . ."

". . . and it's not transferrable. I suppose you'll be coming with me."

His voice rang out in indignation. "I dinna intend to leave."

"Whyever not?"

"My Peigi, my pearl, is here." He spoke simply, but sincerely.

I hugged the shawl around me. "I don't think you have much choice in the matter."

"Ye could leave the shawl behind."

"No!" Our voices, except for that one burst of laughter,

had been quiet, but my startled cry in response to his request stopped the party in progress across the room. Everyone turned to look at me, and the proprietor, Mr. Graham, hurried over to our table. To my table.

"Is something wrong, miss?"

I groped about for an excuse. "I'm sorry, I just read something that startled me. I didn't mean to disturb anyone."

He looked at the table, at my lap.

I didn't have a book with me. Should have thought about that. "On my cell," I said. "On the Internet." I lifted my phone from my purse and waved it in front of me. "I should know better than to read during a meal."

He nodded and hurried away to the other tables, probably to assure them that all was well with the eccentric American. I'd eaten here so many times over the past six years, I felt like I owned part of it, but Mr. Graham still didn't understand me.

I finished my soup quickly, paid, and left with my wee ghostie in my wake.

We walked for several blocks before he said anything. "Why can ye no leave the shawl?"

"I just can't, that's all. I just can't. It would be like leaving a part of myself behind."

Until I said it, I hadn't realized how important the shawl had become to me. I didn't want to be without it. Ever. I glanced down, and the white stripe seemed to shimmer in the moonlight.

It was when we walked in the front door of the Sinclair cottage that I realized there might be a problem.

Bed.

I looked at the broad shoulders of my wee ghostie.

The Sinclairs sat in front of their telly, as they called it, and waved to me as I walked toward the stairs. "Did you have . . ."

". . . a lovely meal?" they asked in their back-and-forth pattern.

I barely paused. "Yes, thank you, but I'm tired. I think I'll go on to bed now," and kept walking.

"Sleep well, dearie, and we'll . . ."

". . . see you at breakfast, lassie."

I climbed the stairs, unusually aware of the ghost behind me. The dimly lit stairs were too narrow for two people at a time, and I was glad he couldn't see my face. We reached the top, and I paused outside my door. "I have to tell you something," I said. "You can't come in my room. I wouldn't feel comfortable with you hovering around while I'm trying to sleep."

"I do believe I know how ye feel. I wouldna verra much like to spend the whole night hovering, as ye say, either."

"Can you stay out here in the hall?"

He looked around him, considering the question. He stepped—or rather, tried to step away from me, but about six feet from me, he pulled up short, as if he'd walked into a wall. "I canna."

"Why not?"

Mrs. Sinclair's voice came up from the bottom of the stair. "What did ye say, dearie?" She climbed a step or two. "I was on my way into the kitchen, and I thought I heard ye call. Are ye alright now?"

I looked over the bannister. "I'm fine, Mrs. Sinclair. I was just . . . humming to myself."

She retreated, and he whispered, "It doesna look verra comfortable out here, and I dinna think I can move verra far awae from you, from my Peigi's shawl."

"You don't have to whisper," I grumped in as quiet a tone as I could manage. "She can't hear you." I opened my door and glanced back at the utilitarian hallway. "This is ridiculous. Okay. Come on in if you must. And close the door, please."

There was a deep silence, and I looked over my shoulder. "I canna," he finally said, shrugging helplessly.

"Sorry. I forgot." I motioned him inside, brushed past him, and closed the door quietly. "You can sit over there," I pointed to a wingback chair of extra-large proportions, "but I'm going to turn it around to face the window. You'll have to promise not to peek."

He rubbed his hand over his chin, and I could hear a faint rasping. I guess his last shave was six or seven hundred years ago, plus about two days. I grinned, but he wasn't looking at me. "Would it no be easier if ye just folded the shawl and set it aside?"

"What?"

"All this day I have been with ye, and ye have been wearing yon shawl. What would happen if ye took it off?"

It seemed such a reasonable suggestion, I was surprised I hadn't thought of it myself. I lifted the shawl from my shoulders, folded it into a soft bundle, and set it on the chair. And he was gone.

I snatched the shawl back up again, and he stumbled into view.

"Dinna do that!"

"I'm sorry. I didn't . . . It was . . . I was . . . Did I hurt you?"

"No, but ye scairt the . . . ye scairt me something terrible."

I folded the shawl once more. "I'll see you in the morning," I said, and laid it gently down.

"Rest ye w—"

I took a quick bath and got ready for bed, but I was too restless. This was crazy. Absolutely insane. How could I have a ghost in my life? Was I imagining it? I touched the shawl with one finger. It was real enough. If I'd gone mad, then this was all pretty convincing. I paced around the room two or three times, sat on the side of the bed and brushed my hair, stood and stretched as high as I could onto my tiptoes. I'd been lazing off. Hadn't gone through my usual yoga routine this morning. If only Mason . . . *Stop it!* I moved the chair to one side and folded myself into

Sukhasana, open palms resting on my crossed legs, hoping it would settle me down.

I guess it helped a little bit. Or maybe it was that, after I'd blown out the candle, I lifted the folded shawl from the chair, pushed Mrs. Sinclair's puffy pillow out of the way, and curled up with my head on an ancient white line.

5

Pitlochry

I ate breakfast without him. It didn't seem fair to subject him to having to watch me eat when he couldn't touch or taste anything at all. A bit before it was time for the shops to open, I went upstairs, freshened my face, brushed my teeth, and opened the shawl.

"Did ye sleep easily?" He stood right before me, almost blocking the light from the window, but I could catch a glimpse of rose leaves behind him. Through him. His eyes widened when he looked down and saw my jeans, but he didn't say anything.

"Yes, thank you. I did. And you?"

He ran his fingers through his silky black hair. "I wouldna call it sleep, exactly. Nor wakefulness, neither. I simply was. And wasna at the same time, if ye know what I mean."

I didn't, but I thought the concept of what he'd gone through might not be an easy one to explain, rather like some of the concepts he was about to encounter—mass transportation and libraries and world history, just to name a few. So I mumbled a platitude or two and set off briskly down the stairs.

We didn't say much walking into town, and when we reached the Atholl Road, I found that I'd come a bit too early, so we strolled until the shops opened.

We passed the World War I memorial. A tall column that had the dates *1914* and *1919* carved on it, and the names of all the Pitlochry men who'd died overseas. I'd seen it often but still was moved by the incredible waste of all those young lives.

He paused and looked it over. "What would this be?"

"It's a war memorial."

"Ah." His hand strayed to the hilt of his dirk, even though I could tell it wasn't a conscious move. He nodded toward the names inscribed around all four sides of the base. "That's many to have died in a battle."

"Not just one battle," I said. "Many. For five long years. They called it the War to End All Wars." I could hear the capital letters in my tone of voice.

"I dinna think it did, for I know a bit about the way men think, and I canna believe they've changed all that much in six hundred years." He paused to watch a bevy of young women pass by.

No. Men hadn't changed much in six hundred years.

They parted and moved around him, oblivious to the energy he must have been putting out to prevent their running into him. Or through him, I thought.

By then the shops were open, and we walked up and down the Atholl Road, looking for handmade items, not the usual run-of-the-mill tourist junk that any shopkeeper could order from a catalog. I had a loyal clientele of leaf-peeper bus companies that brought their customers to Hamelin every autumn to see the riotous fall colors. They generally unloaded their tourists right in front of the ScotShop and directed people next door to the Logg Cabin, Karaline's restaurant, for a meal. Naturally, those people peered in my windows as they walked past and usually returned to browse and buy something after their lunch. Wide-sleeved homespun shirts were a big item with the men, tartan skirts for the women.

Then there were the regular summer residents, most of whom had a house in Hamelin and another farther south, so they could enjoy mild weather year round. They bought mostly gift items for their friends and family. Plaques and postcards, kilt pins and tartan coasters, coffee-table books and clan warrior figurines.

The regular tourists, just passing through for a day or an hour at any season of the year, usually bought a scarf or a tartan tie—I sold a lot of those—but often they'd buy a big-ticket item such as an authentic formal kilt, with kilt hose and matching flashes, a sporran and ghillie brogues, a kilt pin, and they always wanted a *sgian-dubh*, the small knife that is slipped inside the hose. I included a DVD called *How to Put on Your Formal Kilt* with every kilt purchase. No sense having a kilt if you didn't know how to wear it; those things could be confusing as heck to a beginner.

I glanced sideways. He inspected every passing car, probably listening for a horse whinny. His kilt wasn't the military kind, with the pleats already sewn down along the top. No. His was real. Nine yards of tartan. That's where the saying *the whole nine yards* comes from. The fabric had been cut in half and sewn together to make thirteen and a half feet of cloth that he'd have to pleat, lie down on, pull up around him, and belt. Next, he'd stand and arrange the top either around his shoulders or over one of them, securing it with his kilt pin, and finally he would pull up the front corners of the bottom half, tucking them into his belt so they wouldn't hinder his stride.

And quite a stride he had. At first I'd felt I had to keep up with him, and then I gradually saw that he matched my pace, no matter what it was. If I strolled, he strolled, always within three or four feet of me. If I sped up, so did he. I adjusted the shawl, letting it fall open a bit. The day really was quite mild.

I went back to inspecting his garb, trying to do it surreptitiously, as he absorbed all the sights and sounds. His

hose were hand-knit, of course, and the completely utilitarian handle of a *sgian-dubh* showed above the top of his sock.
His left leg. He must be left-handed. I mulled that over.

"When ye have finished inspecting me," he said, and I
raised my head to find his eyes twinkling, "would ye explain
this to me?" He waved his hand at a confectionary store with
stacks of chocolates, boxes of shortbread, and goodies I
didn't even know the names of. Unfortunately, when he gestured, his hand swiped through a nearby man neither of us
had noticed. The man stumbled, and I reached out to grab
his arm. If he hadn't weighed about twice what I did, I might
have been a help. As it was, we both tumbled to the ground.

Passersby, both Pitlochry denizens and tourists, rushed
to help us. By the time the man and I were hauled to our
feet, I'd lost sight of my ghost in the frenzy.

"I don't know what came over me," the man said, shaking
his head and speaking to the crowd. "I don't normally
become dizzy."

A woman standing at my elbow spoke up. "I'll just run
down the side street and ask Dr. McLeod to come take a
look at ye."

I stepped forward. "I don't think that's necessary." I
looked the man straight in the eye, lying for all I was worth.
"I'm afraid I stumbled into you. I caught my foot on . . ." I
looked down at the perfectly even pavement. "Well, I don't
know what I caught it on, but I certainly hope you're not
injured. I think you cushioned my fall."

I tried to smile endearingly, but it must not have worked.
"Ye look a bit sickly," the man said. "Perhaps we should call
Dr. McLeod for *ye*."

"No. Thank you. That's very kind. I'm, uh, I'm fine." I
reached down and rubbed my knee. No blood. My jeans
were sturdy. "I think I'll just mosey along and do a little
shopping."

There was a collective murmur, with words like *elevate*
and *careful* popping to the surface, but I nodded my head

to each of the people surrounding me. "Thank you for helping me," I said. "Thank you. Thank you."

I spotted the ghost nearby, on the edge of the throng, and
headed toward him. When I was sure we were far enough
away, I said, "You're going to have to watch when you throw
your hand around."

"Aye." He crossed his arms in front of his chest. His
massive chest, I noticed. Had he always been that brawny,
or was I only now beginning to see him for real?

"Let's head up that way." I gestured to my right. "There
aren't as many people, and there's a store I want to visit."

"Ye didna answer my question about the wee shop back
there." He thrust his chin in the direction we'd come from.

"They sell all different kinds of candy." When he looked
blankly at me, I added, "Sweets? Desserts? Like shortbread?"

His rather grim countenance lightened. "Ah, shortbread.
The aulde grannies bake it as often as we have sugar. 'Tis
verra dear."

"Expensive, you mean?"

"Aye, that is what I said."

I considered heading back down the street just to pick up
a box or two, but one look at my ghost convinced me not to.
He couldn't eat it, and I couldn't possibly enjoy eating it with
him watching me.

"Here, look at this." I stopped in front of a small store
I'd been in before, where I usually bought notecards, enough
to last me between visits to Scotland. I was old-fashioned
about some things, and writing letters—well, notes—was
something I enjoyed doing. People were always so surprised
when they received something other than junk in their
mailbox.

Maybe I could write Mason a poison pen letter. I
shuddered.

"Have ye caught a chill? Mayhap we should go inside,
out of the breeze."

"Sorry. No, I was just thinking about writing a letter to somebody."

"Ah, a letter?" The awe in his voice was palpable. "I saw a letter once. 'Twas to Father Marcus, from Father Godfrey at the Church of All Hallows by the Tower. In London." I started at the name. I'd toured that church once when I spent a few days in London. It was still in pretty good shape, considering its age. He looked around, almost as if he expected to see the good father sauntering down the street. "Father Marcus let me practice my reading using that letter. 'Twas all about church matters and didna make a great deal of sense to my young mind."

"Nowadays, letters aren't quite so weighty," I said, opening the door.

I nodded to the shopkeeper, who eyed me over her thick glasses. After all, I appeared to be talking to myself. I picked out an assortment of finely crafted notecards with matching envelopes, too good to waste on the likes of Mason Kilmarty, may he rot in hell, but I wasn't going to think about him.

6

A Wee Town of My Own

The rest of the day went much the same, although I was glad we had no more collisions with live people, and I slept well that night, tired from all the walking. The next day we went back into Pitlochry—this was a buying trip after all—and I couldn't help but think how much I loved this little town, almost as if I had some deep connection to it. Well, I did. I'd spent lots of time and money here over the past six years.

The first shop I stepped into, one I'd never seen before, was perfect. Beautifully handwoven scarves and shawls abounded, hung from clever wrought iron racks. A young woman with a dark brown braid that hung halfway to her waist stepped forward. She pushed her hair off her shoulder, and said, "Let me know if I can be of any service to ye."

"She looks like my goddaughter, my niece Lioslaith, my oldest brother's second child." Macbeth's voice was right behind me. "Ask if she's of the Clan Farquharson."

I ignored him. "These scarves are beautifully made." I

ran my hand along one with a particularly vivid purple stripe down the middle.

"They're all natural dyes that I make from plants. The wool comes from sheep in this shire."

"This is your work? How do you ever find the time to do it and keep the store running as well?"

"Aye, weel, the winters are a bit long." She smiled. "I dinna mind the weaving for hours at a time. It soothes me like, and I can make enough to last me through the tourist season."

"I'm looking for a Farquharson tartan." Macbeth—I hated that name—made a slight harrumph, but didn't say anything.

"Like your own shawl, ye mean? That's a fine one. May I touch it?"

"Of course you may." I extended one corner of it. "Isn't it soft?"

"Aye," she said. "Soft indeed." She ran her hand along the white stripe. "Here's the weaver's mark." She must have seen my confusion. "Many of us put one unexpected line in our favorite pieces. It's like a signature." She bent almost as if to smell it, but instead she placed her cheek against the smooth wool. "An old shawl, is it? It feels like it has the years behind it."

I knew what she meant. While I nodded, she turned and lifted a particular scarf from a stack on a nearby shelf. She held it beside my shawl. "See? This Farquharson is bright and springy and new." I nodded again. "While yours"—and she smoothed the flat of her hand along the curve of my arm, tracing the pattern of green overlapping stripes—"yours has more weight to it, like someone has cried over it." She stopped self-consciously. "Laughter, too. That's in it as weel."

"Ask her clan," the ghost urged.

"May I ask what your name is?"

Her smile was sweet, like an early spring dawn. "It's Leslie Gordon."

"Gordon," he sputtered. "She couldna be—not with a chin like that." I ignored him and smiled encouragingly at Leslie.

"My husband's a Gordon, but I"—and she held the blue and green tartan under her chin—"was born a Farquharson."

He gave a grunt, somewhere between satisfaction and vindication.

"That's lovely," I said, and a ripple of something—amazement? delight?—ran up my back. I extended my hand. "I'm Peggy Winn," I said.

Behind me, Macbeth said, "Wynne? I didna know ye were Welsh." I ignored him. Again.

"Wynne," Leslie said. "That's a Welsh name, isn't it?"

I couldn't win. I cringed at the unintended pun. "We spell it W-i-n-n. My dad's family is Welsh," I explained, "but my mother's family left here in the seventeen hundreds."

"Ah, yes," she said. "The forty-five."

"What would be a forty-five?"

This was no time for a history lesson. "No," I said. "They emigrated well before Culloden. Our town was founded in seventeen twenty."

"What would ye be meaning by *before Culloden*?"

I had no intention of telling him about the slaughter of the clans at Culloden in April of 1746. That was one part of history he did not need to know.

By the time I left the shop, I'd bought five scarves—hopefully with nobody attached to them—and arranged to ship a large quantity of her shawls and scarves to Vermont. By being able to order directly from her, I could keep the price fairly reasonable for my customers, and she'd make more money than if she had sold her scarves through a catalog company. We were both delighted.

A few minutes later I detoured off the Atholl Road to

revisit the shop where I'd found my shawl—Peigi's shawl. I walked past several stone buildings, each behind a low stone wall, looking for the arbor and the dark peach-colored flowers with the cinnamon scent.

When I finally found it, the flowers didn't smell the way I'd remembered. I walked in and found, to my dismay, a brightly lit showroom of standard tourist fare. Not an ancient plaid anywhere, and no trio of old women, either. This time, the ripple down my spine was definitely not delight.

That night before bed, I made up my mind. "I have to take the shawl back with me," I told the ghost, "but I'm going to release you."

"Release me?" The moon shining in through the window shimmered just behind, and partly through, his head when he cocked it to one side. I never used the Sinclair's electricity if I could help it. Candles gave such a gentle light, and now it shimmered on the folds of his kilt.

"Yes. Leave you behind. There has to be a way to do it." He frowned, and I hastily explained. "I've thoroughly enjoyed meeting you, but this whole arrangement is a bit, um, unwieldy. I thought if you stayed here, without the shawl, you might be able to . . . to go back . . . to get back, that is, to where you came from."

He looked around. "But I came from here."

"I mean, to *when* you came from. You can't possibly enjoy being so . . . so tied to me."

There was a glint in his eyes, but he turned away and looked out the window.

"If I can figure out a good way—and it must involve a ritual of some sort—wouldn't you be happy to go back to your own time?"

"Only if Peigi . . ." His voice died away to a whisper.

I turned to the dresser and lifted the pewter candlestick. Three years ago I'd read a book about the ancient religions of the world. A lot of it had struck me as nothing but mumbo jumbo, but I had been drawn to something called the Ritual of Letting Go—useful, the book said, when someone was dying a lingering, painful death. That was about the time my twin brother had fallen off the dinosaur skeleton he'd been repairing and broken his back, and I remembered reading the chant and praying I'd never have to use it, but I'd memorized it just in case. He'd survived, even though his legs were useless.

My wee ghostie wasn't leaving life, really. That was for sure, but in a way he was leaving the shawl, and it was a sort of life to him. Anyway, he must be delighted at the thought of finding Peigi again.

So I lit the yellowed beeswax candle. He was astonished when I used a match. Once we got that straightened out, I sang softly about leaving this world behind, about moving into the place where souls go, about cutting the ties that bind. Halfway through, he sat on the chair and looked at me. Finally, he lowered his head.

"Good-bye," I said.

"I thank ye."

I folded the shawl, tucked it in my carry-on, and blew out the candle.

He was gone. And I felt bereft.

7

Home to Hamelin

Mrs. Sinclair was such a dear. She always had a full breakfast ready for me, even though my departure was so early in the morning. I would be exhausted by the time I reached Hamelin, but this trip, what with finding Leslie Farquharson Gordon and her magnificent handwoven pieces, had been particularly rewarding. Ultimately, it would turn out to be highly profitable for both of us. I was sure of that.

Then there was the shawl.

Mrs. Sinclair placed a well-laden plate in front of me and admonished me to "Eat hearty. Ye're as light as duck down."

I did as she said, knowing that the airplane food would leave a great deal to be desired.

With a big dose of regret that my visit was over so soon, I ate the last bites of my sausage, downed my tea, and wiped my mouth. "Absolutely lovely, Mrs. Sinclair. I cannot thank you enough."

I'd paid my bill the night before. I liked my last morning, short as it was, to flow smoothly without interruption.

Instead of clearing the table as was her wont, though, Mrs. Sinclair sat down across from me. "Will ye be careful, dearie?"

"Oh, the trip is nothing. I've done it so many times, I think I could change planes with my eyes closed." I smiled at her sweet concern.

"That is no what I'm talking of, as ye well know." She took hold of my hand across the narrow table and turned it palm up. "At least your life line is long." She traced a line that ran from between my thumb and forefinger and wound around the fleshy base of my thumb and onto my wrist.

I opened my mouth, but she forestalled any comment by pointing to what I can only describe as a starburst of lines that radiated out from my life line a third of the way along it. I'd never noticed it before.

She laid my hand carefully on the table, as if afraid it might break. "In all the years I've read palms, yours is only the second one I've ever seen with this."

"But what does it mean?" I folded my other hand on my lap.

"That I canna say." She tapped my palm. "Ye may not want to tell me what happened on yon mountainside, but I do know 'twas something that will change your life."

I stared at her in some consternation. I honestly didn't know what to say. Had she seen the ghost? Did she know?

"Nae, dearie. I dinna ask that ye tell me anything. All I want is for ye to take care of your sweet self in a way that maybe ye havena thought to do in the past."

I lowered my head, studied my hands, and when I looked up, she'd picked up the plates and moved to the sink. At that point, Mr. Sinclair walked into the kitchen and told me the car was ready for me "if ye be ready for it."

I stood. "Mrs. Sinclair?"

"Yes, dearie?"

"The next time I'm here, I may be able to tell you some

of this." I bent to give old Bruce a good-bye pat on his wiry head, and he woofed gently. "Is that all right?"

She smiled slowly and her eyes crinkled up at the corners. "Whenever the time is right for you."

My thoughts bounced between the ghost—and Mason, damn him—all the way home.

I ran into a heavy Vermont rain soon after leaving the Burlington airport. Even though it stopped halfway to Hamelin, I was a good deal later than usual getting home. Karaline opened my front door and headed toward me as I backed into my driveway. Part of me wanted to talk with her for hours, to tell her everything that had happened. The other part of me just wanted to take a hot shower and sleep for three days.

She bounded down the ramp, her dark pink knee-length sweater bouncing around her black-clad legs. At six foot one, New York–model thin, and with a nose that preceded her in grand style, Karaline always looks something like a wading bird, maybe a blue heron. This evening, in that sweater, she looked like a flamingo. Next to her, I was nothing but a bedraggled wren.

She opened the back door and pulled out my carry-on. "Come on in. I've got dinner ready."

Karaline's idea of dinner is always leftovers from the Logg Cabin. Fine with me. I hoped I could keep my eyes open long enough to taste something.

I bent to scratch Shorty between the ears and run my hand along his silky back. He meowed his welcome. It was good to be home.

The fire crackling in the wood stove drew me to its heavenly warmth. I rubbed my hands together and then turned so my backside could absorb some of the heat. Karaline grinned. "Still a little bit chilly in the evenings."

I looked around my comfy living room at the vases of scarlet long-stemmed roses placed here and there around the room. "What's with all the roses?" Even as I asked, I had a sinking feeling I knew the answer.

Karaline read my mind. "You're right. They're from Mason. No cards, just like before. Ruth's been delivering them every day. I called her and asked her to stop since you were out of town, but she said they'd been prepaid, and she felt obligated to deliver them."

This was all just part of his pattern. The whole time we'd been together, every time he hurt my feelings, said something nasty to me, or forgot something I'd asked him to do, he'd sent me flowers or buy me a piece of jewelry, and he thought that would wipe out whatever he'd done. The roses were another link on that chain. I used to like roses, but I'd gotten to where I hated them—he seemed to think they would make every-thing all better, when what he really needed was a change of attitude. Maybe Andrea had done me a favor at that.

What did he expect—a thank-you note? If he wanted to waste perfectly good money on me, that was his problem, but I didn't have to respond. "I'll take them to the compost pile tomorrow," I said.

I took the carry-on from her, pulled out the shawl, and draped it over my arm. It wasn't that cold here in the living room, but I'd probably need it in the rest of the house.

"Nice," she said. "New?"

"New to me," I said, "but it's really rather old."

She gave it a long look and nodded. "The sixties? You'll look like a hippie in it."

"Older than that," I said, moving away from her. I took a quick look at my bonsai tree and the jade plant. In the kitchen, I headed for the African violets in the window. Karaline always cared for them when I was away. "The plants look great. Thanks."

"You're welcome." She slid my suitcase across the hall to the bottom of the stairs while I washed my hands, then waited for Shorty to settle on my lap. I wrapped the shawl around my shoulders. Shorty snuggled against it and purred.

"Rough trip?" Her voice, rich and smooth as the pure maple syrup she used in her restaurant, settled around me like comfort food.

"Not really. I just spent a lot of time worrying about . . . well, you know." She nodded grimly. I smoothed the shawl, wondering why I felt so reluctant to tell her about the ghost I'd met and left behind.

She ladled a hearty stew into one of my handcrafted-pottery soup bowls. "You look like a crumpled ball of paper. You need some sleep." With each crisp sentence she plopped another ladleful into the bowl. "But first, eat." She lifted a cutting board laden with one of her homemade loaves onto the table and set to work slicing it into good-sized chunks.

If my ghost were here—if he could eat, that is—he'd probably spear a chunk with his *sgian-dubh*. I missed him. Had I made a mistake in leaving him behind? Had he found his Peigi?

We chatted without much enthusiasm. Karaline was right. I felt exhausted. Just eating was effort enough.

She used a slab of bread to sop up the last of the stew juices. "I'm gonna wash these dishes, and you're going to take a nice hot bath and go to bed." She held up her hand. "I know it's early, but you'll probably sleep for fourteen hours."

I grumbled a bit but finally agreed.

She waited for me to finish my last bite, picked up the bowls, and shooed me out.

At the door, with Shorty under my arm, I turned back to thank her. My ghost! He stood behind the chair I'd just left. My ghost. "What are you doing here?"

He shrugged.

Karaline looked over her shoulder at me. "I just told you. I'm washing the dishes. Now, go to bed. You're more exhausted than you think." She flicked her wet fingers at me and turned back to the sink. "I'll lock the door on my way out."

I looked back once as I headed up the stairs. The ghost, trailing behind me, raised his shoulders and his hands in that gesture that said *What could I do?*

"Why aren't you in Scotland?" I spoke even before I'd opened my bedroom door.

"What?" Karaline called from the kitchen.

"Nothing. I mean, good night." I motioned him into my room. "You were supposed to stay there."

"Weel, now." He reached out a hand toward Shorty, who sniffed once and nuzzled his head into the crook of my arm. "Your singing over the wee yellow candle sounded lovely, but I canna see that it did much good."

"It wasn't all that wee," I said, and was appalled at the petulance in my voice. It hadn't worked.

He ignored my whining. "Mayhap ye should ha' asked Mistress Sinclair for help."

I didn't even try to whisper. "I couldn't do that. She'd think I was crazy."

"She wouldna. She is a very wise woman, aye?" He waved his hands at me, palm down. "And hush your voice a bit."

I thought back to her reading of my palm. He hadn't been there then. He'd been in the shawl. "What makes you think she's so wise?" I think I sounded suspicious.

"I do believe she saw me but chose not to talk about it."

"No. She couldn't have."

He frowned, and his very blue eyes seemed to darken, but maybe it was just the shadows. My bedroom drew in the morning light, but it tended to get a bit gloomy in the early evening. And it was downright dark at this hour. I turned on the overhead light. His head jerked up as it came on. "How did ye do that?"

"It's called electricity. I'll tell you all about it later."

A sound that wasn't quite a growl started in his toes and

went right up to his head. "I'm thinking there is far too much to learn in this world ye live in."

"Yeah? You think so?" I dropped Shorty on the bed. "And what if I told you I don't know how to start a fire without matches?"

"What are—"

"Those things I used at Mrs. Sinclair's to light the wee candle." I sounded positively vitriolic. "I also don't know how to skin a rabbit. I don't even know how to kill a rabbit, much less skin it."

He made that growl sound again. "Ye lie. Even a bairn learns early how to skin a rabbit."

"We don't eat many bunnies nowadays."

"Bun—"

"I also don't know how to work a butter churn—"

"That is so sim—"

"Would you hush? Children in this time know how to use a microwave and cook a frozen pizza and blend up a fruit smoothie."

"Wha—"

"And they learn pretty quickly how to cross the street without getting run over."

"Why—"

"Furthermore, they know the Preamble to the Constitution, while you couldn't even find America on a wall map! But children in your time learn about butter churns and hunting and skinning things and starting fires. And if you'd stayed in Scotland when you were supposed to, we wouldn't be having this conversation."

I paused, but only long enough to take a deep breath. "The point I'm making—and there is a point to this—is that you have no more to learn in this time than I'd have if I somehow traveled back to your time, so would you please just can it until I can get you to a library? Then you can learn everything you need to know."

Silence. For a long time. And then he said, rather huffily I thought, "Ye think that will help when I canna even turn the pages?"

He had a point, but I wasn't going to concede. I cast about for a change of topic. "You need a name."

"I have a name, a verra good name." He turned his back on me.

"Yeah, right, but it's unpronounceable, and *Macbeth* has really bad connotations nowadays. I can't call you Mac, because everyone will think I'm talking to our chief of police. Mac Campbell," I added by way of explanation.

He crossed his arms over his chest. I noticed the muscles roping up his forearms. "I dinna trust Clan Campbell."

"Oh, yeah. Because of Glencoe?"

"What are ye speaking of? Glencoe is home to Macdonalds, not Campbells."

I was a little sparse on Scottish history. Maybe the massacre at Glencoe hadn't happened yet. If so, I wasn't going to be the one to tell him about it.

"Never mind. I'm going to call you . . ." I looked him up and down. His long full-sleeved shirt was of a coarse grayish fabric. Homespun, I thought. Well, naturally it was homespun. The Industrial Revolution hadn't happened yet. It took a woman an entire year to spin the thread and weave the kilt material. The blue-and-green pattern matched the shawl I wore, and the top ends were held in place over his right shoulder with a carved wooden circle, threaded through with what looked like a piece of antler. It was primitive and powerful and, somehow, exactly right.

He'd let go of the handle of his dirk, but it was still clearly visible in the . . . scabbard, I guess you'd call it . . . hanging from a heavy leather strap he wore over his left shoulder. I wondered how he managed not to whack people when he walked past them. "Hmm. I'm going to call you Dirk."

"Why?"

I pointed.

"My dagger?"

"It's called a dirk." Why did I have to teach a Scotsman about something as elementary as this?

"Nae. 'Tis my dagger."

Then it dawned on me. A lot of words had changed between then and now. "Nowadays we call it a *dirk*. Anyway, I like the name."

He muttered something unintelligible.

"I have to take a shower before I turn in."

He headed for the bookshelves next to my dresser. "A shower? And what would that be?" His voice was overly polite and only mildly inquisitive.

"I have to bathe." He turned around, and I thought his eyebrows arched, but he turned back away so quickly I couldn't be sure.

"Is the woman out there your servant to carry the water in for ye?"

"She's not my servant. She's my friend. Tell you what: Let me just fold you up in the shawl. You can take a nice little rest, and I'll explain it all later."

His fist clenched. "Ye say that entirely too frequently." His *r*'s rolled so much, I thought his tongue would shake loose.

"Well, I'm sorry, but I just don't know whether I can trust you." Instead of snapping back at me, he began to laugh. I crossed my arms. "What on earth are you cackling about?"

He gasped a couple of times before he could settle down. "I canna pull out a chair. I canna open a door. I canna close it. I canna even decide for myself whither to go because yon shawl pulls me along with ye." He ran a wide, strong hand through his shoulder-length black hair. "And ye wonder what I might do if I see ye in your shift?" He leaned against the dresser and crossed his arms. His face grew solemn. "I dinna like the feeling of . . . of nothingness that I find in yon shawl. If I promise on the honor of my clan to keep my back turned, will ye please just get on with it and let me sit quiet by all these lovely books of yours?"

Chastened, I pushed my comfy red chair over beside the bookcase, facing the window, and draped the shawl on the back of it. I halfway expected him to disappear when I let go, but he sat and leaned against the shawl. "My thanks," was all he said. A daddy longlegs spider crawled up the arm of the chair and paused with just a whisper of space between its nose and Dirk's arm. Fine with me. Spiders ate bugs, and Dirk seemed to attract spiders like a kilted man attracted curious females.

Half an hour later, my skin still tingling from the blessedly hot water, I wrapped my fuzzy blue bathrobe firmly around the green oversized UVM T-shirt I slept in and stepped out of the bathroom. Dirk was bent over the white table near the door where I always kept a coffee-table book. I'd been looking at *Among Trees*, a book of photographs by Sean Kernan, off and on for a couple of weeks, simply relishing the gorgeous black-and-white photos of trees from all around the world.

I walked up beside him. "Lovely, isn't it?" I brushed my hand across the dust jacket, a photo of tall pines, most of them limbless twenty feet up or so, with what looked to me like early morning sun oozing through mist.

"Aye, it is indeed. I have never seen a painting so precise."

"It's not a painting," I said. "This is called a photograph."

He thought briefly. "Drawing with light?"

At my perplexed look, he went on, "I learned some of the Greek and Latin when I was a boy. Father Marcus was a good man, although he sometimes tried to beat the knowledge into me." He rubbed his backside a bit absentmindedly. "My father, though, didna think learning was a' that important."

"How many years did you study with Father Marcus?"

"Until I was twelve, grown enough to do a man's work all day."

"You knew Latin and Greek at *twelve*?"

"Och, aye. Not as much as Father Marcus, but enough to get by." His hand hovered over the book.

"What did you call it? Painting with light?"

"Drawing. That is the *graph* part. 'Tis a Greek word. And *photo*, of course, means light."

"Oh, of course."

I don't think he caught my sarcasm, because he continued smoothly, "So it would be light-drawing. Lovely." He paused, and added, "How is it done?"

"It's kind of complicated." I opened the book at random and flipped back to the introduction. "Here, you can read this while I write in my journal."

My poor neglected journal. I'd written in it only that one night in Scotland. How on earth could I sum up everything that had happened in the past week?

As I settled back against my pillows and pulled Shorty close to my side, I watched Dirk. He wasn't simply reading. He devoured the book. He kept brushing his hands across it, as if it were somehow holy. A treasure indeed. I sighed and examined my journal. I took my journal so for granted. What on earth would I have done if I'd lived in a time when women routinely were not taught to read? Ghastly thought.

I absolutely did not want to write about Mason—no sense having him on paper since he was no longer in my life. I could write about Scotland, the Sinclairs, and Pitlochry. The shawl. Its resident wee ghostie.

Engrossed in writing, I didn't notice Dirk beside the bed until I set down my ballpoint and he appeared in my peripheral vision.

"Since ye have paused writing in the wee book"—his voice went soft when he said that word, and I could hear the awe in it—"would ye mind owermuch coming to turn the page for me?"

"Sure." I moved Shorty off my lap and pushed the comforter back. His eyes widened as I swung my bare legs over the edge. I grabbed my bathrobe.

He readjusted his plaid, pulling it more firmly up on his shoulder. "I have one question, if ye dinna mind."

I looked up at him. "What's your question?" This was no wee ghostie. I don't think I'd fathomed until then just how tall he was. Except in the porta potty, but I'd almost forgotten that. I was a sucker for broad shoulders. My eyes came well below his Adam's apple. It lurched a bit as he swallowed.

"Where did ye hide the inkwell when ye wrote?"

8

Mason Kilmarty

Mason would have kicked himself if Andrea hadn't beaten him to it. Out into the cold—well, all right, so it wasn't all that chilly. Out on the streets, though. The walk home from Andrea's usually took him only a few minutes, but he'd backtracked up to Hickory Lane to take a look at Peggy's house. All those roses he'd sent her. She loved roses. She'd said so when they first started dating. She could have called to thank him. Why hadn't she?

A light was on upstairs. Her car in the driveway. He walked as far as the bottom of the wheelchair ramp before he chickened out. She'd made her feelings pretty clear with that punch she'd given him last week. He rubbed his chin where the bruise was. She sure packed a wallop. Maybe she'd changed her mind, though.

He stood watching from the end of the driveway until the light went out. As he turned away from Peggy's house, back toward his apartment in the middle of Hamelin, he vowed he'd give her something expensive for her birthday; it was coming up soon. He did know it was her thirtieth. He remembered that much. The other two—Gilda and Andrea—they'd just been flings. But Peggy was the real thing.

Once he got to Main Street, the street lamps puddled pale gold circles directly beneath their poles, closehanded as a string of misers, but Mason avoided even the edges of their light.

He paused across the street from Sweetie's Jellybean Emporium. He'd stop by tomorrow and buy a pound or two.

The breeze picked up, swirling his kilt around his legs, and a stray piece of paper skittered across the street and into the gutter. He stepped away from the window, debating whether or not to run after it. Peggy would have. But Peggy was not a factor at the moment. Unless maybe she'd like to have him back. It couldn't hurt. Maybe it would bring him good luck. He darted after the paper and scooped it up. He unfolded it, but here between streetlights, he couldn't see what was written. Looked like a list of some sort. He crumpled it carelessly and stuffed it in his sporran. There.

Mason squared his shoulders and stepped back onto the sidewalk, intending to walk on home, but a glint of moving light caught his eye. Peggy's store. Nobody should be there this time of night. He crossed the street again and stopped at the big display window. Through a tiny crack in the curtains behind the mannequins, he saw the vague form of someone moving near the back wall.

Peggy may have thrown him out—just like Andrea had, damn her hide—but he wasn't going to let somebody hurt Peggy. He felt for his cell phone, remembered he'd left it at Andrea's, and swore under his breath.

Mason eased his way over to the front door and quietly tried the handle. Locked. Just as well, he thought. That bell over the door would have given him away.

He turned left and headed alongside the empty courtyard toward the alley behind the Pitcairn Building.

A single car stood in the alley near the ScotShop's back

door. Mason thought it looked vaguely familiar. He was sure he'd seen it recently. By the time he reached the door, he'd remembered—and it was someone who had no right to be there. The door stood slightly ajar. Mason took a deep breath, straightened his kilt, clenched his fists, and stepped inside.

9

Mirror Talk

The next morning, Dirk was gone. So was the shawl.

I searched frantically through the house. Kitchen, pantry, living room, office, the guest bath. I even looked in closets, which was stupid, come to think of it. He couldn't open doors. Nothing. He wasn't anywhere.

Could he have gotten outside somehow? I turned the handle on the kitchen door, but the thought of Mr. Pitcairn stopped me. My friendly neighbor from the old, old house next door loved to talk over the fence. It didn't matter what time of day I went out, he always seemed to show up, almost as if he'd been waiting for me, usually with helpful advice about landscaping or mowing. I knew he was lonely. His wife used to invite Karaline and me to dinner about once a month, but she died a year ago, and he'd become something of a recluse.

I looked down at my sleep shirt. Would not do. Nothing for it but to get dressed first. I headed upstairs.

And shrieked when I charged into the bathroom. Dirk sat on the edge of the tub, fingering the knobs for hot and cold water. The shawl was thrown across one shoulder, over his plaid. He stood quickly. "I always heard that people cry out when they see a ghost. Now I know 'tis true." He smiled. "Although ye didna cirmest like that when ye saw me the first time."

Keermist? What kind of word was that?

"Why, I wonder. Why did ye no?"

I was still a bit angry with him for scaring me, but after a moment's reflection, I didn't want to admit how relieved I was to have found him. I walked the few steps to the sink and turned on the hot water. Looking at him in the mirror, I matched his smile. "You seemed so natural in that meadow. You didn't scare me, or at least not until I realized I could see through you a bit."

He watched the water running for several seconds, shook his head, and looked at me in the mirror. "How are these made?" He gestured vaguely in front of him.

"How are what made? Faucets?"

"This mirror. I saw only one in my time. 'Twas polished brass. My face looked brown and distorted in it."

"Oh." I turned off the water. No sense in wasting it. "There was this period called the Industrial Revolution. It started in the, uh, the seventeen hundreds, I think, right around the time the steam engine was invented."

"Yes?" He lifted his dark eyebrows in inquiry.

"Um, that was a time when people found ways to make things using machines."

"Things?" He smiled at my reflection. "Like this mirror?"

I turned to face him directly. "Uh-huh, and thread and huge looms so fabric could be made more cheaply."

Before I could keep going with my litany of the wonders of civilization, he looked down at his sturdy homespun shirt and his luscious hand-woven plaid and then at my UVM T-shirt. "Aye, cheaply," he said. "And the people who used to make those things? What happened to them?"

Visions of child labor swam through my head. Soot,

polluted rivers, tubercular factory workers, the Ghost of Christmas Present with two starving children beneath his cloak. I turned and opened the hot water tap. "They had jobs in factories, where the things were made." It was a cop-out, but I couldn't bear the thought of his look if he knew what steam engines and mirrors and fabric had really cost humanity.

He peered over my shoulder at the water. "That must be the source of the waterfall sound I heard last night when ye bathed, but it was louder somehow then."

I turned my head and gestured toward the tub. "That was the shower." This was hopeless. How could I possibly teach him everything I'd spent my life simply knowing? I shooed him out of the bathroom and into the hall. "You go somewhere else. Just stay in the house." He was halfway down the hall before I realized he was more than a yard or so away from me. "Wait! How'd you do that?"

He turned and spread his hands. "Do what?"

"You're not next to me. You've always had to be"—I swept my arms to indicate a wide circle around me—"closer."

He wrinkled his forehead. "Aye. That's true. Mayhap 'tis because this is your house, and your spirit spreads through it." He raised a hand to his chest and fingered the shawl. "Or mayhap 'tis because I hold my Peigi's work so close to me." He spread the edge of it out, and I saw the flicker of the white line. "This is the first thing I have been able to lift, the first thing I can truly touch, since I came into this world of yours, this time of yours."

I felt a totally unreasonable pang of—jealousy. I was jealous of a woman who'd been dead 650 years? Yes. I hated to admit it—even if only to myself. I certainly wasn't going to admit it to him.

"I'm going to get dressed. I'll be out in a little while." I shut the door firmly between us.

I don't know what he did while I was getting ready for the day, but I found him standing at my kitchen sink, looking out the window toward the bird feeders.

I wrenched a banana from a bunch hanging on the banana hook and peeled it. Dirk watched in fascinated silence.

"Go sit over there while I cook me some eggs."

"Ah, eggs. Aye. Where do ye keep your chickens? I saw none outside."

I opened the fridge. "You and I are going to take a little trip to the grocery store in a couple of days. That will explain a lot."

After my usual breakfast of fried eggs, two slabs of pan-fried toast, and two links of extra-hot sausage, I excused myself to brush my teeth. Dirk's teeth were in awfully good shape. I'd noticed that right away—well, in the porta potty. I turned around and leaned my head against the door jam. "Did you have toothbrushes back then?"

"What would be a—"

"Never mind, I'm sure you didn't. I just don't understand why your teeth are so healthy. Didn't everybody back then have teeth that rotted out of their heads?"

His face went through a series of contortions. I couldn't tell whether he was getting ready to laugh or growl. "Nae. Not everybody." I must have looked unconvinced. "My grandmam taught us all to use wee twigs of willow trees to clean our teeth."

"Twigs? How could that help?"

"We mashed the ends until they were soft-like." He made a motion so like an actor in a Crest commercial I laughed.

"Let's go," I called to Dirk a few minutes later. Shorty lay snoozing on the couch. I stroked his back and he fluttered one eye halfway open. "Guard the house," I told him, as I always did, although why I bothered I had no idea. Shutting the door behind us, I stepped toward the head of the ramp and stopped short. Another dozen deep red roses stood in a floral delivery vase. Prepaid. Crap. I pushed the vase aside with the toe of my shoe. More food for the compost pile this afternoon.

"Yon flowers dinna look like any rose I ever saw."

"They're not, I'm sure. These are grown in a greenhouse, and they've been bred for size and color, but they don't smell nearly as nice as the heirloom roses—the kind you must have known when you . . . back then."

"When I was alive."

"Yeah," I said, thinking how very alive he looked right now, with his ebony hair spilling onto his shoulders, catching the morning light. *Stop it, Peggy. He's a ghost.*

He stepped back a pace and studied the blooms. "They are the color of spilled blood before it darkens."

I shivered, although I've never been particularly superstitious. "Let's go. I want to get my shop open. Two tour buses are on the schedule today." I headed down the front walk. "When people come into the store, don't say a word."

Dirk stepped in front of me, and I had to stop so I wouldn't run into him. I didn't even want to think what would happen if I passed right through him. Yuck.

"Ye dinna have to keep telling me that. I am not simpleminded."

"Sorry. I just don't want to look like an—" I stopped myself. Why did I worry what he thought about my language? Dirk was a ghost for heaven's sake. Still, he was more effective than my mother at keeping my mouth clean.

"Like what?"

"Like I'm talking to the wind."

"I dinna think that is what ye planned to say." He wiggled his eyebrows at me. "Am I right, now?" When I didn't reply, he added, "I will try to stay quiet in your wee store."

Mr. Pitcairn's slightly adenoidal voice drifted into my consciousness. I'd been so intent on Dirk, I hadn't thought about my next-door neighbor. "Are you starting to talk to yourself?" He chuckled and wagged his finger at me from his front porch.

I didn't have time to talk, so I just waved and kept walking. Mr. P reminded me of nothing so much as an aging basset hound with his stumpy legs, massive chest, and slightly bowed arms. He had brown hair and baggy eyes. The only things missing were a tail and droopy ears.

His wife, before she died, had been chatty, round, the stereotypical sweet little woman. He'd always been a basset, though. Even when she was alive, he'd harbored an underlying sadness. Two months after her funeral, he'd resumed the monthly dinner invitations, although he never included Karaline anymore. I felt too sorry for him to decline, even though he wasn't much of a cook.

I wondered occasionally if he thought I was a slob. His yard was meticulously maintained, unlike my rather jungle-like assortment of native shrubs under carefully positioned trees. Fat bees bumbled through the clover and dandelions. My weedy yard was sunny in the winter and shady in the summer, and I loved it that way. Mr. P's yard, on the other hand, was golf course quality. Mow, mow, mow. Every couple of days, he religiously deadheaded the impatiens at the foot of his mailbox. Any errant grass blades that dared to come up in his flowerbed were yanked immediately. Heaven forefend that there should be a dandelion in his lawn. I'd seen him wield a hedge trimmer with a vengeance whenever the hedge on the far side of his yard grew any delinquent shoots.

I glanced back over my shoulder. My foxgloves were getting a bit scroungy. I'd have to take a closer look. Later.

Dirk muttered something under his breath.

"What did you say?" I whispered it, trying not to move my lips, still aware of Mr. P watching me from his front porch.

"I asked if ye were a healer."

"Why would you think that?"

He pointed his nose toward the masses of flowers. "Ye have foxglove for the hearts that skip, garlic for ears that pain, elderberry for the flux, and"—here he pointed to where the weeping willow in my backyard towered above the house—"and willow bark for heads that pound. I dinna know any of the others. My Peigi taught me those four."

"I didn't know you could use garlic for earaches."

"And ye call yourself a healer?"

"No, I don't, but what's the garlic for?"

"My Peigi put garlic in the ears of children who wept for the pain, and they stopped their weeping eventually."

Maybe garlic counteracted bacterial infection. I didn't ask Dirk about it, though. Bacteria would have sounded like monsters to him if I'd tried to explain them.

"I'd be happy to mow your lawn for you," Mr. P called out to me. "I have plenty of time."

"Thanks, Mr. P, but I like it on the long side." He'd probably mow down all my native wildflowers if given half a chance, and there wouldn't be any more clover for the bees, either.

His mouth turned down as he compressed his lips. Poor Mr. P, having to put up with me as a neighbor. I know it was rude, and I hated to hurt his feelings—he really was a nice man—but I just ushered Dirk into the car and left with a wave.

"I'll see you for dinner tonight," he called after me.

Rats. I'd forgotten that.

10

Mannequin Down

My favorite mannequin lay sideways on the floor near the back of the shop. I could just barely see it around the vertical blinds on the front door. Why were the blinds and curtains closed? Gilda should have left them open. There was too much reflection of the early morning sun on the glass to see clearly, but that bright splotch of red on the floor had to be the MacKillop tartan kilt we'd buckled onto Percy last week.

Percy was my full-sized one-of-a-kind mannequin, complete with jointed and lockable arms, legs, and neck. He usually posed in the display window, looking out across Hamelin's main shopping street toward Sweeties, the candy store up the way, almost as if he were longing for a handful of their trademark jelly beans. Just last week, though, Gilda and I had moved him to the back, where he seemed to be pointing to the merchandise in the big bookcase. So, who'd lain him down? And why? Probably my crazy cousin, up to another one of his practical jokes. Practical? What a misnomer. There was nothing practical about moving my mannequin.

"Ye seem worrit again," Dirk said.

"Somebody fell over in my shop."

He looked vaguely alarmed. "Should we no go to help?"

I laughed. "It's one of my mannequins." I waved vaguely toward the fake people in the display window. I should have known that wouldn't be enough of an explanation. With one part of my mind I paid attention to Dirk's fashion-industry lesson; with the other half, I looked again. It had to be Percy. We'd sold out of all our other bright red kilts and skirts over the past few weeks, and my latest shipment had been back-ordered. I sent dire mental warnings to that wholesaler. They'd better come today, or I'd be less than happy indeed.

Why did all the purchases come in lumps? One month everyone wanted green tartans, the next month the blues would predominate, and lately it had been red, red, and more red. As red as the dozen roses on my front porch. When Mason first started sending me roses after each of our arguments, I'd persuaded Ruth, the florist, to stop wiring the stems. One less thing to throw away. I now had the most expensive compost pile in the state if not in the entire northeast, and the flower shop was thriving. How much would those dozens of long-stemmed roses have added up to? Mason and I had sure had a lot of fights.

I was dimly aware of Dirk's commentary beside me but didn't register it. I pushed away from the window and smoothed out my tartan skirt. Even I recognized that as nothing more than a nervous gesture. Whatever made me remember Mason and his stupid red roses anyway? I had more important things to think about, like the red plaid on the floor of my shop and the fact that I didn't have any extra red kilts to sell. I'd gone through the storeroom in back twice last week hoping to find one. I rooted around in my purse, looking for my keys.

If a MacKillop walked in today wanting a kilt of his clan, I'd have to undress Percy. I knew, from past experience, that I'd have to take Percy into the back room before disrobing him. Even though he wasn't completely anatomically correct, the clothing change could be disconcerting to my customers. I could dress him in one of the heathery hunting plaids. Maybe the muted Sinclair tartan, I thought, and smiled, thinking of Mr. Sinclair in his kilt. I wished I could have stayed longer this time, but I'd had to get back here for the surprise birthday party Karaline was throwing on Saturday, the one I wasn't supposed to know about.

Without Mason in my life, I'd have plenty of time on my hands. Of course, I had a ghost to fill . . .

". . . not a word I have said, did ye?"

"Sorry, Dirk. I've had a lot on my mind, and I guess I was just thinking of . . . of other things."

"'Tis as weel. I havena been too sure about many of the things I see around me. This town is bigger than Pitlochry, is it no?"

"Well, it's America—that's the name of this country—and we do a lot of things differently here."

"Och, aye? What things?"

I didn't answer him. Instead, I had one of those scary-movie feelings when the alien or the shark is about to attack. Should have been some creepy music in the background. *Get a grip, Winn.*

I shifted my purse higher on my shoulder and scrabbled again for my keys. This was not a good start to the workday. Percy's legs were amazingly sturdy; Gilda must not have locked the joints well enough. I should have double-checked. She was a dependable assistant, but occasionally she would come in dragging her tail and be virtually useless for half the day. She said it was migraines. Still, no excuse.

Business had been thriving recently, but there wasn't any sense in letting perfectly good display items get damaged. The surprisingly aristocratic-looking Percy was my nicest mannequin. I'd bought him at a fire sale in Brattleboro six years ago when ScotShop had been just a baby. My baby.

I ignored my keys for a moment and stepped back a pace

to look up at *1915*, cut into the stone over the door with a tiny American flag etched on either side of the number. I pointed to the hand-carved sign above the number. *ScotShop—A Piece of Old Scotland*. "My dad's a woodworker. He created custom signs for most of the businesses along Main Street."

"Och, aye? 'Tis verra fine workmanship."

I pointed across the street to the Sweeties sign, visible beneath the green of the tall spreading maples that lined the street. Jelly beans of every color imaginable spilled from an astonishingly realistic candy jar and bounced off the bottom rim of the sign. Dad had really outdone himself on that one. Next door to Sweeties, the Hamelin Hotel sign—"best rest this side of Scotland"—sported a set of bagpipes beside a bed. I'd never thought that looked very restful, but Dad said the owner had insisted.

"There's another one. That's Karaline's restaurant—she serves breakfast and lunch."

"The Logg Cabin," Dirk read. "Logg?"

"That's her last name." I looked again at the sign—a jaunty off-center cabin, pleasantly relaxed against a background of dark green fir trees. The Logg Cabin sat back from the corner of the square, where Hickory Lane dead-ended into Main Street, with a small, beautifully landscaped sunken courtyard between it and the ScotShop. Comfortable wooden benches sat ready for the waiting customers. This arrangement left me with an angled front door and two window walls—one that looked out onto Main Street and one with this gorgeous view of the courtyard. The light that flooded my store was a danger to the fabrics—hence the blinds for extra sunny days—but a delight in saving electricity.

"'Tis a verra long queue of people," Dirk said.

"That's called the breakfast rush. Right after it's over they'll have the lunch rush. The Cabin's very popular with locals and tourists alike." The smell of good cooking wafted across the courtyard and down the street, enough to lure

people in for Karaline's maple pecan pancakes. The line
snaked around the corner of the courtyard, almost all the
way to my front door. A few not-so-patient folk looked at
watches, fiddled with cell phones, and generally put out an
aura of gloom. What good was a vacation if you brought
along your city schedule? The early morning air was still
chilly enough for them to need jackets, but many of the coats
were open. Just the thought of Karaline's meltingly good
food warmed their bodies as well as their hearts. She knew
more about good Vermont home cooking than anybody's
grandmother.

I was willing to bet she'd be over to chat after the Logg
Cabin closed at three. *And me with a ghost to talk around.*
I waved to a few folks I knew, smiled at the others—never
knew when one of them might wander in to look for Scottish
mementos.

The shop was a natural in Hamelin, Vermont, a town
founded by Scots in the early 1700s, where most of the men
wore kilts on an everyday basis. The rent for my third of the
building was steep but well worth it, considering the tourist
trade that came through here. Known to the locals as the
Pitcairn Building, the stone-faced structure was named after
a fellow who was some sort of town big shot a hundred or
so years ago. This end of the building used to house a now-
defunct clothing store, insurance office, hardware store—the
tenants kept changing. I'd transformed it into a small patch
of Scotland.

The ScotShop was quite a bit of work but worth all the
effort. I thoroughly enjoyed my buying trips to Pitlochry
and a half dozen other lovely towns scattered around Scotland. I could import catalog items, of course, and so I did,
but I needed to go there at least once a year to see the tartans
in their natural setting, to see the lamps and statues and
intricate souvenirs in the so-to-speak flesh. You just couldn't
tell from a catalog picture. A case in point was the brooch
on the shoulder of that fallen mannequin's plaid, a running

stag that had looked chintzy in the wholesale catalog but was quite simply stunning pinned to a tartan. And occasionally I found a local crafter, like Leslie Farquharson Gordon, whose work wasn't in the catalogs yet.

I squinted against the light and looked again. Between the bright glare of sunlight and the fingerprints on the outside of the glass, I could hardly see anything, just that splotch of red, but something else looked wrong. Something was missing, but I couldn't place what it was.

The dead bolt lock stuck—again—and I swore softly. The ghost of my diminutive, loudmouthed, and very much alive mother always seemed to hang around right over my shoulder, shaking a finger at my epithets, mild as they tended to be. "Margaret," I could hear my mother saying—she never called me Peggy—"do watch your language." I did try to hold my tongue usually, especially now with Dirk in tow, but Percy was down, and who knew what Percy, heavy as he was, had knocked over. The cranky front door plus the fallen mannequin added up to more than I could take.

Mother faded into the background, though, as the lock cooperated and the bell over the door jingled. I looked around for Dirk. He stood a few feet behind me, eyeing the people in line at the Cabin. I cleared my throat and motioned to him when he turned around. Several of the people in line had turned, too. "Come on in after you finish breakfast," I said, to explain my arm-waving. "I'll be open by then." I ushered Dirk inside, locked the door behind me, and automatically pulled open the blinds to my left.

My six-foot-wide antique hard rock maple bookcase lay facedown on the showroom floor with Percy right beside it. Well, crudbuckets. I dropped my keys and purse onto one of the rocking chairs and scampered across the room. I thought fleetingly that I should be grateful Gilda and I had done some rearranging, so the round table with all the castle lamps on it hadn't been in the line of fall.

"Damn! What happened to you?" As if the bookcase

could tell me. It was my pride and joy. I occasionally wished the bookcase had removable shelves, so I could adjust the height of them, but it worked pretty well. Gilda and I were both good at picking the right-sized merchandise to fit in the right places.

"This isna supposed to be lying down, is it? Is it a sideboard?"

"It's a bookcase."

"A case for books?"

"Yeah," I said, but my mind wasn't on Dirk. I hated to think about the fragile figurines, the bookends, and the mugs lying smashed now beneath the heavy wood, to say nothing of Percy's leg where the bookcase had fallen on it. I tried to lift the bookcase, but the darn thing was way too heavy. "Damn." I didn't know if I was indignant, disgusted, angry, or a little bit of all three. Would insurance cover this?

Sam and Shoe. I'd have to get them to help me. Cousins came in handy at a time like this. I felt real pity for people who moved away from family—until I thought about my mother. There was something to be said for a mobile life. Maybe I could move to Scotland. The winters there couldn't be any colder than the ones here in Vermont, could they? Dirk would enjoy going back. But what would I do there? How could I support myself?

Dad was okay, though. I'd miss him if I left. Ditto with Drew. How could anybody move away from her own twin? And Sam and Shoe were useful. Tall, slightly juvenile at times, salt of the earth, they were both good with our customers, and they looked rather imposing in their kilts when they were working for me. I looked at my watch. Could I call them this early in the morning? Darn right I could.

I made my way back to the front door and rummaged through my purse for my cell. A would-be customer tapped on the glass, and I mouthed, *Sorry, not open yet—nine o'clock,* and pointed to my watch. She smiled, checked her own watch, and nodded. Good. She wasn't mad about it. I had to get this bookcase upright before I let people in. There would most likely be glass to clean up. Heaven only knew what all had broken. Probably everything except the heavy bookends and the guidebooks, and they would have their corners bent. If Percy's leg was badly damaged, I was going to scream. Too bad Dirk couldn't help.

I scrolled down to Shoe's name. He was the more lucid of my two cousins at this time of day. One ring, two. I glanced out the plate glass window. It needed cleaning. Fingerprints. By the fourth ring, when I was readying my brain to leave a voice mail, Shoe answered.

"Yeah?"

Not the world's best communicator.

"I know this is your day off, but can you and Sam come help me pick up the bookcase?"

There was a brief pause as Shoe digested my question. "Pick it up? Where'd it go? Out gallivanting? Has it been arrested?"

"Very funny. It fell over last night."

"Fell over?" I could practically hear the wheels turning, but Shoe couldn't seem to think of a smart-aleck reply to that one. "Fell over," he repeated.

"Yeah. On top of Percy's leg." I tried not to whine, but that was what it sounded like.

"Peh-eh-gee," he whined back at me, making three syllables out of my name, "that bookcase couldn't possibly fall over. I know. I helped you move it in there, and it's as sturdy as . . . a tree," he finished—without much imagination, I thought.

"Yeah? You think? Like Grandpa's beech?" Our Grandpa Winn had lost half his roof a few years back when a sturdy old beech tree succumbed to a heavier-than-usual snowfall. The fact that Grandpa had backed into it with his pickup truck a number of times over the past five years might have added to the tree's stress. But no truck had hit my shop. I was sure of that. "So," I said, "are you going to get over here and help me?"

"Is . . . uh"—his voice took on a studied nonchalance—"is Gilda there yet?"

We'd all grown up together—my cousins, my brother, Andrew, and I from the Winn crowd, and Gilda Buchanan, whose parents lived four doors down the street from our house and three doors up from Sam and Shoe. Andrea was part of that crowd, too, but I wasn't going to think about her. Gilda was just another kid to play with back then. Blonde pigtails, snub nose. But now Gilda, Sam, and Shoe worked for me. A couple of months ago, Shoe sort of woke up and realized the girl of his dreams had been right there all along. I grinned as I remembered. I'd seen it happen. One day when Shoe and Gilda were on the same shift, Shoe looked at her, did a double take, and took a step backward. I thought it was funnier than heck, especially since Gilda paid about as much attention to him as she would to an overzealous puppy.

"Soon," I said. "She'll be in at her regular time. Looks like I'm going to have to keep the shop closed until we can get the mess cleaned up." I hoped the woman who had tapped on the glass earlier would be patient. I walked between two racks of tartan skirts, placed far enough apart to allow for wheelchair access. "How soon can you get here?"

"Will you let me put on my kilt first?"

I stuck out my tongue at him, even though he couldn't possibly see me. I knew he couldn't. His apartment above the hardware store up the street was not in a line of sight from here. Sam lived there, too, to the left at the top of the stairs. Shoe lived to the right.

"Quit sticking out your tongue. It makes you look cross-eyed."

He knew me way too well. "Bring Sam with you," I told him, and looked up as my store manager tapped on the door.

She must have forgotten her key again. "Be right there, Gilda," I called. I heard a muffled gasp on the other end of the phone line and knew that my cousin would be on my doorstep within moments. "Don't forget Sam," I hollered at him, but heard only that vacant nobody-there sound in reply. I started to stick my tongue out at him again but changed it to licking my lips when Dirk cleared his throat.

11

Death by Bookcase

I unlocked the door. Gilda stepped in, and her already-wide eyes came close to popping out of their sockets. In a voice almost as high-pitched as the bell above the door, she asked, "Whatever did you do to the bookcase?"

"Thank you," I said. "I'm glad you think I'm strong enough to knock a three-hundred-pound bookcase over all by myself."

"It weighs three hundred pounds?" Gilda sounded a bit breathless as she closed the door and followed me toward the back, but then, she always sounded breathless. Dirk walked behind the two of us. Even when I was ignoring him, I was aware of him.

"I was guessing, Gilda. Exaggerating." I pushed my toe against the bookcase, just beside where Percy's leg disappeared beneath the wood. "It might as well weigh that much. The point is, it's very heavy."

"Why would the bookcase fall over? I thought it was pretty secure."

"So did I."

Dirk clambered over the bookcase. I supposed he couldn't hurt it. How much did a ghost weigh? "Wood as sturdy as this doesna fall on its own. This—'twas pushed over." He knelt next to Percy.

"That's what I was afraid of."

Gilda gave me a look. "Huh?"

"Nothing. Just thinking out loud."

"'Twas moved away from the wall before that."

He must have noticed the confused look I gave him. He pointed to the base of the bookcase. "This part is several feet awae from the wall. The other side is close."

He stood abruptly, and I missed one or two of his words while I pondered the strength of those leg muscles that had propelled him so quickly to his feet. Of course, he was a ghost, so maybe it didn't take as much muscle power for him as it would have for me.

". . . ye had to use a key on yon door."

I shifted gears. He was right. There was that heavy dead bolt lock on the front door. The trouble was, the back door had a rather questionable lock, but I'd never advertised the fact. I'd meant to replace it, but one thing had led to another, and I had to admit, I'd never worried much. I trusted the people in this town.

Shoe was the only one I knew of who had taken advantage of my lock lapse. Well, he and Drew, my twin brother. They'd squeaked the door open several times and left some rather dubious "gifts" for me—a plastic mouse once just beside the cash register, a rubber snake on the rolltop desk in the back room as a birthday present, and a disgustingly realistic-looking puddle of fake vomit—I was pretty sure that was Drew's idea—draped artistically over my measuring tape on the shelf underneath the counter. The jokes finally quit three years ago, right after Drew's accident, when I hired Shoe and he began to take more of an interest in the ScotShop. No. He wouldn't have done this. He never would have hurt Percy. Neither would Sam; and of course, my brother couldn't have done it. But who? Was there some-one who hated me enough to mess up my shop like this?

My ex-boyfriend crossed my mind. No. Despite the fact that I'd slugged him, I couldn't imagine that Mason Kilmarty would want to harm my store.

The bell jangled, and Shoe charged in. I glared at my assistant. "Gilda, what happened to the rule about locking the door behind you when you come in?"

"Oh, gosh, I forgot. I'm sorry."

"Yes, I know, but *sorry* doesn't help when an early cus-tomer barges in and we're not ready. Why don't you go ahead and get the cash register open? It shouldn't take too long to clean up this mess." I turned to Shoe. "Lock that door." I shouldn't have had to remind him. "Did you call Sam?"

"Uh . . ."

I whipped out my phone again and went through much the same conversation with Sam as I had with Shoe a few minutes earlier, except without the reference to Gilda.

Gilda opened the curtain behind the display window and headed toward the disaster. I watched her curly blonde hair bob around the bookcase, as she picked up odd broken bits as she came upon them. Shoe followed her, hands out-stretched, and she passed the pieces to him.

He walked past me on his way to the trashcan.

"Finding any treasure?"

He held out his large cupped hands and rolled his eyes. "Buncha crud, mostly."

I glanced at the mess. Besides my twenty-five-foot tape measure, what he held was mostly junk—some broken bits of a Culloden stone replica, pieces of shattered crockery from the hand-thrown bowls a local craftsman had made for us—I hated to lose those; I never should have put them on the top shelf like that—two keys, several curlicues of carved wood that I recognized as the top border of a fancy bookend. This was going to be expensive. "Where'd you find the tape measure?"

"On the floor behind the bookcase. Must have fallen off the counter and bounced, but it shoulda been on the shelf underneath."

That was my fault. I could have sworn I'd put it away after I'd used it to measure the distance between some of the racks we'd moved. I like to keep everything as accessible as I can. Most stores are so crammed, nobody in a wheelchair can get farther than three feet from the front door. "Well, put it back where it belongs. I shouldn't have left it out."

I stepped away from the counter while Shoe dumped the junk into the trash. He returned to where Gilda held even more broken bits for him.

Dirk had lain flat on the floor beside the bookcase and seemed to be peering under it. "Ye need to pull Master Percy out of there."

"Why?"

"Why what?"

"Nothing Gilda. Just wondering why this happened."

She grinned. "Maybe we had an earthquake."

"Ye maun do it now."

Maun. That meant *must.* What was the big deal? "Shoe, lift the top of the bookcase a few inches, just enough for us to drag Percy out."

He flexed his biceps. "I'll pick up the whole thing."

"He doesna need to lift it."

"Huh, why not?"

Shoe paused. "Why not what?"

"The case of books isna resting on the leg."

I bent to take a closer look. He was right. There was an inch or two of air above Percy's leg. "Shoe, help me here." We dragged Percy a few feet, and left him behind a rack of poet shirts. The top edge of the bookcase still hovered above the floor.

Dirk muttered something that I didn't catch.

"Looks like something else is caught under there," Shoe

said. "You didn't have a second mannequin standing over here, did you?"

"Don't be ridiculous." The granite bookends shaped like Urquhart Castle were the only items sturdy enough to hold half the bookcase off the floor like this. I had visions of the dents they'd leave on the shelf edges.

"Are ye not going to lift the bookcase?"

"Not yet. Where the heck is Sam? We need him before we can lift this thing."

"Aye. I suppose ye do. It doesna appear that 'twill matter."

What was he talking about?

Shoe grabbed up a small, unbroken plastic statue of the Loch Ness Monster. "Maybe Nessie did it." I sold those hokey things because of Hamelin's nearby lake, Lake Ness, named by a long-ago resident with a warped sense of humor.

"And maybe you have a screw loose, Sh'muel." The only time I ever used his given name was when I was upset with him. My mother's twin, my aunt Minnie, had been in one of her phases when she had twin boys. Named them Shadrach and Sh'muel, and not a Jewish bone in the family anywhere, or not that we knew of. Of course, even before grade school, they'd become Sam and Shoe. If they'd been triplets, we'd probably have a Methuselah in our midst. I shuddered to think of what his nickname would have been. Whatever had Aunt Minnie been thinking? Still, in a town where old Scottish given names like Stenhouse, Macaslan, Ruskin, and Macourlic abounded (with first names like that, you could tell there were loads of Buchanans and Camerons in this area), what was so unusual about Shadrach and Sh'muel?

I headed past the bookcase, intending to see if anything had fallen over in the storeroom. Maybe there *had* been an earthquake. As I approached that door, though, I glanced to my left and noticed the wall behind the bookcase. Behind where the bookcase should have been, that is. A long gouge ran down the wallpaper where a strip of wallpaper had been torn and left dangling.

"Dammit," I yelled, and Gilda came running, Shoe right after her. "Look at this! Whoever upended the bookcase ripped my wallpaper." I don't know why I hadn't noticed the damage right away.

"You never liked it that much anyway," Shoe said in a disgustingly reasonable voice.

"That's not the point. Now I'll have to replace it." I looked at the forty-foot expanse of wall and groaned. "I don't want to spend that kind of money."

"You could just patch it," Gilda said. "Don't you still have that roll of paper in the back?"

"I suppose I could." The thought of trying to match those swirling flocked flowers gave me a touch of vertigo.

Shoe reached beneath the cash register to the shelf where we kept all the odds and ends a shop needs but doesn't want the customers to see. "For now, just tape it up."

I took the roll of tape with some reluctance. Of course, the bookcase would cover the damaged area, but it seemed distinctly shoddy to do this to the old-fashioned wallpaper. I lifted the strip and was surprised to find a hole in the wall near the top of where the wallpaper had been ripped down. About an eighth of an inch in diameter, perfectly round—as if it had been drilled—a bit above the level of my knees.

I ran my hand over the wall and found four—no, five more holes. What on earth was going on? I looked up, ready to call the others, but the phone rang and Gilda went to answer it. Shoe had apparently lost interest and was bent down picking up more of the mess. Dirk peered over my shoulder.

"The wee holes look as if something was nailed there."

"They weren't there when I bought the place," I said.

"What?" Shoe straightened up and squinted at me. Did he need glasses?

"Nothing. Just talking to myself."

Dirk grinned.

I set the tape down and walked into the employees-only part of the shop, intending to step into the small bathroom and see if the holes came through back there. Dirk followed me.

The back door. That was how whoever had done this had gotten in. I forgot the bathroom and headed toward the door. Not only was it not locked, it wasn't even closed all the way. Why did I have a good dead bolt lock on the front door and a puny thing like this on the back? Why was I thinking about this now instead of two weeks ago?

Dirk wandered around the room, gazing at plastic bins, cardboard boxes, metal drawers. Life must have been a lot simpler way back when he lived.

I poked my head outside. Nothing suspicious in the alley. The Dumpster, the rear doors of other businesses, the privacy fencing that separated the backs of the stores from the backyards of the homes on Beech Street. The usual stuff. I ran my hand over the outside of my door. No sign of a crowbar or anything like that. Well, heck, of course not. Shoe had told me all he and my brother ever had to do was lift the doorknob to make the whole thing pop open. I closed the door and pushed the little button. I'd send Shoe to the hardware store later for a real lock.

I looked around. The old rolltop desk that had been here forever—or so I assumed—was still piled as high as before. The practical joker should have stolen my paper monster. I would have been eternally grateful. I had a fairly good idea of what was in my inventory, and nothing seemed to be missing, but I had to admit it was hard to tell in a space as crammed as this was. It wasn't enough that I had to store all my own stuff—inventory, repair items, file cabinets with all my financial info—but Shoe still hadn't picked up the things he'd left here when *last* year's baseball season ended. I pushed his second-best glove away from the edge of a table and walked back into the showroom, pausing to let Dirk through before I let the door swing shut.

Sam showed up fairly quickly, ready for work, wearing a Gordon kilt. "I like it better than the Winn tartan," he'd told me a couple of years ago. "As long as I have to wear a kilt, it might as well be one that matches my eyes." And he'd blinked his lashes in a parody of a 1930s showgirl.

I took a discreet look at him. Had to admit, the blues and greens set off his blond hair better than our Winn burgundy would have. "Anyway," he'd added, "the customers won't care what I wear, as long as it's a kilt." He was right about that.

Gilda locked the door behind him. Good. "Point me to this moving job," he said.

Gilda pointed. Sam gaped. Typical reaction. The bookcase was such a sturdy presence in the shop, its demise—because that was what it looked like—was downright disconcerting.

"What's the damage?" He spoke in an awed whisper.

"I imagine everything is at least dented, if not smashed," I said. "Everything except the Urquhart castles."

"Urquhart?" Dirk sounded confused. Of course.

"Those little statues of the castle are pretty sturdy," I explained.

"Ah," said Dirk.

Shoe rolled his eyes. "We know that."

Sam smirked at the supine mannequin. "He's come down in the world." He wiped his face clear when I frowned at him.

"I'll thank you to remember he's one of a unique line that's been discontinued. Worth a lot to collectors."

"Somebody would have to be out of their gourd to collect mannequins."

I pushed him aside. Dirk was strangely quiet. I suppose he felt bad about not being able to help. "Come on, you two. Let's get this bookcase upright." Shoe stepped to the counter and put down another handful of the odd bits he'd been gathering. They looked rather woebegone next to the cash register. "Try not to step on anything," I said. "There may be a few items that didn't break." Fat chance, I thought, but I could always hope.

Shoe pushed past me. "We can handle this." Macho, I thought. Still, I was perfectly happy to let them do the lifting. "One, two, three." They hauled the bookcase to an upright position and manhandled it into place back against the wall. I wondered if I could rig up some sort of brace that would keep this from happening again.

Gilda screamed.

"I do believe ye have a problem here," Dirk intoned.

My stomach roiled, and I slapped my hand over my mouth. I couldn't throw up, I couldn't, I couldn't.

Shoe reached out and pulled Gilda toward him. He sort of tucked her under his arm and she shut up. I turned my attention to the reason the bookcase hadn't lain flat.

He was definitely dead, but books and movies said you had to be sure, so I bent gingerly beside him, careful not to touch the blood, and felt the wrist on his splayed-out hand. I was fairly sure the carotid artery was a better place to feel for a pulse, but there was no way I was going anywhere near his smashed-in face.

His skin was cold. Clammy. Nothing moved. No breath, no pulse. Nothing.

"Shoe, that's your bat." Sam stood still, bracing the bookcase as if afraid it might fall again.

Shoe cleared his throat. He cleared it again. "It's only my spare."

Sam mumbled something, then said more clearly, "Who is it?"

A muffled sound came from Gilda, her face still buried in the front of Shoe's shirt.

I took a deep breath, swallowed the bitter fluid inching its way up my throat. Even with his face caved in, I knew it was Mason. I recognized his tartan. And the length of his hairy legs. His kilt was hiked up almost indecently. No mistaking that small reddish-purple birthmark, shaped like a comma, quite a ways above his knee. If it had been on his knee, everyone else would have known about it. That's what happened when you lived in a tourist town where most of the men wore kilts all summer long. No knees were ever sacrosanct. But I was probably the only person in town who knew about this birthmark. I and his mother. And Andrea, damn her.

Gilda seemed to choke. "It's Mason."

Shoe made a dismissive gesture. "You can't be sure."

"Yes, I can. I recognized his . . . kilt."

Was it my imagination, or had she paused a moment too long before that last word? I reached out to pull his kilt down a couple of inches.

Why would anyone want to kill Mason Kilmarty? Other than the fact that he was an obnoxious bastard, that is. Of course, I hadn't always felt that way.

Thank goodness Percy hadn't landed in the blood, I thought, and was instantly ashamed of myself. Mason was dead. A baseball bat lay next to him. A dark red blotch stained several inches of the rounded end. Blood, I assumed. Mason's blood.

"There isna enough blood," Dirk said, and I looked at him in some confusion. "I've seen a man bludgeoned near to death, when Caw McFarlane ran awa' wi' John Mac-naughton's wife. John caught up wi' them that night and went after Caw wi' a hoe handle. Struck him many times. The blood near covered the walls of the shed, and John as well." He spread his arm. "There should be blood every-where here." He paused. "Unless only one blow was struck."

I was still having trouble controlling the contents of my stomach, but I could see the sense in what he said. "Some-body would have had to hit him pretty hard to do this much damage in one blow," I said.

Shoe grunted as if he'd been struck. "You can do that with . . . with a baseball bat," he said. "You'd have to have a good windup though."

Sam pantomimed swinging a bat. There would have been enough room. The counter with the cash register stood a good seven feet from the bookcase.

Mason's face wasn't the only thing bashed in. His shirt looked like it had been pushed an inch or two into his chest in a narrow stripe right across the front of his body. What could have done this kind of damage? I thought for a moment. My bookcase would have done him in if the baseball bat hadn't killed him first. The edge of one of the shelves, right across his heart, as the bookcase crashed down on him, could inflict this kind of wound, could leave this kind of mark. Death by bookcase? What a ghastly thought. His knees, completely untouched, must have lain under an open area above a shelf. There were bookends and clan plaques on and around the body, around Mason, where they'd slid off the shelf when it came crashing down on him. Guidebooks lay scattered around his head and shoulders.

But why had Mason been in my store at night? And why would he have stood still while somebody hit him with a bat and dumped a bookcase on him?

Sam touched my shoulder. "We have to call the police, Peggy."

I held out a hand for him to help me to my feet—I did feel a bit shaky—and reached for the counter where I'd set my phone. I gritted my teeth and called.

12

Napoleon of Hamelin

Moira, Hamelin's sassy and thoroughly southern police dispatcher told me Mac Campbell was out of the office.

Thank goodness. I didn't need his officiousness this early in the day, especially when I had a dead body to worry about.

Moira told me she'd send someone. It came out: *Ah'll sin suhm-won raht awaee, sugah.* "You just sit tight, don't touch anything, and don't let anybody else in that store of yours. Do you know who it is?"

"It's . . . it's Mason. Mason Kilmarty."

"Your boyfriend?"

"My former boyfriend. I broke up with him last week."

"Well, honey, somebody finally done him in for you." She paused, and I heard her voice in the background issuing orders. When she came back, there was a distinct clink as her ringed fingers cupped around the phone. "Was it you who did it?"

"Moira!"

"Well, honey," she said, giving up her whispering, "everybody knew you two had problems."

"Everybody did not."

"They sure did after you asked to have the town books audited. Harper's on his way there. You hold on."

My hands were shaking so hard, it took me two tries to hit the End button.

Rather than just wait for someone to show up, I called my brother. He and Mason were—had been—friends. That's probably why I got hooked up with Mason to begin with. He was always hanging out at our house, almost as much as Sam and Shoe.

"Where are you, Drew?" Mobile technology is great, but I never know where anybody is when I call. Andrew travels a lot. He has a specially equipped van that lets him go practically anywhere. And Tessa to help him with all the details he can't do himself.

"Manchester. What's up?"

"Are you sitting down?" Rats! Of course he was sitting down. "What I mean is, are you okay to hear some bad news?"

"Just a sec." I heard him drop the phone into his lap, and his wheelchair squeaked the way it does when he lifts himself to reposition his legs. "Okay. Shoot."

"It's Mason. He's . . . he's . . ."

"What's he done this time?" It was more a statement than a question.

"No. Hush. He's . . . dead."

"Did you say *dead*? He's awful young for a heart attack. Are you sure he's dead? Maybe he just passed out."

"Drew! Shut up and listen. Somebody . . . killed him . . . last night . . . in my shop."

"What was he doing in your shop?"

"I don't know. Look, Drew, I have to run. There's a cop at the door. Just wanted you to know . . ."

"When's the funeral? I can be back for it."

"Are you nuts? How would I know?"

"Call his mom."

"No! The cops can tell her."

"Peg." He was using his big-brother voice, even though he's only five minutes older.

"I can't call her. I broke up with him just before I went to Scotland."

"He finally pushed you too hard, huh?"

"He cheated on me. I don't want to talk about it. Give Tessa a big pat for me. Be good."

I hit End and opened the front door.

"I'm Captain Harper, Hamelin Police. We got a call that there was a body in here."

"Yes. That's right. I'm the one who called. He's . . . he's . . ." I gestured over my shoulder. "He's back there."

I opened the door a little wider, and he stepped past me. There was the tiniest suggestion of citrus in the air around him. Aftershave?

I locked the door and led Harper to where Mason lay. Harper didn't know there was a ghost preceding us.

He took a searching look at the body, keyed the mike on his collar, asked Moira to contact the medical examiner and "the rest of the crew. You know what all we need." She should know. Moira had moved up north to Hamelin when I was just a kid, and she'd been attached to that *po-leece* phone ever since.

Harper moved all four of us to the side of the store away from the windows. I could see a few gawkers looking in— they must have wondered why a cop would go into a closed store—but the body wasn't in their line of sight.

Two more officers showed up and began stringing yellow crime-scene tape out beyond the sidewalk, all the way around the corner. Good, that would keep people from peering in either the front windows or the side ones next to the courtyard. The cops had attracted a crowd. I saw Andrea, notepad in hand, questioning people. Most likely she was making up sheer drivel for her so-called news blog. Bunch of petty gossip if you ask me. My next-door neighbor was there. So was Sweetie, from across the street.

Ethan Dorman, who owned the Auto Shop, stopped one of the officers and held a brief conversation with him. Ethan was a good guy. I knew from past conversations that he was something of an insomniac who took frequent walks at night. Maybe he'd seen something.

Harper introduced himself to the others and quickly established: 1) what the problem was—a dead body; 2) who we all were—Peggy, Gilda, Sam/Shadrach, and Shoe/Sh'muel; and 3) what had happened—we'd found the body after we'd moved the bookcase.

"Let me get this straight: You didn't know there was a body under there when you saw the bookcase on its side?"

"No," I said.

"We saw Percy lying down," Gilda added helpfully.

"Percy?" He looked at her for an explanation.

She dimpled. "Peggy's favorite mannequin."

She made it sound like a perversion.

He turned back to me. His dark eyes—not quite the color of charcoal, but close—narrowed a fraction. "Your favorite mannequin." Not quite a question.

How do you explain something like this? I opted for the unembellished truth, no matter how weird it sounded. "I bought Percy, the mannequin, when I opened ScotShop six years ago. He has sort of a Mona Lisa smile, and shoulders that broad," I spread my hands apart to show him and saw that the officer's shoulders were just as wide. I lost my train of thought. "Where was I?"

"Mona Lisa." His voice was a deep, resonant bass.

"Yes, well, he looks really good in a kilt." My eyes strayed down the length of the blue uniform in front of me, and I wondered briefly what a kilt would look like there. I caught myself. "It seemed natural to give him a name, since Gilda and I got into the habit of talking to him, asking him where he thought a particular item should be displayed."

Shoe piped up. "You can see he gave very good advice." He waved his arm to indicate the layout of the store.

"Thank you, Shoe," I said. "Now shut up, please."

The officer looked from Shoe to me. "Brother?"

I shook my head. "Cousin."

"Close enough," he muttered, and wrote something in his notebook, which he held at just enough of an angle that I couldn't see what he was writing. Another officer came in snapping a camera. He conferred briefly with Harper and walked back toward the body, taking more pictures as he went.

I took Captain Harper through my actions starting with when I'd looked in the window and seen the red plaid on the floor. He took a few notes but mostly just listened to me. His eyes were very dark, and I kept getting sidetracked.

"Who else knows about this?"

"Nobody. Except the murderer, I suppose."

"You haven't mentioned it to anyone else?"

"I haven't had time to. I just called Moira a few minutes ago."

He looked decidedly skeptical. "Is that who you were talking to when I knocked on the door?"

"Oh, I forgot. That was Drew. But he and Tessa are in New Hampshire."

What makes you think he doesn't count? I could almost see the thought go across Harper's face. "And Drew would be . . . ?"

"My brother, Andrew."

"Yes," Gilda said, as if she were tired of being left out, "They're fraternal. Not identical."

Harper kept a straight face. Shoe didn't. "Gilda that's nuts! Of course they're not identical. Drew's a guy, in case you hadn't noticed."

"I noticed." Gilda glowered as Shoe gave one of those *go figure* gestures. Can't say I blamed her. Too bad he didn't see it.

Harper studied the two of them briefly and turned back to me. "Is Tessa your brother's wife?"

I looked at him in some surprise.

"Or his girlfriend?" he added.

"Tessa is my brother's dog," I explained. "She goes everywhere with him. He lost the use of his legs when he fell off a dinosaur three years ago. She's not trained as a service dog, but she helps him out a lot."

"Fell off a . . . dinosaur?"

"Well, the framework around it actually."

"What," Dirk asked, "would be a dynasore?"

"Not a live one. It was a skeleton."

"What would be a—"

"A dinosaur," Harper repeated slowly.

"Yes. In a museum."

"What would be—"

"I'll tell you later," I said, hoping that Harper and Dirk would both stop asking questions.

Harper took a deep breath, as if he had to reset an internal mechanism. "Uh, where is this mannequin"—he looked at his notes—"Percy?"

We were interrupted by the entrance of the medical examiner. He carried a black bag that made him look like an old country doctor. That was fast, I thought. "Didn't he have to drive all the way from Burlington?" I spoke before I thought about it.

"Dr. Gunn was vacationing in Arkane," Harper said. If he hadn't been leaning so close to me, I wouldn't have heard him. "I guess people with his sort of job never really get a vacation, do they?" His words tickled my ear, his breath was so soft.

Dr. Gunn ignored our group and walked slowly toward the body, looking up, down, and around as he went. Thinning gray hair tonsured his pointy head.

I turned to Harper. "Don't you have to go with him?"

"No, no, no," he said, and backed up a step. "I made the mistake of trying that once and got my tail feathers flayed. Dr. Gunn wants the body all to himself. He hates when people mess up his evidence."

Uh-oh. I looked at Gilda and my cousins. We were in trouble.

He must have seen that look. "Was there something you wanted to tell me?"

"Oh, uh, nothing much. I just think maybe you should know that I pulled down Mason's kilt—it was . . ." I made a gesture and Harper nodded. "And then I checked the back door and pushed the button a couple of times. I think that's how the . . . murderer . . . broke in. And we picked up a bunch of broken stuff that was lying around the bookcase."

A muscle on the side of his face contracted. Hard.

I put one hand on my hip. "You really shouldn't do that, you know."

"Do what?"

"Grit your teeth. It wears down the enamel."

He stared at me for such a long time, I felt a need to run my tongue over my teeth, checking to see if they still felt solid and healthy.

"Thank you for that piece of advice," he finally said, "but we were talking about how you opened the back door and disturbed possible evidence when you shouldn't have."

"I know I shouldn't have," I said, feeling a desperate urge to defend myself, "but I didn't know there was a body. I thought it was just a prank."

"Hmm," he said, and wrote another note. A lock of light brown hair fell onto his forehead. "What did you pick up?"

I thought for a moment. "Well, Shoe and Gilda did it. They found a lot of broken merchandise, bookends, figurines, and such."

He turned to Shoe. "Where did you put them?"

"In the trash basket under the counter."

He said something under his breath. Maybe it was just as well I couldn't hear it.

"What else have you not told me?"

I was saved from replying by the grand entrance of Police Chief Mackelvie Campbell, self-styled Napoleon of

Hamelin, otherwise known as Mac. He may not have been short like Napoleon, but he was a tyrant. He generally made up in noise what he lacked in subtlety. He listened to Harper's recitation of the facts. He did listen; I'll give him that. But then he raised one side of his Brillo Pad eyebrow—he had only one; it stretched all the way across his face like the fifty-yard line on a football field. "Now, just remind me, Peggy," he said. "How long have you hated him?" He tilted a massive head toward the back of the store where the medical examiner bent over the corpse.

I widened my eyes. "I don't hate Dr. Gunn."

Mac screwed his mouth to one side. "You know I'm not talking about him. I heard you broke up with Mason."

Damn you, Moira. I bet you told him.

"Well?" Mac's voice broke into my thoughts. "Did you?"

"Did I what?"

"Kill him. I know you considered him with some contemptuousness."

Ah, I thought, the big words, three or more syllables. I glanced around to see just whom he thought he could impress. Nobody was within earshot except a couple of cops, my cousins, and Gilda. Hmm. Bouncy, bubbly, cute-as-a-button Gilda. Was the show for her benefit?

"I haven't spoken to him since before my trip," I shot back. As an afterthought, I added, "And you know that perfectly well." Of course, he had no way of knowing that, but it sounded good.

He grimaced and asked me where I was last night.

"Home," I said, aware that I had no way to prove it.

"Alone?"

Just the ghostie and me. "Alone."

"You're pretty calm for someone who's just seen your boyfriend dead."

"Ex-boyfriend," I said with more than a little venom.

Harper closed his pad and opened it again.

Mac glanced over his shoulder, probably wondering what

I was looking at. He turned back to me. "Are you going to answer my question?" His supercilious tone irked the heck out of me.

"I dinna care for this constable."

Me, neither. I looked Mac square in the eye, which was a bit difficult considering how he was six foot four and I was only five foot six. My nose was level with his armpit. "You didn't ask me anything," Only a small note of asperity crept into my voice. Before he could contradict me, I said, "All you did was comment that I was pretty calm under the circumstances." I knew quite well I'd most likely fall apart when I got home, but this wasn't the place or the time to be squeamish. I certainly wasn't going to give Mac Campbell the satisfaction of seeing me squirm.

"Your shop is closed, you know."

I didn't roll my eyes at him, even though I wanted to. "I know. It's a crime scene now."

"We'll be going over it for fingerprints."

"What would be a finger prince?"

I grimaced at Dirk, hoping he would be quiet. I'd answer all his questions later. Didn't he realize my tongue was tied right now?

Mac leaned closer to me. "Care to tell me what you're worried about?"

Harper leaned closer, too. I threw him a glare, turned back to Mac, and said, "When I came in this morning, all I saw was the bookcase lying down where it was pushed over." I may have sounded a bit peevish. "Naturally I touched it. I had no idea there was a . . . a body under it. Anyway, we all work here, so you'll find all our fingerprints, here in front and in the back, too."

"My, my, aren't we being defensive?"

"Also, I looked out the back door this morning." I raised my chin and refused to blink when he began to grumble.

Dr. Gunn called him over. It was a good thing. I wanted

to scratch Mac's eyes out. Impertinent, pompous butthead. I stomped after him, determined to find out what had happened to Mason, but Harper put out a hand before Mac could tell him to get rid of me.

"Don't go anywhere," Mac growled over his shoulder.

"I need some air." I reached for the door handle, hoping to push my way out through the crowd of onlookers that stood outside the semicircle of yellow crime-scene tape, but Harper's firm hand grasped my arm.

"I think you'd better stick around," he said in an undertone.

Mac bellowed after us, "You leave and you're under arrest! And hand over your key to this place."

I didn't make a scene, but only because of the crowd outside. And maybe just a little bit because of Harper's shoulders and his charcoal eyes.

Everything inside me felt raw. How could this have happened? How could Mason be gone? Why in my store? What was I going to do about the blood? I took a deep breath to quell the panic that rose now that I wasn't doing anything. Why him? Why me? Crudbuckets.

Officer Harper placed a hand on my elbow and steered me to the carved bench in front of the shoe display. "Sit," he told me. "Stay here."

Did he think I was an Irish setter? I sat.

I looked at the ghillie brogues and tried to imagine that I was a customer trying on a pair of those no-tongue shoes. I tried to remove myself from this scene. It didn't work. I stared at the curtains that hid three little dressing rooms where customers could try on kilts and shirts and tartan skirts.

Harper came back with a glass of water. I took a sip and then another and another. Good grief, I felt dehydrated. Maybe finding a body does that to you; all the adrenaline uses up resources . . .

". . . ing better now?"

"Huh? Oh, yes. Yes, I am." I looked back at the dressing rooms. "Maybe the murderer's back there."

He followed my gaze and shook his head. "Joe already checked it out."

He pulled a card out of his shirt pocket and wrote something on it. "I want you to call me if you think of anything else."

I glanced at the card and stifled a grin when I saw his first name. He'd written his cell number below the e-mail address printed on the card.

"Anything at all. You call me."

Mac bellowed his name, and Harper touched me lightly on the shoulder. "Sit here and rest. I'll be back."

I never knew a morning could drag by so slowly. Gilda and the guys ended up sitting with me, Gilda on the bench and my cousins on the blue-and-green tartan carpet that covered that half of the ScotShop. Harper didn't seem to be in a hurry to come back. It felt like hours later—although it may have been a lot less.

"I'm afraid you'll have to go to the police station to be fingerprinted," he said. "It's for comparison only." He herded us through the shop and out the back door, "so we can avoid the crowd out front." It took some deft footwork on my part to be sure nobody ran into Dirk as we walked down the alley and up two blocks to the station.

The desk sergeant, a redheaded Irish Murphy in this town of Scots, ushered us into a bare conference room. "I need to collect the keys to your shop," he told me. "All of them. Chief's orders."

I looked at Gilda, remembering that she'd forgotten her key this morning. That was why I'd had to let her in. We both had spare keys, too, but we didn't need to mention that to Murphy. I pulled my key off my ring. "Here you go," I said, nodding to Murphy. "That's it."

"Anybody else here have a key?"

All three of my employees spread their hands in the time-honored gesture of innocence.

When Murphy's back was turned, I winked at Gilda. Sam and Shoe grinned. Dirk looked faintly disapproving. Murphy paused at the door. "The chief will be here in a minute or two."

I'd watched enough TV to know you shouldn't leave a bunch of witnesses together in one room because they might bend their stories to match one another's. Of course, we didn't have anything to worry about, so I relaxed back, as much as possible, into one of those molded plastic chairs that never fit anybody's anatomy.

Despite the gravity of the situation, Shoe kept us in stitches with his straight-faced imitation of Mac Campbell. With his index finger stretched across his brow line like Mac's one eyebrow, Shoe leaned over me and intoned, "You leave and you're under arrest, because I need to arrest somebody, and it might as well be you."

"You wouldn't dare," I countered. "The town needs the tax money my shop generates." As an afterthought, I added, "Maybe he'll arrest you instead."

Sam wound up and threw an imaginary pitch. "Can't arrest either of us. We're needed for the Fourth of July game." Hamelin and the nearby town of Arkane took turns hosting the annual baseball game between the Hamelin Pipers and the Arkane Archers. This year it was our turn. The teams may be strictly amateur, but the competition is fierce. Sam's our best pitcher, and Shoe is our star batter.

"That reminds me," Shoe said. "I think I left some of my old gear at the shop a month or two ago. Do you know where it is?"

"What?" I said with mock ferocity. "A month or two? Ha! Your stuff's been cluttering the storeroom all winter. It's a wonder I didn't throw it out."

Shoe staggered back as if he'd been hit. "No! No! Not my glove. Even if it is my spare one."

I laughed. "I've been storing your spares? Should have burned them all. Your glove is there for sure. I saw it this morning when I went in the back. And your smelly old shoes." It was on the tip of my tongue to mention his bat, but of course I didn't. That was nothing to joke about.

I swallowed hard and lightened my voice. "Don't forget you're supposed to pick up a dead bolt lock and install it on the back door. Get four keys."

Shoe started to answer but stopped when Mac strode into the room and paused, like a Force 1 hurricane that couldn't make up its mind which way it was headed. Harper was right behind him. Mac swung around and barked at me as he moved in my direction.

"I'm splitting you up." He pointed at me, his index finger coming uncomfortably close to the heavy weave of my sweater. "Come with me."

I went. Harper spoke to Gilda, and two more officers waited in the hall, apparently one for each of my cousins. Dirk, muttering Gaelic imprecations under his breath—what was he whispering for?—followed me down the hall.

Mac was going to have to get his hearing checked. I told him my story, not once, not twice, not even three times. The first time, Dirk put in little additions here and there, so I stuttered a bit. The next time it went smoother.

After about the fifth repetition, Mac peppered me with obnoxious innuendos about my love life going to pot and my jealousy of Mason and Andrea. "If I'd wanted him back," I told him, "I'd have killed her, not him." If I'd been into murdering somebody, I probably would have knocked off both of them, but I didn't say that out loud.

Mac finally took me back to the first room. The others were already there. Harper was nowhere in sight. As we stood shaking out legs cramped from so much sitting in awful chairs, an officer stuck her head in the door and motioned to Mac. I'd seen her at the shop but couldn't recall her name.

He turned back to us. "Stay here. I'll tell you when you can leave." And out he went.

A quarter of an hour later, Sergeant Fairing—that was her name—came back. "Mac says you can go to the Logg Cabin for lunch, but you're not to talk about what happened here."

As if we'd want to. I kept seeing Mason's face—what was left of it. Harper walked in then and gestured toward the door. "I'll be going with you."

Shoe grunted. "Babysitting us?"

"You're grown-ups. Ought to be able to behave yourselves, but this keeps it official."

As we walked past the ScotShop, the few people hanging around the crime-scene tape wanted to know what was going on. Harper, who accompanied us as far as the restaurant door, stepped forward. "I can't comment, and these people"—he gestured to the four of us—"will get in big trouble if they talk about it, so don't even ask them."

They oozed away. "Enjoy your lunch if you can," Harper held the door open for me. "Try not to think about it."

Right.

Nothing on the menu looked good. I settled for a salad.

Gilda had been strangely silent. I felt sorry for her, but there was nothing I could do to help. Her hand shook as she lifted a soup spoon to her lips. Not surprising. It's not every day you get questioned about a murder. It's not every day you see a corpse, for that matter. I wasn't feeling so chipper myself. I held my hands out over my salad and lowered them quickly to my lap. They weren't shaking quite as bad as Gilda's, but they weren't too steady, either.

We need a change of mood. I whipped out my phone and scrolled through the photos. "Gilda, do you want to see a picture of Bruce?"

"Bruce?" She sounded almost strangled. What was going on? "Who's Bruce?"

When I showed her the Sinclairs' dog, she brightened a bit. "I always wanted a Scottie."

"Yeah, me, too, but I think Shorty wouldn't like the idea." I passed the phone around the table. Thinking about a dog was much happier than thinking about a murder.

13

A Wee Cup of Coffee

"He *what*? Why would Mac arrest Shoe?" Outside my kitchen window the next morning, two male cardinals chased each other around the bird feeder, red feathers flickering in the early morning light. I knew how they felt. I wanted to peck Mac's eyes out.

Gilda bellowed at me—not her usual breathy voice at all. "It was his baseball bat!"

"Well, of course it was." I shifted the phone to my other ear. "We have to get him a lawyer."

"It's already done." Gilda was back to her breathy voice. "Shoe called Sam, and Sam called Bart, and Bart went over to the jail right away, and Bart said Shoe would be out of jail as soon as we could get bail raised."

"How much is bail?" I eyed Dirk. He and Shorty seemed to be having a conversation.

"Forty thousand."

I choked on my tea. "Dollars?"

"Yes." She sounded awfully prim. "The judge said the crime was *hee-nus*. It's right here in the morning paper.

Andrea wrote the artic—oh, I'm sorry, Peggy. I shouldn't
have mentioned her name."

"That's okay, Gilda. Not a problem." *My blood pressure
is skyrocketing; my teeth are gnashing; my fist is clenched;
not a problem at all.* "I have to get dressed, Gilda. See you
at the shop." I dropped my spare shop key into my purse.

Dirk looked up from where he knelt beside my cat. "Ye
dinna sound cheerful."

"Of course I *dinna* sound cheerful. Shoe's been arrested."

"That is verra poor luck for him. Will they hang him,
d'ye suppose?"

"Hang him? Of course not. We don't hang innocent
people in Vermont."

"Then why are ye worriting?"

Hmm. "Good thought, Dirk. I'm gonna go get dressed."

Twenty minutes later, Dirk and I walked out to the driveway
and found my neighbor, Mr. Pitcairn, sweater-clad and
slightly stooped, standing by my car. Dirk fingered his knife
and I put out a restraining hand, remembering at the last
moment to switch the movement into a quick check of my
hair.

"When you're through waving your arm about, would
you give me a lift to the Auto Shop?"

I laughed and reined in my arm. "Your car isn't working?"

"I don't drive it very often, and wouldn't you know it, the
one time I want to go somewhere, I can't find my key. If
you'd just drop me off there, Ethan keeps the information
on file."

"Of course. Happy to." Spouting the Auto Shop's slogan,
I said, "'We have most everything, know most everything,
and repair most everything.'" I popped the locks and held
the back door open for Dirk. Mr. Pitcairn stared over the
car at me as I stood there. I bent and looked into the backseat

as if to check for something, being careful not to bump heads with Dirk.

Mr. P chatted interminably all the way into town. He talked about his yard, the weather, what a shame it was to have had a murder in my store, how much he liked my new shawl, and the increase in traffic on our road in recent years. I tried to be polite, but I was too aware of Dirk's scowl in the rearview mirror and all too aware of his comments. He didn't seem to like poor Mr. P. Of course, he didn't seem to like anyone. Any man, that is. I'd caught him watching Gilda rather closely, but with an air of—of what? Pity? I wondered why.

"I'm sorry I missed your dinner last night. Mac kept us at the station and I just forgot to call."

"Don't worry. We'll find another time." He thanked me profusely as he got out.

"It's nothing, Mr. P. You'd do the same for me if my car weren't running."

"Yes." He slapped the car roof. "I suppose I would at that."

"Yon man isna good," Dirk commented as we watched Mr. Pitcairn's receding back.

"I feel sorry for him. He must be awfully lonely. I wish he'd get a hobby or something." I made a U-turn and headed back the few blocks toward the police station.

"What would be a hobby?"

"Something to occupy his time, like collecting stamps." Dirk opened his mouth, but I waved him quiet. It's not easy to explain philately to someone who's never written a letter.

The station was housed in a squat building near the center of town. I'd never thought it looked particularly ominous, but now it did. Shoe was somewhere in that stark brick edifice, locked in a cell. Did they have visiting hours? Or could I just walk in and say I wanted to see him? I sure did hope Bart Cartwright was a good lawyer, since nobody had enough money to bail Shoe out. Just before I reached the door, I looked over at Dirk and muttered out of the side of my mouth, "Quit scowling. You look positively grim."

"And who is to see it except your own self?"

"Let's hope nobody else can, or we'll have a riot on our hands." I reached for the door, but it banged open and practically pushed me off my feet. I felt a momentary shiver, as if I'd walked out my front door into a misty morning.

When my head cleared, I found Police Chief Mac Campbell in front of me with a particularly nasty sneer on his concrete face. "Nice footwork, Peggy. Where'd you learn that? In tap dance school?" He looked over his shoulder to be sure his minions had heard his cleverness.

Dirk stepped toward him, holding his small but wicked-looking *sgian-dubh*. "Don't do that," I told Dirk.

Mac sneered again. "Do what?"

"Did ye see?" Dirk snarled. "Did ye see what he almost did? He was ready like a fighting boar to run ye over. I'd slit his throat had I half a chance."

Just as well I'd stopped him, although I doubted a ghost knife could have done any true damage. Remembering that feeling of being enveloped in a mist, I asked him, "Are you the one that kept me from falling?"

"Yes," Dirk said, at the same time a deep voice just behind my left shoulder said, "I'd be the one who did that." I turned to see Harper glare at his chief. "Seems to me she needs an apology since you almost ran her down."

Mac flexed his fingers. Dirk saw it and raised the knife a bit higher.

"Don't," I told Dirk again.

"Why not?" Mac sneered again. "You don't want me to apologize? Do you enjoy being pushed around?" He made it sound like an indecent proposal.

Harper's grip tightened on my arm. "Let's go somewhere for a cup of java." Mac opened his mouth, but before he could say anything, Harper scowled at him. "Interview. I'm the detective on this case."

He turned, pulling me with him. Dirk came up on my other side, and asked, "What would be a detecktiff?" His knife still glinted in the morning sun.

"So," I turned to Harper and pulled my arm free, "you're the one who's going to investigate the murder and detect who did it, since you're the detective?"

I felt more than saw Dirk nod at my side. "I thank ye." He bent to tuck his knife away.

Harper's face went through a series of contortions as he seemed to try out various answers to my inane comment. Finally he settled for "Yes. I am," and steered me up the street toward the Logg Cabin.

The ScotShop looked so forlorn, with the curtains once again pulled shut behind the display windows. Dirk paused to stare at the mannequins in the window with that look of utter incredulity that made me see the display through his fourteenth-century eyes. Clothing in the fourteenth century must have been so much more utilitarian. I doubt any man back then owned more than two shirts, and a woman who had three dresses was probably minor royalty. Seeing it through Dirk's eyes, my window looked like a travesty—a caricature of life.

I slowed my pace so Dirk could catch up to me. Harper strode along toward the Logg Cabin with his head down, lost in thought, unaware that I had dropped behind him.

Karaline stepped through the swinging door at the back of the restaurant, saw Harper and me at the end of the short line, waved, and took a quick look around the room. I knew she could take in everything at once—every table, every guest, and every single one of her staff. She came forward and spoke a few words to Geraldine, the hostess, picked up two menus, and motioned us toward the back, where Dolly had just wiped off a square table. I looked back at the people we'd preempted. "Won't they be upset?"

"No. They're waiting for a table for six. We're moving fairly fast this morning. Everybody's hot to get out of here and shop."

"And my store's still closed."

"Quit whining. It could be worse." She put down one menu, looked Harper up and down, winked at me, and set the other one kitty-cornered to my left. "Dolly will be right back to take your order."

Harper held my chair, ignored the menu, and sat across from me with his back to the wall. Dirk stood looming over me on my right. Dolly placed our silverware, wrapped in napkins, and whipped her order pad out of her brown uniform's capacious pocket. "Hullo, Officer Harper, Ms. Winn. What can I get for you this morning?"

He raised his eyebrows. Unlike Mac, I thought, Harper has *two* eyebrows. I stifled a giggle.

"Coffee okay with you?"

I nodded. Dolly knew I liked it black, so I didn't specify.

"That's all then." He smiled at Dolly, and she dimpled. I wasn't the only one intrigued by his eyes.

Dirk still stood close to my right arm with his kilt swishing as he shuffled from one foot to the other. "I twisted my ankle while I was in Scotland," I said. "Do you mind if I elevate my foot?" I didn't wait for his answer, and pushed a chair away from the table. I waited until Dirk sat, then raised my foot and balanced it on the rung. Wasn't much elevation, but Harper couldn't see it, and anyway, my ankle was just fine.

"Are you okay," Harper asked, "apart from your ankle?"

"Of course I am."

"That was a nasty shove you got from the chief." When he narrowed one eye, he looked downright piratical. "I don't think he meant to do it; he doesn't always watch where he's going. Just assumes everyone will get out of his way." His charcoal eyes got even darker. "But he didn't have to enjoy it so much."

"Aye. I wanted to rip out his heart."

I nodded and unrolled my napkin. "Thank you for keeping me from falling."

"Ye are most welcome."

"Sure. Happy to do it."

They spoke at the same time, sounding like lopsided stereo at a symphony concert.

"Why aren't you wearing a uniform?"

He shrugged. "Detectives usually don't."

"But you had one on when you came to the ScotShop."

Dolly poured the coffee into two enormous mugs. I'll say this for Karaline, she really knows how to keep people liquefied.

"I was filling in that evening for one of the other guys on that shift. His wife just had a baby, and I had some extra time on my hands."

"Paula had her baby? I hadn't heard. Girl or boy?"

He shrugged.

Men.

"Did the mother live?" Dirk's question was almost breathless.

I looked at him. "Of course," I said. Dirk looked at me funny.

"Of course what?" Harper was looking at me funny, too.

"Sorry. I get lost in thought sometimes."

"Sounds like you answer yourself, too." His eyes crinkled. It was a good thing. If he'd been complaining, Dirk might have decked him.

He set down his mug. "Your twin brother called me."

"He did?"

"I didna know ye were a twin."

"What did he want?"

"He offered me advice on how to do my job." Harper's voice was dry.

"That's Drew. He likes to manage things."

"Aye. What would be wrong with that?"

I started to kick Dirk under the table and then recalled that I probably wouldn't be able to. And didn't want to find out for sure. I'd either break my toe on the chair leg or run into his dirk. Dagger. "My brother and Shoe are good friends. They grew up together."

Harper nodded but didn't say anything.

I looked over at Dirk. He was studying Harper intently but seemed to sense my stare and looked back at me. "What's that ye twa are drinking?"

"Ah," I said. "Coffee."

"That doesna answer my question. What is coughee?"

I looked back at Harper. "I wonder when people here first learned to brew coffee from ground-up roasted coffee beans. Do you know?"

"What?" I was pretty sure he thought I'd lost my mind, but he put on a gentlemanly pose. "Coffee. Right. It had to have been well after Columbus. Coffee didn't reach England until the late fifteen hundreds."

"What would be a klumbus?"

I gaped at Harper. "How on earth would you know that?"

He grinned. "Social studies project in seventh grade."

"What would be a klumbus?" Dirk was louder this time.

I interrupted. "How is Shoe doing? Have you seen him?"

"I've talked with him several times. Just like your brother says, Shoe swears he's innocent."

"Well, of course he is. Why can't you look for somebody else, the person who really killed Mason?"

"Ms. Winn," he said in an exceptionally patient voice, "that's just what I'm doing. But you know as well as I do that our chief is the one who arrested Shoe, so he insists that Shoe is guilty."

"Yeah, but Mac's an—" I stopped abruptly when Dirk cleared his throat at my side. "He's all wet," I added, rather lamely.

Harper laughed out loud. "Whatever you were intending to say is probably more to the point." He pushed his coffee mug aside. "Do you have any idea whatsoever, no matter how farfetched it may be, as to why"—he looked around the restaurant, and I turned to follow his gaze. Most of our near neighbors were engaged in animated conversation. He turned back to me and lowered his voice—"any idea why Mason was in your store at night?"

A tiny spider skittered across the table toward Dirk. Did all ghosts attract spiders or just Dirk? Or was it a coincidence? "I've thought about it, but I can't come up with anything." He had no reason to be there." He used to have plenty of reason, but that time was quite simply dead.

Dirk spoke up. He, too, watched the spider. "Mayhap he was meeting someone, and that person killed him."

"I doubt it," I said.

"Doubt what?" Harper was looking at me funny. Again. He scooped the spider onto his napkin and transferred it to a nearby potted plant.

I propped my elbows on the table and leaned my chin into my hands. My head was disconcertingly close to Dirk's. I pulled back a few inches. Dirk gave me a look I couldn't identify. I cleared my throat. "Maybe Andrea knows."

"Who would this Andrea be?"

Harper twirled his coffee mug around. I think he was trying to figure out how much to tell me. "She said she had no idea. She'd just kicked him out that night."

"She did? That's the best sense she's shown in a long time." I hated to give her credit for anything.

Harper snickered, I'd swear he did, but he covered it well by converting it into a cough.

"I wonder why she threw him out?"

"She said she'd found out he'd been cheating on her."

"Really? With who?" He didn't answer me. I guess I understood why. It wasn't any business of mine. I wished I'd slugged Mason twice.

"Mayhap Andrea killed him."

"Yeah. I mean, too bad we can't nab her for the murder, but she doesn't have enough sense to plan something like that."

"You're right," Harper said. "Mason's murder looks like it wasn't planned, though."

"You can't dump a heavy bookcase like that over on somebody without planning how to do it. It had to have been moved away from the wall first—"

"Aye, did I not say so?"

"—and that's not an easy job," I finished. "Maybe the other woman killed him. She might have found out about Andrea." *And me, too. Who else?*

"No. She has a cast-iron alibi."

"I thought alibis could be faked."

"Not this one." He fiddled with his coffee cup again. "That blow to Mason's head . . ." He seemed to be choosing his words carefully.

I thought back to the scene that morning. When we lifted the bookcase off him, there was a deep indentation right across his chest where the front edge of one of those heavy, immovable hardwood shelves had landed. "My bookcase killed him?" My stomach twisted, and I clenched my teeth to keep the coffee down.

Harper leaned across the table and pried my fingers off my coffee mug. "No. Absolutely not. He was killed by a person, someone who slammed him brutally and then dumped the heaviest thing he could find on top of his victim."

He was right. Technically. Murder is done by people. Still, it could have been my bookcase. Maybe I could sell it to that store up in Montpelier . . .

"Peggy?" His hand tightened on mine. "Are you okay?"

I focused my eyes with some difficulty and looked down at my hand, where Harper's fingers gripped hard. Dirk's hand clutched my arm. Maybe that's why I felt so cold all of a sudden.

Harper held up his other hand, and Dolly scooted over. "We need a glass of water."

Between all the fussing, first from Dolly and then from Karaline, I managed to get enough water in me to float a boat. Talk about being *liquefied*. I did feel better, though.

Finally, I was back to normal, or as close to normal as I could get, considering what I'd just learned. "Did you notice that the wallpaper behind the bookcase was damaged?"

"I know. We checked behind the bookcase during our examination of the crime scene. Any guess as to what happened?"

"I'm sorry. All I know is the wallpaper was in fine shape when I installed the bookcase three years ago."

"And then there were those holes," Harper said.

"Do they go all the way through into the bathroom on the other side of the wall?"

He raised an eyebrow. "Is that what you call it?"

"There's a toilet in there and a sink." Of course there also were all those shelves of stuff. I didn't have a very good inventory system. "So, did the holes go through?"

"No. I wasn't sure at first. It was hard to see considering all the . . ."

He seemed to be looking for the least offensive word. *Junk*. That was what he was thinking.

". . . merchandise in there."

When I'd first opened the ScotShop, there'd been a sink in the back but no hookup for a toilet. I moved in a composting toilet—it worked just fine, although the little separate room walled off around the sink had been awfully crowded already, what with built-in shelves along the wall it shared with the showroom. Still, the toilet didn't take up too much space.

I'd been meaning to reorganize those shelves for months—years—but never seemed to find the time. I wasn't about to apologize for it, though.

Harper didn't seem to expect an apology. "We shifted around some of the stuff so we could get a clear look at the wall from that side, and there weren't any marks, which isn't all that surprising. Thin drill bits won't go through seven or eight inches."

"What would be thindril bits?" Dirk's first question in quite a while. I'd almost forgotten about him.

"Why would a . . ." I groped for a way to explain to Dirk without setting off the barm-alarm, but couldn't think of a thing. "I thought interior walls were only as deep as a two-by-four."

"A what? What would be a *to-before*?"

"They usually are," Harper said. "But then again, this building probably has two-by-six studs. It was built a hundred years ago."

"Is that all?" Dirk sounded incredibly haughty. "The chapel in Edinburgh Castle is nigh on three hundred years old. 'Twas built near the start of the twelfth century."

I was about to retort, but then I thought about it. A building built in the early twelfth century would have been—I did a quick calculation—a little less than three hundred years old in Dirk's time, but now it would be nine hundred and something. "A hundred years isn't really all that ancient, is it? I read once that the difference between Scots and Americans, is that *they* think a hundred miles is a long way, and *we* think a hundred years is a long time."

Harper just looked at me and couldn't seem to think of what to say.

"Does it still stand on its verra high hill? Edinburgh Castle?" Dirk sounded wistful.

"Edinburgh Castle has huge, thick walls," I said. "I've visited it several times."

Dirk sighed with relief. "Ah, 'tis nice to know."

Harper leaned his elbow on the table and propped his chin in his hand, mirroring my own position. He gazed at me, and I felt lost in those charcoal eyes. Before I could go too limp, he asked, "What are you talking about?"

I sat up straighter. "Thick walls?"

Dolly, bless her heart, chose that moment to refill our cups. "You doing okay now? Do you need more water?"

I shook my head and then smiled at Harper. "You were talking about how thick the back wall of the shop is."

"Uh-huh." He eyed me with some concern. "Is that wallpaper something you put up yourself?"

I shuddered. "Not hardly. I inherited it from the last owners. That kind of pattern is awfully old-fashioned. I thought it made the place look . . ." I recalled the dark shop between the rowan trees in Pitlochry, and glanced at Dirk. ". . . look sort of old-world and authentic, so I kept it. I like that kind of store." *But not that horrible flocked wallpaper.* Would rowan trees grow in Vermont?

"Anyway," I went on, "it was in pretty good shape. I think it was the original wallpaper, which would make it antique, and I didn't want to spend any extra money on replacing it. The shop setup was expensive enough as it was."

Harper turned his mug around and around. "You must have paid a fortune for that bookcase."

"It's nice, isn't it?" I started to smile, but then I remembered what that bookcase had done. Damn. Why had I ever bought it? "I got it at an estate sale. Cheap."

Dirk was drumming his fingers on the table without making a sound. I laid my hand flat on the table but couldn't feel a vibration. "What would be a nestate sale?" He sounded peeved.

Poor Dirk, but I was getting tired of trying to answer him without getting myself committed. "It was one of those old houses down in Brattleboro. The owner died and they had to sell everything."

Harper didn't pay attention to that. He looked at my fingers splayed out beside my coffee mug and shook his head ever so slightly. "Was anything missing from the shop?"

"Not that I noticed, but I didn't even think about it at first. I was just busy getting the bookcase righted. And then Mac kicked me out of there before I had a chance to do any sort of inventory."

He motioned to Dolly. "We'll go there now. I want to know if anything was taken."

14

A Wee Mess, but Not My Own

As Harper ushered me out the door, I paused long enough for Dirk to scoot through the opening. Wouldn't want him to get stuck behind. Against the bright glare of the sun in my eyes, I could just barely make out a few people looking in the window at the ScotShop. Not that they could see much. Those privacy curtains were still pulled tight shut just behind the display—dammit! I needed my customers to see all the wonderful merchandise inside.

I inhaled sharply. That sounded so crass. He'd been my boyfriend, my fiancé—well, almost fiancé—for way too long, and here I was worried about my bank balance.

Still, Mason might be dead, but I was alive, and I needed the front door wide open. The next rent payment would eat into my savings if the shop stayed closed much longer. The building might be old, but the real estate was considered prime.

I felt like a heartless heel, but I asked anyway. "How long before I can reopen?"

His charcoal eyes widened. "We released the scene this morning."

"What?" I yelped. "Why didn't anybody tell me?" I put on a bright smile as I approached the small group of people milling around the crime-scene tape. "Folks, we'll be opening up this afternoon. I hope you'll come back."

"You bet," said a voice from the other side of a fairly large woman. A kid, maybe her son, stepped out from in back of her. "I wanna see where the guy got creamed."

"Watch your foul tongue, ye wee gomerel."

My sentiments exactly.

"Now, Robert, you behave yourself." His mother didn't sound like she meant it. The avid gleam in her eye made me certain that she'd come up with the idea first.

I let just the three of us in the door, closing it quickly in the woman's face, barely managing to miss slamming the end of Dirk's plaid. Not that anything would have happened—could a ghost plaid catch in a door? Maybe it could. I'd never seen Dirk walk through a wall or anything. It was too much to think about. I leaned back against the window frame, waiting for my eyes to adjust to the dim light.

After a few seconds I flipped on some lights and took a long, hard look at my shop, hoping all the blood was gone. The bookcase wasn't aligned right. The tiered tables near the back were twisted askew. The two circular racks, one of pleat-sewn kilts and the other of full-sleeved shirts that could make any man look like an eighteenth-century poet, had been shifted to one side, probably so the police could move the body—Mason's body. I'd designed the layout of the shop with my brother's wheelchair in mind but had never thought a stretcher would need to get through. I swallowed a bitter taste and saw Harper watching me from in front of the tie display. He started toward me, as my ghostie stepped between us, hand on the top of his dirk. "Are ye aright, now? Ye still look a bit peaked."

"I'm fine. Don't worry."

"I'm not worried," Harper said. "Seeing a crime scene can be a hair-raising experience, though. Are you sure you're okay?"

"The bookcase is off-center." Without thinking, I added, "I'll get Sam and Shoe to help me move it."

Harper cleared his throat. "Maybe I could help instead."

"Damn. I forgot about Shoe." I hadn't really forgotten about him. The fact that he was in the town jail—thank goodness they hadn't carted him off to the state prison—had been in the back of my mind most of the time since he'd been arrested.

"I would help ye if I could." Dirk paused before a particularly obnoxious plastic Nessie. "What is this?"

I moved his way and shifted the little statue a bit to the right. "The Loch Ness Monster never looked so good, did it?"

"That is no wha' she looks like."

When that sank in, I couldn't help myself. I gaped at him. "Have you seen her?"

"Och, aye. Once. When I was a child and my family went to a gathering at the Loch." His left hand clamped onto the hilt of that wicked-looking dagger of his. "But once was enough for a lifetime."

"Seen who?" Harper fingered a shirt. I wondered which clan he was from.

"Nothing. I'm going to call Gilda and Sam. No reason why they can't help me open up."

"You were going to check to see if anything was missing."

"After I call. Gotta get this shop open for business." I shifted the shawl higher on my shoulder and pulled my cell out of my purse as I walked toward the back, but I stopped dead before I pressed the contact list. "What on earth happened here?"

Harper and Dirk both headed in my direction. A fine, dirty-looking powder covered the display tables, the lamps, the bookcase, the cash register, the counter. "Good lord, I can't open the shop if it looks like this."

"Fingerprint powder."

"What is finger prinpowder?"

"Shh," I said to Dirk, but they both looked offended.

"I'm sorry," I said to Harper, hoping that Dirk would guess the apology was meant for him as well. "I guess I'm just feeling the strain." I swept my arm in an arc that took in the devastation.

Harper opened his mouth, closed it, and ran a finger along the smooth head of one of the less obnoxious Nessie statues. This one sported a sprightly green spray of artificial seaweed dangling from its jaw.

Since he didn't seem to be planning to say anything, I jumped back in. "I hope you found something worthwhile."

He paused. "No. Most everything had been wiped clean. The prints we found were what we'd expect to find in a store that most of the townspeople and a lot of tourists visit."

"Well, they won't visit unless I can get this cleaned up." I called Gilda, told her to bring Sam, and turned to inventory my messy store.

As it was, I couldn't find anything missing. And we didn't open that afternoon, even with Harper helping us. Fingerprint powder is a bear to remove. So were the dried blood and bodily fluids.

As we worked, I couldn't help but examine Gilda. She looked like heck. Several times I asked her if she felt okay, but each time she just shrugged me off. "Headache." Still, she kept doggedly at the cleaning, although I saw Sam and Harper—and Dirk, too—staring at her occasionally. I wasn't the only one wondering what was going on.

The obnoxious Robert and his mother came back around two o'clock and pounded on the door. I unlocked it and told them we were still cleaning.

"Aw! I wanna see!" Robert pushed his way past me before

I could stop him. I blocked his mother and called to Sam to catch him before he did any damage.

I'd forgotten about Dirk, who stood smack-dab in the middle of the aisle.

"Och, no, ye wee feond." He didn't sound particularly angry, but he did sound resolute.

I was sure Robert, "fey-ond" or not, couldn't see or hear my ghost, but he pulled to a sudden stop, and only I could see that he had seemed to collide with Dirk. He shuddered from his head to his feet, made a U-turn, and shoved me aside to get back to his mother. "I wanna go home," he whimpered.

I closed the door, not even caring how she handled the boy. Dirk stood, openmouthed, as bewildered as I was. "How did I do that?"

"I was wondering the same thing," I whispered. "Did you feel it when he ran into you?"

"Not feel, precisely. But—ye ken when ye have a bad dream? Someone's trying his best to kill ye, and ye dinna want it to happen, but ye dinna seem to be able to stop it?"

I nodded, not sure where this was heading.

"I didna like that young brat, and when he pushed ye aside, I wanted to stop him, but didna know how I could, and then . . ."

I waited for him to go on, but he just stood there. "And then . . ." I prompted.

"Who are you talking to?" Harper looked concerned.

"The resident ghost," I said without thinking. How much had he heard?

"Right." He shook his head. He reached out, almost as if he were going to touch my arm, and Dirk bristled beside me.

"Keep your hands off her, ye miswenden manny."

I wondered what "meswinduhn" meant but didn't ask. After all, Dirk had lived just before the time of Chaucer. I wondered how I could even understand him. Some sort of trans-time auto translation, maybe. Memories of *The*

Canterbury Tales in high school senior English came back: *Whan that Aprille with his shoures soote,/The droghte of March hath perced to the roote,/And bathed every veyne in swich licour,/Of which . . .*

Dirk reached in front of me. Harper's hand hung in mid-air about three inches from my elbow. He shook his hand, the way someone whose hand has gone to sleep will shake it to get rid of the pins and needles.

I glared at Dirk. "Did you do that?"

He just smiled.

Harper rubbed his hand down the side of his pants. "Do what?"

"Um. Nothing. Did you need me for something?"

He leaned to one side and looked around in back of me, shook his head, rubbed his hands together, and motioned me toward where Sam stood in the back. "We had a question about where you want the bookcase."

I followed him, with Dirk on my heels. "The bookcase has to be placed exactly, with its center twenty feet from that wall."

Dirk asked me why, and Sam snorted. "Picky, picky, picky."

"Can it, Sam."

Harper waited for the inanity to stop. "Why?" he asked.

"Why what?"

"Why does it have to be centered?"

"If it's not, it looks unbalanced from the front door."

Sam rolled his eyes, but Harper—and Dirk—turned and walked back to the front of the store. They stood side by side. "Aye, ye are right."

"I see what you mean."

I put my hands over my face. Stereo. This was ridiculous.

"Are you okay?"

I spread my fingers apart to see Harper looking at me yet again with some concern. "Yeah. Sure. Let's get busy here." I started to reach under the counter but pulled back. "Don't need the measuring tape. I'd almost forgotten—I marked the baseboard at seventeen feet. That's where this edge of the bookcase goes."

After the Logg Cabin closed at three, Karaline came to help, bearing gifts.

"Good grief," she hollered as she breezed in. "Looks like a funeral home in here." She carried a large tray of doughnuts— I could smell them even from across the room. Or maybe I only imagined that I could. She balanced the tray on a rack of tartan skirts and opened the vertical blinds a bit. The light did make it brighter. Not happier but definitely brighter.

Even with her help and lots of coffee from the oversized pot in the back room, we didn't finish the cleanup until well after closing time and into the wee hours. Opening time at nine o'clock was going to come way too soon.

Still, late as it was, we gathered at the table in the back room. Karaline's edible gift had been almost decimated over the course of the afternoon and evening, but there were enough doughnuts left to lure us into sitting down. Dirk watched Harper take a seat across the table from me before he leaned against the edge of my desk. I could see him directly between Harper's right shoulder and Gilda's left. Gilda looked marginally better. Maybe hard work dissipated migraines?

Sam snatched a jelly-filled. "Aren't you supposed to be at the station interviewing somebody or canvassing door to door or testing blood samples or investigating something?"

"What would be kanvasing?"

Harper looked back over his shoulder. Surely he couldn't have heard Dirk's question?

He said, "I *am* investigating," but he looked just a wee bit uncomfortable as he said it, and I could have sworn he glanced at me. Was he . . . no, he couldn't be here just because of me . . . but he *had* spent the major portion of the day here—I shook myself. He was not interested in me. He was not. He couldn't help it if those charcoal eyes of his drew me into them.

"I think we can assume," Karaline said, waving a long arm around the table and grabbing a doughnut as her hand passed over it, "that nobody in this room is the murderer, right?"

"Are ye sure of that?"

"Yes," I said in the general direction of the desk before I remembered. "I'm sure it wasn't one of "—I waved around the table. Harper cocked his head at me but didn't say anything—"so I don't know why you're investigating us . . ."

"Maybe he just wants to get to know us all better."

Karaline crossed her eyes at Gilda's comment.

I continued despite the interruption. ". . . and we know Shoe didn't murder . . . Mason." His name caught in my throat, but only Harper and Dirk seemed to notice.

Gilda reached for a maple-glazed. "What I want to know is why Mason stood still long enough to get a bookcase dumped on him."

I looked at Harper. Was he going to answer her? Apparently not. "He was knocked out first, Gilda. With Shoe's baseball bat, remember?"

She shrugged. "I didn't want to think about it." Her voice was even breathier than usual.

"But why, can ye tell me, was yon case for books moved in the first place?"

"I don't have a clue," I said.

"About what, cuz?" Sam asked between chocolate-covered bites.

"Why the bookcase was moved."

"Maybe it was an accident," Gilda offered.

"Nay."

"No." The stereo effect again. Dirk quieted down, but Harper pointed out that the bookcase was too heavy to have moved or fallen on its own.

Dirk crossed his arms—his muscular arms, I noted yet again—and his plaid drooped lower on his shoulder. "There must ha' been something behind it. Something our wee murderer wanted."

"That may be, but why kill Mason?"

Karaline swiveled her head to her left and curled her lip at me. "Did you kiss the Blarney Stone over there? Who're you talking to?"

"The Blarney Stone's in Ireland," I snapped.

"To her ghost," Harper said.

I shrugged. "It's still a good question—what did Mason do to get himself killed?"

"Ye're not listening to me, woman!"

I stared at Dirk. I didn't know he could shout like that. For a dead man, he had quite a set of lungs on him. "I was, too—" I caught myself and improvised. "I was too worried before to think about it much, but . . ." I couldn't come up with a way to end my sentence.

"What, I asked ye, was behind the case that the murderer wanted?"

I nodded to let him know I'd heard. ". . . but what do you think was behind the bookcase?"

Karaline laughed. "Crappy wallpaper, that's what."

"Dead bugs?" Sam suggested.

"Nothing." Gilda sounded definite for once. I was so used to her tentative groping for words, I gaped at her. "There wasn't," she said. "There wasn't anything back there. The bookcase was just a way to throw us off the scent." She nodded her head as if to say *so there*.

"Mayhap your Mason was the one who moved it."

"He's not my Mason," I muttered under my breath, but I had to admit Dirk had a point. "Maybe Mason was the one who moved it," I said to the group.

"You need a good night's sleep," Karaline said. "Maybe then you'll stop talking to the wall."

"He couldn't have moved it," Sam said. "He was under it."

Gilda touched his forearm and left her hand there. "Maybe it fell on top of him while he was moving it."

Harper shook his head but stayed quiet.

"Mistress Gilda's horse isna hooked to her plow, is it?"

Before I could giggle, Karaline filled in the silence. "Gilda? Hello? Second time, here. Remember the baseball bat?"

"Oh. Yeah."

"The holes," Dirk said. "Dinna forget the wee holes."

I was getting dizzy. I took a deep breath. Sam broke in before I could say anything. "It takes two to move that case." He flexed his arm. "Two men."

Karaline threw her napkin at him.

He fielded it and threw it right back at her. "Or a man and a strong woman," he amended. "Maybe Karaline is our culprit."

"I wouldn't touch Mason Kilmarty with a ten-foot pole, much less a short baseball bat." She met my eyes, and I knew she was remembering how I'd cried off and on for an hour the night I'd found Mason and Andrea in bed together. The night I'd rushed to her house, blubbering like a drama queen, swearing one minute that I was brokenhearted and the next that hell couldn't burn hot enough—freeze cold enough—for a rat like Mason.

Dirk interrupted my little trip down nightmare lane. "The holes. Ask about the holes."

I reached for a double-glazed. "Anybody know why there'd be holes in the wall behind the bookcase?"

"They looked like they'd been drilled," Sam said. "Three-sixteenths," he added with authority.

"Three what?" Dirk strode around the table, his kilt swirling as he walked, until he stood to my right, behind Karaline—probably so he could get a good look at Sam's face across the table. "What sort of number is that?"

Harper shifted in his seat but remained silent.

"Besides Peggy and Karaline," Gilda said, and I could have sworn she added *and me* under her breath, "who else would want to kill Mason?"

Harper gave a minuscule shake to his head. Or maybe he didn't. I wasn't sure.

"Good question," said Karaline.

"That still doesna explain—"

Karaline stood, and Dirk backtracked quickly to get out of her way. "I have to get some sleep."

". . . the wee holes," Dirk added with a glare at my friend.

A faint buzz sounded from across the table. Harper pulled out his phone, looked at it, and stood. "Gotta run. Duty calls." He cringed. "How trite is that, I ask you?"

"Treit? What would be this treit?"

"T-r-i-t-e. Commonplace, unoriginal," I muttered, and Harper's shoulder's tensed.

"That was trite when I was alive," Dirk observed.

"You're working days and nights both?" Gilda sounded awestruck.

Harper looked a bit sheepish. I thought he was going to answer, but he must have decided against it. Either he was mad about my "trite" explanation or maybe he wanted out of here. All this was my imagination. He didn't really want to spend time with me. He was working. He was investigating. I was insane.

I let him out the front door, and Karaline, too, locking it behind them before Sam and Gilda could leave. "Would you two help me move the bookcase?"

"Again? How many times you gonna move that sucker?"

"Those holes bother me, Sam. Maybe if we take a closer look at them, we can tell what's going on and help Shoe out."

Sam looked at Gilda and shrugged. "You mind waiting a little longer, sweetie?"

Sweetie? Sam and Gilda? I thought Shoe was—

"That's fine, honey. I'm not in a hurry."

Without waiting for me, they both headed toward the back and began removing items from the shelves. Good idea. I'd hate to break anything else moving that sucker, as Sam called it.

Movement to my left caught my eye. My own reflection
in the shop windows where Karaline had opened the blinds.
As dark as it was outside and with these overhead lights on,
we might as well be spotlighted. The thought of Harper
walking by and seeing us still here brought a momentary
qualm, but I squashed it decidedly. I backtracked, closed
the blinds on the courtyard side, and drew the curtains
behind the mannequins on the street side. We didn't use
them often—only when the sun was exceptionally bright—
but tonight we needed privacy for what I was planning to do.

"Sam," I said, "be sure you go by the hardware store in
the morning and get a dead bolt lock. We need four keys, too."

"Don't have to." He dug into his jeans pocket and pulled
out a bedraggled white paper bag. "Harper took care of it.
I'll install it in the morning."

"You can install it tonight." I took the bag. "That was so
nice of him."

"Yeah. Here's the receipt." He grinned fiendishly. "He
said you could pay him later."

15

Hidden

Between the three of us, after Sam installed the dead bolt, and with Dirk watching and muttering under his breath, it took a lot longer than I'd expected. Maybe it should have been two big men struggling with it, I thought. We managed to rock the bookcase away from the wall, far enough that we had room to stand behind it.

I couldn't help it. I imagined the effort it would take to get that bookcase falling. If I leaned against the wall and put one foot up against the back of it . . .

"Why are you just standing there?"

"What are you looking at?" Gilda and Sam spoke at the same time, her voice coming from somewhere behind him. She peeked around Sam, whose arm was braced against the wall at a spot higher than my head.

I peeled back the Scotch tape I'd put there this morning, and a strip of antique wallpaper drooped down like a brown-flocked retriever's ear. The Sheetrock, when I touched it, left a white trace on my fingertips. I remembered the Easter Sunday two years before, when Mason had shown up at my house right at dawn toting rolls of wallpaper as a birthday surprise for me. For a week or two before that, I'd been halfheartedly stripping off the wallpaper in the downstairs half bath, but I'd kept getting sidetracked. He helped me steam off the rest of the old paper, and when I asked him how long it was going to take—because, even though the shop was closed on Mondays, I did have to open it on Tuesday—he waved away any answer. It took us all day Sunday and a great deal of Monday; that old Sheetrock was spewing dust at the slightest touch. It stuck to our hair, our clothing. We ended up having to replace one sheet of it, and that was a job from hell. I'd never want to do that for a living. Mason was, had been, so nice in so many ways. Except when he was stealing town money. Or pawing through my purse. Or messing around with Andrea and whoever else.

I loosened my clenched fist. It took some effort.

Dirk was fascinated by the Sheetrock. "What is this?

Sam and Gilda seemed to be paying no attention to me, except that I heard Sam say something about la-la land. I poked him in the ribs with my elbow. "See the holes?"

He looked over my shoulder. "Yep. Drilled. That's what I said."

I ran my finger carefully over one of them. "Why on earth would anyone do this?"

Dirk peered over my other shoulder. "What is behind the wall?"

"There's nothing behind the wall," I said, "except the storage area and a little bathroom."

"We know that," Gilda said.

"I meant, ye wee stubborn lass, what's behind *this* wall and in front of the one on the ither side."

"You mean, what's in between the walls?"

Sam reached over my shoulder and cupped his hand under my chin, pulling it toward him. "Her eyes are clear. Her jaw is firm." He snapped his fingers beside my head with his other hand and I flinched. "Her ears seem to be working just fine." He looked at Gilda and back at me. "Why do I get the feeling she's going bananas on us?"

"Bananas?" Dirk sounded confused.

Gilda poked her head under Sam's arm again, like a yellow mushroom springing up after a rainstorm. "Because she's not making any sense?"

"Stop it, guys. I'm perfectly sane. I'm not going bananas—going crazy." I glanced at Dirk, and he nodded his understanding. "I'm just . . . answering my own thoughts." *And those of the resident ghost.* "Doesn't it make sense that maybe something is in the wall? Something the murderer wanted?"

"Maybe Mason surprised him in the act."

Gilda poked Sam in the side. "What act?"

"I dunno. Whatever he was looking for."

That wouldn't hold up grammatically, but I got what he meant. "You think Mason saw him somehow or other?"

"Mayhap he was in on it himself."

I stared at Dirk. "Ohmigosh, I never thought of that."

"Thought of what?" Sam said, as Gilda said, "Huh?"

"Maybe Mason was the one drilling the holes." Even as I said it, though, I didn't believe it.

"But why?" Gilda sounded as plaintive as a mewling kitten.

"I dinna ken."

"I don't know."

"Beats me."

After that little trio, we were all silent for a minute or two—even Dirk, who ran a finger up and down over the strip of wallpaper without moving it a hair.

"I know what we have to do," I finally said. "Let's cut into the wall and see what's back there." I will admit to a momentary qualm about destroying a wall that didn't belong to me, but the qualm didn't last long. Curiosity wins every time.

A circular saw is not one of those tools I normally keep around the shop. Nor did I have a drill. But I did have a hammer. Sheetrock would be easy to put a hole into. Picking a likely spot between two of the drilled holes, I gave it a good whack.

And about broke my arm. The hammer bounced off something solid. Behind the Sheetrock, as we soon found out, was a layer of unappetizingly gray wallpaper and a solid wall of tongue-and-groove wooden slats fitted together.

"Who built this?" Sam shook his head in disgust. "Can you imagine how much it musta cost?" He grabbed the wallpaper strip and ripped it off, all the way down to the floorboard. "I say we find out what's behind all this."

"And how were ye planning to do that, wee manny?"

"Good question," I said. "Maybe we should start by stripping off the wallpaper?"

"What question?" Sam twirled his finger around his ear. "I still say she's going barmy on us."

I ignored him. "Pull it off carefully. We don't want to damage anything that's going to show when the bookcase is back in place. Just from here"—I drew an imaginary line in an arbitrary spot about a foot inside the limits of where the bookcase sat and just to the left of the first hole—"to here." Another line on the other side.

"No," Sam said. "Leave on the wallpaper. It'll help hold the Sheetrock together."

He fetched a knife from the workroom and slit the Sheetrock along those imaginary lines. As we worked, I had to push Dirk out of the way. Well, not *push* him exactly, because there was no way to do that, but I kept making little shooing motions.

"What is this sheet of rock? It is no like any rock I have ever seen."

I just shook my head. I wasn't going to try to explain the building industry. I'd had enough trouble with horses under a hood. "No higher than six feet. We don't want the bare wood to show over the top of the case."

I'd forgotten how dusty Sheetrock is. My bathroom at home was nothing compared to this. Of course, this Sheetrock was probably five times the age of my house. This was not going to be fun to clean up. Dirk kept sticking his head in where I was just about to pull on the Sheetrock, and I shooed him away a couple more times.

"I'm not in your way," Gilda complained.

"Boy, are you cranky," Sam said. Not to Gilda. To me.

I pulled out one more chunk of Sheetrock, about waist high, and ripped away the gray wallpaper behind it. "Would ye look at that?" Dirk had stuck his head right in front of me. "Look at these lines." He drew back and turned around, keeping his hand hovering in front of the wall behind him.

I leaned around him. "You're right."

Gilda stopped pulling on her section. "Who's right?"

"Look at this." A clear rectangle of solid wood, set into the tongue-and-groove boards, looked amazingly like a door, but without a handle. The top of it was just a bit lower than my waist; the bottom went all the way to the floorboard. Its right-hand edge was maybe three feet from the door into the back room, about a foot from where the edge of the bookcase would have been.

Sam reached past me and spread his forearm along the upper line of the door. "Eighteen inches wide," he said.

"How do you know that?" Gilda sounded awestruck.

"From here to here"—he indicated two spots: his elbow and the bony protuberance on his wrist—"is exactly thirteen inches, and from here to here"—he pointed to his wrist and then to the middle joint of his little finger—"is five inches."

"You measured all your body parts?" Gilda's eyes widened suddenly and she blushed furiously. So did Sam. I just rolled my eyes and looked away from the two of them. Dirk snickered. Even the ghost got that one.

"Let's get back to work," I said. "I'm beginning to think that whoever broke in here was maybe looking for this door. Does that make sense?"

"What's on the other side?" Dirk tapped noiselessly on the wall.

"I think we need a screwdriver or something." I headed toward the back, but Sam grabbed my arm.

"You need to call the police, Peggy. There was a murder, remember?"

Damn him. "But if we knew what was back there—"

"Peggy." I'd never heard Sam sound so forceful. "Call Harper."

"I'll call him tomorrow." I looked at my watch. "That is, later today."

Gilda laid her hand on Sam's arm. "Aren't you the least bit curious about what's in back of that door?"

Bless her. Maybe I should give that breathy little minx a raise. Sam furrowed his brow for a fraction of a second. "We . . ." His brow cleared. "Do you really want to know, little sweetie?"

I ignored his unctuous gushing and concentrated on letting her convince him.

It didn't take long. A few batted eyelashes and he was a goner.

Sam took up the hammer. "Gotta get all these nails pulled, or we'll rip our hands."

The Sheetrock nails were spaced fourteen inches apart—I measured them before he started pulling. "I thought studs were eighteen inches apart."

"Yeah, they are nowadays. Back a hundred years ago, buildings were built to last. Today, a two-by-four is really one and a half by three and a half."

"It is?" Gilda sounded bewildered. "So, why did they need closer studs if they had wider two-by-fours? And why," she went on doggedly, "are the studs fourteen inches apart, but the door is eighteen inches wide?"

"That is a verra good question."

Sam looked at Gilda, then at me.

"That's what we're going to find out," I said, and Sam went back to pulling nails.

I sent Gilda to clean up the coffeepot and the table while

Dirk and I watched Sam. Not the highlight of my day, but Dirk looked fascinated. Didn't they have nails back then?

Sam dropped the nails on the floor as he pulled them. I thought about reprimanding him, but then I saw the force he needed to wrench them out with the hammer and held my tongue. I could pick up nails just fine with precious little effort.

Dirk bent over and inspected a nail. "Ridges. It has ridges. The nails I made never had ridges. How does the maker do that?"

I asked Sam and received a veritable lecture about the different kinds of nails.

"And they're made with machines," I said, knowing I'd get one of those sideways looks from Sam. I did.

"Do ye mean like with the wee horses under the hood?"

"Something like that," I muttered, and bent to pick up more nails.

Gilda popped out of the back room with—oh lordy—a mug of coffee in each hand. I was going to float home once this was done. I took a sip.

Dirk shook his head. "I dinna ken what is so wonderful about that brew that ye imbibe it at all hours."

I couldn't figure out how to answer him without keying another *barmy* from Sam.

"The coffee's good, Gilda. Thanks. But let's get this done and over with."

Sam groaned. Gilda placed a hand against his chest and he shut up.

Once all the nails were out of the way, Dirk offered his dagger to help pry open the door, but, because that obviously wouldn't work, I sent Sam for a screwdriver.

Within moments I was watching him try to force the door open. The trouble was, it was fitted so tightly, he couldn't get a handle on it. A handle. *A handle?* "Wait a minute, Sam! I'll be right back."

I scooted into the storage room, with Dirk right behind me, and rummaged in a junk drawer until I found a small package of sturdy three-inch screws. I tipped some out onto my palm.

"What are those?" Dirk sounded baffled.

"They're called screws." I held my hand out so he could see.

"These are made of metal?" His voice was full of wonder. "The only ones I have ever seen were carved from wood."

I looked at them with a deeper appreciation. "Handy little things," I said. "Come on. Let's put them to use."

I handed Sam three of them. "Screw these in about half an inch." I waited for congratulations but met only blank stares from the two of them.

Sam rubbed the top of his head. "Why?"

It seemed so obvious to me. "So we can each hold one and pull the door outward."

The light dawned. The operation continued.

My intention had been for all three of us to pull at the same time so we could share the fun, but Sam put in two and stepped back. "It's your wall," he said.

Technically, it wasn't, but this was way too late to bother with the legality of putting a big hole in somebody else's wall. Who owned this building anyway?

"You don't suppose there's a"—Gilda took a deep breath—"a body in there, do you?"

I hadn't thought she had that much imagination. "Don't worry, Gilda. A body wouldn't fit in a space that's only six inches deep. Anyway, even if there were a body, it'd be nothing but a bunch of bones after this long." She didn't look particularly reassured.

I'd been told that the wallpaper was the original, ordered all the way from New York City a hundred years ago by Mrs. Emelinda Pitcairn, whose husband had built the structure, the largest building in Hamelin at the time. Come to think of it, it still was the largest.

As I reminded Gilda of all this—and of course, Dirk as well—I rested my hands on the two screws, almost afraid to see what was back there. Maybe it *was* a skeleton. What would I do if . . . *Get a grip, Winn*, I told myself, and pulled on the screws, with Dirk urging me on from behind my right shoulder.

Nothing happened. The door was tightly wedged, as if the wood had swollen over the years. Sam and I both pulled. He inserted two more screws, one for each of us. We found gloves in the back room so we could hold on tighter.

Finally, after more than a few cuss words from me, the door moved. Sam let go, waved me on, and I lifted it out and up, over the ledge formed by the baseboard.

No body.

No bones.

A safe, looking like something out of an old B-grade movie. This wall was obviously deeper than six inches.

The safe, festooned with cobwebs, was gunmetal gray with gold curlicues at each of the corners and fancy lettering in red and gold that proclaimed *Thos. Barnes, Pittsburg, PA.* Holy crap, what were we going to do with this? Naturally, I tried the handle. Naturally, it was locked. The combination dial spun easily as I twisted it back and forth.

We stood there in the Sheetrock dust, congratulating ourselves on our find, berating ourselves for not having known about it sooner, and drinking Gilda's coffee like crazy.

"This sure did take a long time," Gilda said around a yawn.

I looked at my watch. Dirk cleared his throat before I could swear. "Yikes! We have to open in two hours."

We replaced the door, threw out the broken Sheetrock, and vacuumed up all the dust—moving considerably faster than the ache in my muscles called for—and pushed the bookcase back into place moments before nine o'clock. I looked carefully. There was no sign of Sheetrock, damaged wallpaper, or a hidden safe. Gilda and Sam arranged the display items as I opened curtains and unlocked the front door right on time, all three of us harried and dragging our tails but putting on a good show for the tourists.

I called the station at ten. Moira answered, her southern drawl stronger than usual. "Hamelin Po-lice Station. What kin I do fer yeuw?"

"Good morning, Moira. It's Peggy. I need to talk with Harper."

"He's not in right now, Peg." *Raht naow.* "He's gone to the funeral." *Feeoon-ruhl.*

"What funeral? Who died?"

There was a long silence. I could hear male voices in the background. "That would be the funeral of your former boyfriend, remember?"

"No, I didn't re-mem-buh." Good grief, why was I being so sarcastic? "I'm sorry, Moira. Shouldn't have grumped at you."

Damn. I'd honestly forgotten about the funeral. I hadn't wanted to go anyway. I'd have to watch Andrea crying, although she might not be too devastated, since she'd thrown him out. That's what Harper had said. "Harper didn't even know Mason," I said. "So what's he doing at the funeral?"

Another silence. "Honestly, Peg. I should think you'd be able to figure that out." She lowered her voice, and the background sounds diminished. She must have cupped her hand around the receiver. "Your boyfriend—"

"Ex," I said. "Very much ex."

"Don't get your britches twisted. Your ex-boyfriend . . . was . . . murdered."

I thought about it. Oh. Sometimes the murderer attends the funeral. Fine. I'd tell Harper about the safe later.

"Shall I take a message, sweetie?"

"No. It's nothing much." Just a major surprise in an already muddled case.

16

A Wee Puzzle of My Own

The shop was busy, and I spent most of the morning surreptitiously moving daddy longlegs outside. I'd scoop one up, carry it through the back door, and deposit it on the fence across the alley. As soon as I returned to the ScotShop, I'd have to field questions about finding Mason's body. There were enough purchases to make the morning worthwhile, but I got awfully tired of the ghouls who came in to absorb the aura of murder without buying anything. At least Robert—the wee fiend, as Dirk would say—didn't show up again. Maybe his mother got smart and disowned him.

Gilda asked me if I'd tried Harper again. "Not yet, but I will as soon as we get a break." An hour later, Sam reminded me to call him. "Yeah, yeah," I told him. "I'll do it." But visions of the shop closed clouded my judgment, and I kept putting off the call.

I was still so tired, it took me a while to see what was happening, but just before noon I noticed that wherever Dirk stood, not only did spiders spring out of nowhere, but customers seemed to avoid him. They couldn't possibly be doing it consciously. No one ever gave any indication that they saw anything, but I'd see someone start toward him, stop, turn around, and head the other way. When he wandered toward the tartan ties, some of the best-selling items in the shop, I hurried over to divert him.

Pretending to straighten the display, I spoke as quietly as I could. "You've got to go into the back room and stay there."

"Why?"

It's hard to talk without moving your lips. "You're scaring my customers away. They don't want to get near you."

"They dinna know I'm here."

"Yes, they do. They don't know it, but they *know* it, if you get what I mean."

"Ye are making no sense whatsoever."

"Were you talking to me, young lady?" I looked to my right. A white-haired woman peered anxiously at me.

"Not at all, ma'am. I tend to talk to myself whenever I straighten the ties." *And whenever my ghost is around.* "It passes the time."

She gave me a befuddled smile. I motioned Dirk out of the way. "Just what were you looking for, ma'am?"

"I'd like a Graham plaid tie for my son-in-law."

Dirk hadn't gone as far away as I wanted him to. "Would she be wanting Graham of Monteith or Graham of Montrose? They're verra distinct, ye ken."

"How would I know?"

"Well, don't you work here, young lady?"

"I'm sorry, ma'am. I meant, would you happen to know if he's Graham of Montrose or Graham of . . . uh . . ."

"Monteith. Can ye no remember the twa?"

"Yes, Monteith. Which one?"

"Oh dear, I'm not sure. Does it make a difference?"

"Well," I said, "Graham is Graham, after all. . . ."

Dirk snorted. "Try telling that to Bonar Graham of Clan

Monteith and Macgilvernock Graham of Clan Montrose. They wouldna thank ye."

I cleared my throat. "Let's move along, right down here to the Gs. The ties are in alphabetical order, see?" I helped her find a lovely green plaid tie and a matching tartan scarf for her daughter.

Dirk pounced as soon as she walked away from the register. "She purchased a Monteith. Let us hope he is not of Montrose. Ye had a Montrose right next to the Monteith. Could ye not have sold her both so he could have a choice?"

"You're turning into quite a marketing expert, aren't you?" Dirk gave me a long, level look. Guess I hadn't kept the sarcasm out of my voice. "They were both green," I said. "She didn't know the difference."

"Aye, but he might."

He was right, damn his hide, but I was too tired to think about it.

As soon as I could, I ushered Dirk into the stock room and draped the shawl over the back of the desk chair. "Stay," I said, as if I were talking to my brother's dog. "If Gilda or Sam come back here, keep out of their way."

"Ye could at least have brought me a book."

I rummaged in the desk, pulled out a dog-eared paperback, and propped it open. "Read slowly. I'll come back when I can to turn the page." And remove spiders, too, most likely.

"Talking to your ghost again?"

I spun around. Harper stood just inside the door, notebook in hand.

Dirk moved in front of me as if to protect me, although I couldn't imagine from what, except maybe Harper's ridicule for my habit of talking out loud to the thin air. I glimpsed Harper's face through Dirk's shoulder for just a moment and quickly stepped to one side. That was just too bizarre for words, the two of them melded together like that.

"I tried to call you," I told him, "but you were at the funeral. We found something last night."

"I know." He crossed his arms. "Gilda called and said you had a surprise for me."

"Gilda? That little—" I took a deep breath. "Yes. I'm glad she did."

Was that a smirk on his face? Whatever it was, he wiped it clean immediately. "So, what do you have to show me?"

"Can it possibly wait until after closing time? Business is fairly good, and I don't want to have to close early."

"Why would you have to close early?"

"There was something behind the bookcase, and you're not going to want to look at it when there are customers around."

"We missed something?" He looked incredulous.

"Aye, ye did." Dirk positively gloated. I wanted to kick him.

"It wasn't that obvious," I said. Probably the understatement of the year.

Harper looked at his watch. "Is it something that will hold a few hours?"

"Och, aye. It will that, and mayhap another hundred years or so."

"I think so," I said. "It seems to have been there for quite some time."

"Are you always this enigmatic?"

Dirk's hand flew to his dagger. "He insults you?"

I thought back to Chaucer. Maybe *enigmatic* wasn't a word back then. "I do tend to be mysterious at times," I said, and flicked my fingers at Dirk.

Harper watched my hand. He cleared his throat, entirely unnecessarily. "I'm interested in seeing this mystery behind the bookcase, but there's something else. Something I'd like to talk over with you." His eyes had gone a deeper gray. Maybe it was just a shadow cast by the light from the high window over the desk.

"Fine. What's up?"

"I want to show you something."

You can show me whatever you'd like. I put an instant—well, almost instant—brake on that thought. "What is it?"

He glanced around the workroom and right through Dirk. The shawl was, thank goodness, invisible to others when Dirk held it. Apparently satisfied that we were alone, Harper opened his notebook and extracted what must have been an evidence bag. I'd seen enough of those on TV and in the movies. He laid it on the desk, carefully avoiding the daddy longlegs strolling across the surface. I bent to look. Dirk stepped closer. The bag held a wrinkled piece of paper with scratchy old writing on it. "What is this?"

"Do you recognize it?"

"No." I glanced at the handwritten column of words and numbers. "The ink looks old-fashioned," I said, "but the words are nothing but nonsense."

L side 18 to wl

       ,000 dentists

L

4

      _& 10

_ _ stars

     /100 %

1 R

brother against brother

     ended just in time

I read it aloud again. "Dentists?" I said. "Stars? What on earth is this?"

He took it back and returned it to his pocket. "I hoped you could tell me. We found it in Mason's sporran."

The last time I'd seen that sporran . . .

I felt woozy and reached for a nearby table. Harper grabbed my arm just as the bell over the front door jingled. I straightened quickly and looked out into the showroom. A busload of middle-aged women fanned out among the displays, and I heard Gilda and Sam greet them. I sure hoped they'd find lots to buy. Maybe good sales would take my mind off Mason's bloody face.

Harper came back half an hour before closing time and wandered around the store, fingering a tartan here, a knick-knack there. My ghostie, carrying the shawl—he would not stay put—stalked after Harper, until I caught Dirk's eye and motioned him away. "He's not doing anything wrong," I hissed. "Leave him alone."

"I dinna trust him."

"You said that about old Mr. Pitcairn, too, and look how harmless he is."

"He's nae so aulde as all that."

"Don't argue with me. Just leave Harper alone, okay?" I looked past Dirk's shoulder. Harper stood there, watching me. I hummed a little tune and broke out into a song. The only song I could think of at the moment. Straight out of that scary scene in *Jaws*.

"What are ye doing for aye?"

"*Show me the way to go home, dum, dum, I'm tired and I wanna go to bed, doop-de-doo.*" I certainly was tired, if that was the best I could do. I moved away from both of them, hoping neither one would follow me. It was all I could do to keep from looking back to see if three yellow barrels popped out of the water behind me. *Peggy, you're being ridiculous.*

A few minutes later, right before closing time, I helped a young woman find a weathered Keith tartan tie for her fiancé. "The brown matches his eyes," she told me with a fair amount of moon dust in her own. I wrapped it in the

ScotShop signature paper, placed it in a tie box, and sent her on her way, thanking her, and locking the door behind her.

When I turned around, Gilda straightened up quickly but not fast enough. She looked decidedly off-kilter. "You," I pointed at her, "are going home now."

"But I want to watch."

"Not a chance. You look like you're asleep on your feet, and your hands are shaking." I patted her shoulder, surprised at how bony it felt. Had she been losing weight? "Get a good rest, and I'll see you tomorrow."

Sam stepped up beside her. "I'll take you home."

"You will not," I snapped. "I need you here."

Gilda pressed her cheek against Sam's chest, narrowly avoiding poking her eye out on his kilt pin. His arms went around her. "I'll be fine," she said. "I'll just go to bed." I saw his arms stiffen. "That's all."

I must have missed something. She sounded like she was trying to convince him of something unspoken but thoroughly understood between the two of them. I looked at Harper, wondering if he'd caught whatever was happening. He stared at Gilda and a line formed between his eyebrows.

She stepped away from Sam and opened the door. "I promise," she said, looking directly at Sam.

I locked the door behind her. "What was that about?"

Sam shrugged but wouldn't say anything. I made a mental note to grill Gilda tomorrow.

I glanced at Harper again, but his arms were crossed on his broad chest. I couldn't help but notice the ripple of muscle down his forearm. "So," he said, "what do you have to show me?"

I motioned to Sam to close the blinds and shut the curtains—we needed all the privacy we could get—and led Harper to the bookcase. "We have to move it one more time." Sam let out a loud groan, but it was just for show.

Harper looked from Sam to me but didn't say anything.

"After you and Karaline left the other night, we got to wondering why those holes had been drilled in the wall."

Sam let out his breath audibly. "You mean *you* got to wondering. I wanted to call the cops."

Self-righteous twit. "Right. Sure you did. And all Gilda had to do was bat her lashes at you once or twice to convince you otherwise."

He grumbled but had no way to contradict me—I was right, doggone it.

"We thought—I mean *I* thought—the murderer might be looking for something behind the wall."

Harper tilted his head to one side. He looked awfully intent. "Go on."

"So we tried to break through the Sheetrock, but there was solid wood behind it." Harper frowned at me, but I kept going. "Behind the Sheetrock," I explained. "You'll just have to see for yourself."

"You do know there's a penalty for destroying a crime scene?"

"What right do you have to grump at me? It's not a crime scene." My indignation was about as strong as my sense of guilt. "I mean, it was a crime scene, but the yellow tape is gone and you released it." I really should have called him first, but I wasn't about to admit it.

"That's splitting hairs, and you know it."

"I do not. I mean, it isn't. I mean . . . damn it, do you want to see this thing or not?"

"I don't think I'm going to like what I see."

"Mistress Peigi, I would be most happy to rip his heart out and hand it to ye on the tip of my dagger."

I growled at Dirk. He was entirely too protective. I don't think he liked Harper at all.

"What's wrong with you, cuz?" Sam slapped me on the shoulder and practically sent me sprawling. I rounded on him, ready to fire him or at least clop him upside the head, but Dirk jumped in between us. His plaid swept through me and I staggered sideways.

Harper's notebook clattered to the floor. He grabbed me,

and I was surrounded with the subtle scent of citrus and a whiff of soap—the kind my mother always bought when I was growing up. I looked up at him. What kind of guy used little-kid soap? I had a brief vision of me in a bathtub when I was about five, holding down the bar of Ivory. Every time I let go, it would shoot up out of the water, like a dolphin at SeaWorld. *Pure Ivory. It floats.* Still, the smell felt ordinary and comforting, with not a hint of a ghostly presence anywhere, as I stood there with Harper's arms around me.

I heard the ominous whoosh of Dirk's knife sliding out of the scabbard. "I'm okay. Nothing to worry about." I pushed myself away from Harper's chest, wishing I could stay but not wanting to see what might happen if my ghost tried to impale my cop. *My* cop? Where had that idea come from?

Harper gazed at me steadily for a long moment. I straightened my shoulders to show him how good I felt. "You're not going to fall again, are you?"

"No. I just stumbled, that's all."

His eyes darkened, as if he didn't quite believe me. "Let's see what you have to show me."

Anything you want, I thought. *Stop it, Peggy. Stop it right now.*

Harper's lips twitched. I sure hoped he couldn't read minds.

Between the three of us, with Dirk hovering protectively in the background, making suggestions and threatening to skewer both my helpers, we shifted the thing away from the wall. Harper whistled when he saw the gaping hole in the Sheetrock.

Sam had been quieter than usual for a few minutes, but now he spoke up. "Why would anybody build a solid wooden wall as nice as this one is and then put Sheetrock on top of it?"

Harper stepped back a ways and scanned the wall. "You said the building was a hundred years old?"

"Right around there," I said. "It says 1915 over the front door. It's been divided into three separate stores, but originally it was just one business, and this"—I swept my arm around in an arc—"was the front office."

"The wooden dividing wall was the original," he mused.

"But why the Sheetrock, too?" Sam sounded more aggrieved than curious.

"The Sheetrock was put in later," Harper said. "Sheetrock wasn't in use a hundred years ago."

"Messy it is," Dirk muttered, although why he was bothering to keep his voice down, I had no idea.

"The wallpaper, though," I objected. "I found an old dated receipt for it from 1915 in the rolltop desk. Made out to Mrs. Josiah Pitcairn. Described it in detail and gave the number of rolls, which would have been just enough to do this one wall."

Harper ran his hand through his hair, leaving one unruly tuft sticking up, like Dennis the Menace. "They may have bought the paper a hundred years ago, but they didn't put it up until the Sheetrock went on. I can guarantee that."

Maybe he was right. It wasn't worth an argument anyway. "There's more." I stepped away from the wall and pointed to the outline of the door—the door I'd been standing in front of. Did I have a sense of drama or what?

17

Safe Assumption

Harper moved closer, and I caught another faint whiff of citrus. He'd missed shaving a tiny patch of beard on his jaw, just below his earlobe.

"Excuse me," he said, and I took a step backward. He ran his finger along the outline. "Does this open?"

"It lifts out," Sam said as he headed toward the back room. "I'll get the gloves."

We'd left the screws in place, and the door came loose more easily this time. Harper whistled again when the safe came into view. He pulled a handkerchief from his pocket, placed it over the handle, and pushed down. Of course, it didn't budge.

"It's locked," Sam said, and I saw a muscle twitch beside the little patch of beard Harper had missed.

"Anyone know the combination?"

Sam snorted in derision. "If we'd a known that, we'd a had it open by now."

Harper crouched beside the safe and touched the dial very gently with a forefinger. He brushed some of the cobwebbing away, leaned closer, and placed his ear against the red-filigreed door. He turned the dial to the right a hairsbreadth at a time.

How much safecracking experience had this man had? I held my breath.

After a few minutes that seemed like an hour, he sighed and straightened up. "Old safes like this usually had complicated dialing systems for the combinations. You'd spin the dial to the right first to clear everything and stop on the first number. After that, these Barnes safes required four turns to the left, three turns to the right, two turns back to the left, and a final turn to the right to get to the last number. Sometimes the owners would dial all but that final number. That way, they could open the safe quickly."

Oh, crapola. I'd wiggled the dial back and forth. Luckily he wasn't looking at my face.

"So," Sam said, "you thought you might be able to hear the number click?" He sounded dubious.

Harper rubbed his right hand along his jaw, faltered when he connected with those few stray bits of beard. "Yeah," he said. "It was worth a try."

"But it didn't work," Sam pointed out unnecessarily.

Harper gave him a level stare, and I could almost smell the increase in testosterone. "Not this time, it didn't."

"It wouldn't have anyway," Sam snapped. "Peggy played with the dial."

Thanks, traitor.

Harper whipped his head around and narrowed those beautiful eyes at me. "Is that true?"

"Uh-huh. I'm sorry."

He positively glowered. I lifted my chin a bit higher. "I didn't know there'd be a problem. I only moved it a little each way." *And spun it around a couple of times.*

"Yeah," Sam put in. "Enough to ruin the sequence."

"You don't have to be so sarcastic," I grumped at him.

Dirk stepped forward and thrust his face close to Sam's.

"Ye didna know either, and here ye pretend to be so learned." Sam took an involuntary step back and wiped his face with one hand. Good for Dirk.

If Sam hadn't been goading me, I think Harper might have stayed angrier longer. As it was, he turned on Sam, much as Dirk had done. "It was a logical error. Most people would try turning the dial." He took a deep breath and swiveled his head back to me. "You mentioned the wallpaper receipt in the rolltop desk. There wasn't a piece of paper with just five numbers on it, was there?"

"I'm pretty sure there wasn't," I said, although a shade of doubt entered my mind. "No. No, there wasn't. The woman who owned the dress shop, the one that was here before me, said she'd cleaned out the desk when she opened her store, and that was ten years ago."

"But she kept the receipt for the wallpaper?" Harper looked skeptical indeed.

"She didn't keep it—she just overlooked it. It was stuck way back in one of the pigeonholes. I found it shortly after I opened."

Harper moved to his left and studied the four drilled holes. About six inches apart, they formed a ragged line a foot or two above the floor. He pulled out his wallet and extracted a loop of thin wire, which he straightened and poked into the holes. Who carries wire in his wallet? In each case, the wire went way in with no resistance.

Harper worried his lower lip with his upper teeth. They were very white. Maybe that was why his smile was so arresting. My eyes, I swear I couldn't help it, wandered down the length of him. Dirk cleared his throat, and I popped back to reality in time to hear Harper say, ". . . would he have drilled here?"

"He was looking for the safe," Sam said, and the words *you dope* hung in the air unsaid.

Dirk threw up his hands in disgust. My sentiments exactly.

"You're right," I told Harper, pointedly ignoring my cousin. "It does seem strange. . . ."

"He was so close . . ."

". . . but not quite close enough . . ."

"Almost like he was following directions . . ."

". . . but the directions were wrong."

Dirk uttered a couple of words I'd never heard before, but I could tell he was exasperated. "Ye sound, the twa of you, like Mister and Mistress Sinclair."

I just looked at him, too surprised to say anything.

Harper followed my gaze, back across his right shoulder. "What are you looking at?"

"Oh, nothing." *Except for my not-so-wee ghostie.*

A loud knock on the front door startled us all. Dirk spun around and headed for the front, followed closely by me and the other two. I peeked through the blinds that covered the window. "Mr. Pitcairn?"

I opened the door a crack.

"I saw your lights on, Miss Peggy, and just wanted to be sure you were okay." He glanced over my shoulder. "May I assist you in any way?"

"That's kind of you, Mr. P, but we're just doing a little cleanup work."

"I'd be happy to help you."

He sounded so hopeful, I almost let him in, but Harper stepped closer. "Everything's under control here." His tone was brusque; he was a different man altogether. "Thanks for checking, but we need to get back to work now." He nodded, pleasantly enough, pushed the door firmly shut, and turned the lock.

"Are you sure you're okay?" Mr. P's voice was faint through the heavy door.

"I'm fine," I called. "Don't you worry." I pulled the curtain more firmly into place. "My neighbor, Mr. P. He worries about me."

Before we were halfway back to the safe, another knock sounded on the door. This time it was Ethan, the owner of the Auto Shop. "I saw Mr. Pitcairn looking in the window, but he walked away when I asked him what was up." His gaze flicked over Harper and back to me. "Your lights aren't usually on this late. I thought I ought to check."

"I'm doing fine, Ethan. Thanks for asking. Harper and Sam are helping me with something, that's all."

This time Harper closed the door with finality. "Does everybody in town keep tabs on you?"

I really didn't think that question deserved an answer, but I said, "They're friends. They care about me."

"Ye have entirely too many men"—that word came out like a growl as Dirk fingered his dagger—"worriting themselves about ye." I looked at the knife. Wickedly sharp, I could tell. Of course, knives are supposed to be sharp. Less chance of a ragged wound—the kind created by dull blades. Or so they said.

"That's fine," Harper said, "but we don't want people seeing the . . ." He waved his arm at the scene before us.

"The crime scene, now with mysterious wall safe included?"

He nodded. "There has to be a connection."

Dirk must have felt the same way, because he nodded, stepped between us, and followed me back toward the bookcase, leaving Harper to trail behind.

We asked more questions that didn't have answers and threw out more theories that didn't have any chance of being proven. Eventually, though, my yawns got to be too much. "I'm going to go home and go to bed, so you nice folks can all leave," I said.

"That isna polite. The host should stay until the last guest departs."

"They're not guests." I turned majestically. I hoped it didn't look like I was drunk. Drunk with tiredness, I guess. "You're here at the behest of the ownership." *Good grief. I was absolutely potty.* "So I give you my permission to pack up and go 'way."

Harper just nodded and headed for the bookcase. "Sam, take that end."

They heaved and shoved and wiggled it until the left-hand edge lined up with the seventeen-foot mark on the base-board.

By that point, though, I didn't care.

18

Amy

The next morning's dawn light barely made it through the curtains. Rain. I'd been halfway aware of it all night long in that dreamlike state that recognizes the real world without fully acknowledging it.

I stumbled into the bathroom and cringed at my reflection. I was going to need major help today. For one thing, I must have slept on my left side all night. My hair on that side was plastered to the side of my head. I closed my eyes and felt for my brush. Maybe if I didn't look, it would go away.

Usually I wore a tartan skirt with a simple blouse and a matching plaid scarf. Today I'd go full Scot—or rather full Welsh, but most of my customers wouldn't know the difference. A quick shower first, and then I donned an off-white linen chemise, navy overskirt, burgundy bodice, and my Wynne tartan arisaidh. I added a linen kerchief so my lopsided hair would remain nicely hidden all day and wouldn't wilt in the rain.

In a tourist town, rain could help or hurt sales. Sometimes people either stayed away altogether or else they crowded into the stores to get away from the downpour, but with no intention of buying anything.

I hoped today would be one of the other kinds of rainy days, where customers inundated the store and kept finding more and more ways to spend their money, the longer they avoided the drenching rain outside.

The books on my bookcase gave me an idea. I pulled one out and stood it on the dresser. The pages fanned open. Hmmm. That works.

Dirk stood in the front bay window, the shawl folded over his right arm. He frowned in disapproval as I walked down the stairs. I couldn't tell if it was because of my burgundy-and-navy Welsh arisaidh or whether he'd figured out that I was leaving the shawl—and him—behind today. It was neither.

"The rain is lovely," he said.

"Then why are you frowning? Anyway, it's cold and wet."

"Aye, but it remembers me of home."

"Remembers? Oh—reminds you."

"Ye look quite bonny today."

I gaped at him. It was the first compliment he'd ever given me. "Thanks." I twirled, feeling the arisaidh billow around me. Come to think of it, I felt bonny.

"Even in a Welsh plaid," he added, and I rolled my eyes.

"Dirk, listen. I've decided to set up an at-home library for you."

He cocked his head to one side. "What would that be?" His long black hair spilled over one shoulder and distracted me for a moment.

"Um, I'm going to prop open a whole slew of books so you can go from one to another and read the first three pages. Then, when I come home, I'll switch the pages to the next set."

"Three pages? And how would ye be planning to do that?"

"Easy. I'll stand the books up and prop them open at the first page, leaving it stuck out a bit, so you'll be able to look in back of that first page at pages two and three." His eyebrows pulled down a bit, and I went on quickly. "You can tell me what sort of books you're interested in. I still have a bit of time before I have to leave."

"Ye were planning to leave me behind?"

"Aye. I mean yes. You and the shawl. You can keep it with you."

His right hand came up to his chest, pulling the shawl closer against him. "What did ye intend to do if the murderer"—lots of rolled *r*'s in that word—"happens to come into your wee store?"

You can't even open a door, I thought, but I didn't dare say it out loud. It would hurt his feelings. "I'll be okay," I promised. "There are always plenty of customers, and Gilda and Shoe will be there."

"Shoe? Isna he the one in prison?"

"Oh, crudbuckets. This is Shoe's usual day. I guess it'll be Gilda and Sam." Making a mental note to call Sam just to be sure he was up, I headed for the kitchen. Rainy days always made me want scrambled eggs and stove toast. Comfort food. Of course, the rain also made me wonder whether Shoe could hear it from his jail cell. I needed to go visit him, but when was I going to fit it into my schedule? That was ridiculous. He was in jail for heaven's sake. If I were the one in there, wouldn't he have come for a visit? *Yeah*, said a little voice inside me, *and he would have spent the whole time wisecracking.*

Dirk watched as I assembled my breakfast and sat across from me as I ate it. He was good at keeping me civilized. Usually—pre-Dirk—I ate standing up by the kitchen counter. Why did I even care if a ghost thought me civilized?

"We'd best select a goodly number of books," he said as I finished my last bite. "I read quickly."

"Right." I folded my napkin—yes, I'd even set out a cloth napkin.

He must have already studied the titles, because he seemed to know precisely which books he wanted to start with. I used forks to hold the first page in place and knives or spoons to brace the other pages back out of the way. After I'd used up all my utensils, I improvised with whatever I could find. Finally, I just opened the rest of the books to page one and lay them around on the living room floor. For the ones that wouldn't lie flat, I weighted them down with crystals, the edges of flower pots, and other books he didn't care to read yet. The living room looked like some sort of historic archive after an earthquake. I pulled the top of my arisaidh up over my head. "Are you sure you'll be okay with this?"

He'd already started on my old British history textbook from college. "Aye," he said distractedly. I'm not sure he even heard me leave.

The steady downpour was wreathed in fog. I dashed to the car, grateful that I never had to lock it. I set the windshield wipers on high and backed out of my drive directly into the fog-obscured path of an oncoming garbage truck. Damn. I had a split second to register that something bad had happened before the front end of my poor little car spun from the impact and slammed against the right side of the truck. I watched in slow motion as my right hand, entirely without my cooperation, lifted in a dance-like arc to the right and then headed left across my field of vision. My head whipped around, cracking against the side window. I heard glass shatter. The windshield wipers continued their inane *swish, swish, swish*. Didn't they realize the world had stopped?

The truck driver materialized a moment later, pulling the door open and yelling, "Are you okay? My God, you're bleeding! I didn't mean to hit you, lady!" Rain poured in on me, as hard as the man's exclamations. I could feel it, but my eyes must have been closed.

"You've killed her." A nasal voice that sounded vaguely familiar penetrated the fog around me.

I felt a hand on my arm and heard multiple voices shouting

in the background. None of them made any sense. A door slammed. Someone's fingers touched the side of my neck. I knew there had to be a reason why, but I couldn't fathom what it was. "She's alive. Move back," this new person ordered, and the other voices receded behind the pounding of the rain. "You. Pitcairn. Call an ambulance. Now." A what? What was an *amlance*?

"Can you open your eyes?" The voice was gentle. I'd heard it before. At least I thought I had. "Squeeze my hand if you can hear me." Somehow my hand felt warm, safe. I squeezed. That much didn't hurt, even though everything else did.

I blinked and raised my other hand to my head. An egg sprouted just above my left ear. I felt like I'd been put through a Vitamix one limb at a time. Someone's head swam into view. "Don't move," it said. As if I could. "Help is on the way."

"Call Gil," I croaked. That didn't sound right, but it was the best I could do.

The face wavered a bit. "Gil? Do you mean Gilda?"

It took too much effort to answer. I closed my eyes for a moment.

When I opened them, my neck was in a brace, and I was being lifted onto a stretcher. Someone held an umbrella over my face. Good. Too much rain. The stretcher moved toward the ambulance—that was what it was—and I saw the front of my house through the swirling fog. Someone stood at the bay window, someone waving his arms and shouting. I saw a flash of metal brandished high over his head, and then the ambulance ate me.

The face at the window bothered me. There was something I needed to do, but the fog outside had penetrated my brain. I shivered. *I'm cold*, I said, but the woman bending over me didn't seem to hear me.

"We're taking you to the hospital," she told me. "You're going to be just fine."

How would she know? Why was I being held down?

"Don't move like that. You have to lie still. All you need to do right now is just wait for the doc to take a look. Stop thrashing." More fog slid into me.

When I woke, a nurse immediately hit the call button and announced my waking state. I'd never seen her before. You'd think in a town this small, I'd know everybody who lived here. I reached up to my head, where an ache the size of Montana had settled in with a vengeance. "You've had some stitches," the nurse said. "Don't fiddle with the bandage. It needs to stay in place. The car window shattered, and we had to pull glass out of your head."

"I thought cars had safety glass."

She looked inordinately pleased. What was there to smile about?

The door opened, and a vaguely familiar face bent over me. "We've had quite a morning, haven't we?"

We? He wasn't even making eye contact.

"You have a concussion, and we're going to keep you quiet until we're sure you're okay."

"I have to work. The ScotShop."

His face twisted but so quickly righted itself, I thought I might have imagined it.

"The what?"

"I own the ScotShop. In the old Pitcairn Building."

He held out a hand, and the nurse placed a clipboard in it. My chart? I thought they did everything on computers nowadays. "Looks like you're from Hamelin."

Where am I?

"You just stay quiet." After that pronouncement, he left.

The nurse stepped closer to me and touched my hand. "You're in Arkane Hospital, Ms. Winn. We have a better trauma center than the clinic in Hamelin, and it looked like your injuries might have been extensive. It's better to be safe than sorry, wouldn't you say?"

On that platitude, she patted my arm, told me her name was Amy and that all I had to do was push the button if I needed anything, and left.

I took a good look at my left hand, where an IV line snaked in, delivering its cold fluids. I stretched gingerly. Everything hurt. A padded brace of some sort encased my neck. I felt the side of my head, wincing as my left shoulder objected to being moved. A bandage, just like Amy had said, covered what I could tell was a rather substantial lump. My fingers met with stubby bristles where they'd cut my hair. Oh crap! Now I'd be even more lopsided than usual. Looked like I'd be wearing my kerchief for a good long time.

I pushed back the covers, lifted the blue-dotted hospital gown, and examined some rather spectacular bruises along my left side. I must have slammed into the door when the car spun. Luckily, my heavy arisaidh had cushioned the blow somewhat.

I looked around the room. There was a narrow closet on the opposite wall. It couldn't have been ten feet from where I lay. I gauged the possibility of making it over there. I could do it. I pushed the sheet to one side and hit the buttons to lower the bed and raise the back of it. I turned my back to the door and swung my legs over the edge, on the side next to the IV pole. I could hang on to it while I shuffled across the room. My left thigh protested. That was where the bruises were the worst—why didn't they make softer armrests on cars?

A throat cleared. "Shouldn't you be staying in bed?"

The cold air wafting across my bare back where the johnny gapped wide open froze me almost as much as the voice. I twisted around, gasped in pain, and immediately felt an arm across my back—my bare back—supporting it as a hand grasped my right shoulder and held me still. The hand slipped down my arm and slid beneath my knees, lifting me gently back into place. He could do all that leaning across the bed? I sincerely hoped he wouldn't get a hernia. "Hello, Harper."

"You were planning an escape?"

I studied his face but couldn't detect any sarcasm. "No." I pointed across the room to the closet. "I wanted to see if my arisaidh survived the crash."

He pulled the sheet up over me and nodded. Keeping a wary eye on me, as if worried that I might bolt, he opened the closet door and pulled out a plastic bag. Without any prompting, he opened it, laid the contents on the bed for my inspection. Thank goodness I'd worn pretty underwear, but he didn't seem to pay any undue attention to it.

The kerchief, for which I'd paid an inordinate amount of money, even at wholesale, had a fat line of dried blood along one side. He picked it up and held it out in front of him. "It's only on the right side," he said.

"That's the left side," I told him.

He frowned. "It's the right side as I'm looking at it."

"It's the left side when I'm in it."

He compressed his lips and stepped to the sink.

"Cold water!"

"I know. Grew up with sisters."

Hmm. I watched him saturate the kerchief, agitate it gently, scraping one layer against another, squeezing and rinsing several times. He repeated the process twice more, adding soap the third time through. After that, he ran a sinkful of water and left the kerchief to soak. "It'll be good as new."

I glanced down at my chemise. "Is there blood on anything else?"

He took a moment to look carefully, and then reached for a coat hanger. "Nope. Everything else is okay. Just wet from the rain." He hung the chemise and overskirt from hooks on the wall, put my underwear back in the closet, and picked up the arisaidh. "And how are you doing? Other than wanting to leave, that is."

"I'm okay."

He raised an eyebrow, and his eyes ran the length of me.

"No, really, I'm fine. I just want to get home."

"You're fine?" There was a quizzical twist to his words. "Do you know what *fine* stands for?"

I shook my head as much as the brace allowed.

"It means Freaked out, Insecure, Neurotic, and Egotistical."

I could hear the capital letters. I laughed, but that hurt, so I took a deep breath instead.

"There," he said. "That's better."

"How is the truck driver? Was he hurt?"

"He's fine—I mean he wasn't hurt at all. He told me that he'd been wondering for some time about whether or not he should sell the garbage business." A funny expression, one I couldn't interpret, flitted across Harper's face.

"He owns it? What was he doing driving a truck then?"

"Well, that's the funny part. His business started small, here in Arkane, but then he was so successful, he expanded into Hamelin and a couple of the other towns around here. Usually he sits behind a desk, shuffling paper, but some of his men are out with the flu, and he decided to take one of the runs. That's the only reason he was in the truck." He paused, sliding my arisaidh, which he'd been holding all this time, onto the coat hanger.

He was quiet so long I prompted him. "So, what does this have to do with selling his business?"

"He said that running into you made up his mind. All because he filled in for somebody else." He held my gaze for a second or two and then looked away. "Amazing what can happen when you do that."

"Do what?"

"Fill in for somebody."

That didn't make sense, but I let it drop. "Does Gilda know? Is the shop open?"

He cleared his throat. "Yes. I called her. She said she and Sam would be there all day. They're planning to stop by this evening during visiting hours."

"My car?" I hated to ask, but imagining the worst was no fun.

He shook his head. "Back end is crumpled. Frame is bent. Totaled."

"Oh, jolly." Why hadn't I taken that old '57 Chevy when my dad offered it to me? It would have been dented but still drivable, although it probably would have gotten about twelve miles per gallon. "How's the garbage truck?"

The man actually snickered. "You think your little car could damage a garbage truck?"

"Whew. At least my insurance won't have to pay for truck repair."

He smiled. "Martin, the guy who owns the garbage company, told me at the scene that it was entirely his fault. He was going too fast. He said he thought his insurance should pay for the whole thing."

"You're kidding." I remembered the voice that had pulled open my door, terrified that I might have been badly injured.

"Gave him a ticket."

"You gave that nice man a ticket?"

"He was practically asking for one."

The door opened and Amy, the nurse, bustled in. Why do nurses always seem to bustle? She winked at Harper. I had the distinct feeling that these weren't visiting hours. He'd probably just smiled at her and she'd let him in. "Hi, Harper. Don't worry; she's doing just fine." She turned to me and lowered her voice. "My friend here has been sitting in the waiting room for the past two hours, ever since he got through doing his cop stuff."

"Buzz off, Amy; I'm working."

She stuck out her tongue at him. "No, no, no. I'm the one

who's working here. Out you go." She lifted my hand, inspected the IV site, and winked at me. "I'd be willing to bet my patient has to use the potty."

Harper blushed a bright red. I didn't know he could blush. Amy looked at me and giggled. He left hastily as she pulled back the sheet. "Close the door on your way out," she called.

After I took care of the essentials, Amy helped me rinse the kerchief and wring it out.

It wasn't long before I was inundated with visitors. Well, only two, one on each side of the bed, but it felt like a crowd.

"They made us wait out there in that dreadful waiting room, when I should have been in here with my baby the whole time."

"Hi, Mom. I'm doing just fine." Harper's definition rang in my head and I grinned.

"What's so funny?" She reached back and pressed her hand into her lower spine. It was a movement I'd seen her make so many times, I almost didn't notice it anymore. "Here you are almost dead and I haven't even been able to stay with you, and now you're laughing?"

"Not laughing, Mom." I was tired already. "I just thought of something funny, that's all."

She didn't ask what—not that I expected her to—she was too caught up in her monologue. "We're taking you home as soon as Doctor Carrin says you can leave. Your old room is still just the way you left it. You can move in there for a week or two. Maybe three. However long it takes my baby to heal. You certainly don't want to go out in public with your hair looking like that. I don't mind waiting on you hand and foot, even though it will be hard on my back. Whatever it takes to get you well."

Oh my God, I'd forgotten about Dirk. "Mom, I need to go back to my own house." *He must be frantic.* I remembered seeing him in the bay window, shouting and waving his dagger. "I need to get there right away." I pulled back the sheet and swung my legs to one side, more successfully than the first time.

"Now, honey." Dad sounded reasonable and absolutely adamant at the same time. He reached for my legs, had second thoughts inches from my bare skin, and simply stood in front of me, leaving me no room to haul myself to my feet.

Sighing, I pushed the call button. Amy's voice came through loud and clear. "What do you need, Ms. Winn?"

"I need to go home. How soon can I get out of here?"

"I'll be right there."

"Your brother is absolutely frantic. I told him he could stay with us while you're there. That way we'll be a cozy, happy family again."

"Mom, I don't need cozy," I said as the door opened. "I need to be home in my own house. Call Drew back and tell him I'm okay. He won't want to stay there, either. You know you don't like Tessa."

Amy must have had years of practice reading body language. She very kindly but firmly ushered my parents out. "I need to check her vitals," she said. "We may be able to release her early. You'll need to go to the waiting room."

"Better yet," I called after them as Amy pulled the curtain between the bed and the door, "go home and wait for me to call you."

I could hear my mom's objections fading as the *tap tap tap* of her high heels receded down the hallway. "Thanks for saving me," I said, and Amy chuckled.

"I really do need to get your vital signs," she said. "You're doing pretty well, but we have to be sure. Any headache?"

"Nope. The stitches hurt, but no headache."

"Difficulty swallowing?"

I gave it a try. "None."

"How's your vision?"

"I can see just fine," I told her with some impatience. "I really do have to get home. There's somebody there I need to check on."

"Cat? Or dog? You look more like a dog person."

I couldn't very well say I needed to check on my ghost.

"His name is Shorty," I said. Amy bent over me and pulled my lower eyelids down as she looked at my pupils or something. She checked the computer readout and noted some numbers on a chart. Then she typed something on the console that sat, like a broody hen, beside the bed. An apt image, since I felt like a plate of scrambled eggs.

I did my best to look alert.

"Who's going to take you home? Your parents?"

"Heavens, no! I'll call Sam. They'd haul me across town to their house. I need to be at my own place. Sam can take some time away from the store to come get me."

"Boyfriend?"

"Not hardly. Cousin."

"Hmm." She looked pleased.

"And employee," I added. I'm not sure why I wanted to clarify that point. "I own the ScotShop in Hamelin."

"I know. I love that store. I bought my dad a tie there a couple of years ago."

"You're welcome to come back anytime." Every tie helped.

"We have to get you out of here first, though." She tugged absentmindedly at the corner of the blanket, straightening it. "Is there someone at your house who can stay with you for a couple of days, just to be sure you don't fall? With a concussion, your balance may not be the best right away."

Did Dirk count? "Yes," I said. "There's somebody there. My, uh, housemate."

"You shouldn't do any bending, either. Keep your head above the level of your heart, and let your housemate walk the dog."

"I have a fenced-in backyard," I told her. *And Shorty is an indoor cat.*

"That's good. Just be sure you take it easy. Let other people wait on you. Does your housemate cook?"

I had a brief vision of Dirk gutting a squirrel and roasting it over an open campfire. "Not exactly, but my friend Karaline will bring me food from her restaurant."

"Oh? Which one?"

"The Logg Cabin."

"I love that place. We go there a lot on Saturday mornings."

"Yeah. It's great having a friend like that."

"You let her pamper you, okay?"

"Fine with me. I love being spoiled. I'll be just fine." Fine. Right. Freaked out, insecure, and . . . something or other. I couldn't remember the rest. Neurotic. That was it. What was the *e* for?

"I'll call Dr. Carrin and see if he'll release you."

"Just don't let my mother know you're releasing me until I can get Sam here."

"Don't count your chickens. Call Sam after Dr. Carrin agrees. He might not release you, you know. And you might not need Sam anyway."

"Why not?"

She ignored my question and said something about a brolaw, whatever that was. "I'll go get the doctor."

I nodded, and she left the room. A minute or so later, the door opened and Harper walked in. "You doing okay?"

I shrugged. "Why are you still here? Don't you have something else to do? Like finding out who killed Mason?"

"Just thought you'd like to know Shoe was released about an hour ago."

"Really? That's great! Did you catch the guy who did it?"

"No, but that lawyer of his convinced the judge to reconsider the fact that all the evidence was completely circumstantial. He pulled in affidavits from leading town citizens saying that Shoe was a young man of upstanding character." His smile was wry.

"The baseball game, right? Those leading citizens all want Shoe to be able to play against the Arkane Archers on Independence Day?"

"Probably. The charges weren't dropped, but he's out on bail." Harper frowned slightly, and his eyes seemed to go darker. Maybe it was just the shadow from his eyebrows. "It didn't seem to occur to the judge that a number of convicted serial killers were thought to be of upstanding character before they were caught."

"Shoe is not a serial killer. He's not any kind of killer. He's—"

"Don't get your britches twisted. I'm just stating an obvious fact that the judge missed."

"My britches twisted? That's what Moira says. Did you ever live in the south?"

He avoided the question by asking one of his own. "You ignored my first question. How do you feel?"

"I feel like I've been run over by a truck."

"A garbage truck."

"Just my luck. But what about Shoe? He had a forty-thousand-dollar bond. He couldn't possibly pay that."

"Reduced to ten thousand."

"Yuck. That's still way more than he can afford."

"Uh-huh. Karaline Logg put up the money."

"Karaline? You've got to be kidding." This was getting more bizarre every moment. "I didn't know Karaline had that kind of money." Why would she bail out Shoe? Surely there was no romantic interest there. Karaline was way too sophisticated for Shoe, and he was goofy over Gilda, anyway. I wondered what was going to happen when he found out Sam had moved into his territory. We'd probably have a testosterone war on our hands. I could only hope that it didn't invade the ScotShop.

". . . could take you home."

"Huh?"

Harper narrowed his eyes, but the corners of his mouth curved up. "You haven't heard a word I've said, have you?"

I screwed up my mouth. "Guess not. I was thinking. Did you say you'd take me home?"

He nodded. "Amy told me I needed to feed your dog for you."

"I don't have a dog."

"I know. You look more like a cat person. So, I'll feed your cat. She said you weren't supposed to bend over until your head had a chance to heal."

"Get me my chemise," I said. "Is the arisaidh dry?"

"How are you planning to get dressed with that needle in the back of your hand?"

Crud. I'd forgotten that. "Well, we can at least get everything ready."

"We can, can we?"

"I have to get home right away."

He lifted the chemise and shook his head. "What's the big hurry anyway? Don't you enjoy"—he gestured around the room—"the ambiance?"

"Poop," I said, and Harper grinned. Where was Dirk when I needed him to keep my mouth civilized? He was stuck in my house, frantic with worry, that's where he was. "I'd rather go home," I said, and took the chemise from his outstretched hand.

He reached for the arisaidh, but Dr. Carrin walked in, followed closely by Amy. He looked so goshdarn familiar, but I still couldn't place where I'd seen him before. He looked at my clothes spread out on the bed. "A bit premature, aren't we?"

"Anxious," I said. "I'm getting prepared, just in case."

He flitted his fingers at Harper, a completely inappropriate gesture if there ever was one. Harper raised one eyebrow but turned to leave. He paused at the door. "I'll be in the hall."

Dr. Carrin held out his hand, and Amy handed him my chart. He spent a few long moments looking it over. I inspected the ropey muscles of his forearm. He took the stethoscope from around his neck. "Let's take a listen." Amy pulled the privacy curtain. I leaned forward, gasped when that cold circle hit the skin of my back, and breathed deeply when instructed.

"Can I leave now?"

He ignored me, scribbled something on the chart, and

handed it to Amy. When he turned back toward me, something in the way he moved reminded me of Mr. Pitcairn, my
neighbor. They held their shoulders the same way. The doctor was more pit bull than basset hound, though—straighter,
younger, and stronger than Mr. P. Maybe they were related.
At least that would solve the problem of why he looked so
familiar to me.

". . . as soon as the paperwork is completed."

"I can leave?"

"That's what I just said, isn't it?" He sounded a bit
peeved. Harper had seemed amused when I wasn't listening.
I decided Doc Carrin was a grump. Despite what I thought,
though, he seemed to relent. "You need to be more careful
in that car of yours. We wouldn't want anything to happen
to the lovely owner of the ScotShop."

Lovely? What kind of sexist remark was that? But then I
looked at his concerned-looking face and decided he was
just a little bit old-fashioned. I wondered how he knew about
the ScotShop. Did they put things like that on hospital charts?

After he left, Amy fussed around a bit, removing the IV,
tapping away at the computer keyboard, and giving me
instructions about the care of my bandaged head. "Your
roommate will have to inspect the bandage once each day."

I nodded, more intent on finding my underpants than
anything else. Karaline could look at it. If she wasn't fooling
around with Shoe. I had to find out what was going on.

". . . see you back here in a week."

"Um, right. A week."

"I've written it all down." She handed me a clipboard.
"Sign here." She gave me the pink duplicate. "Do you need
help getting dressed?"

"No. I can manage. Thanks, though."

"Push the call button when you're ready." She opened
the door. "Not yet, Harper," I heard her say. "She's not
even . . ." I lost the rest as the door closed.

19

Archives and Arachnids

As it turned out, I still had to deal with my parents, but Harper ran interference—isn't that what the football people say?—and assured Mom that he was required to take my statement about the accident. "I'll just do it on the way as I drive her home," he said, and I couldn't believe my mother accepted that. Dad gave me a quizzical look, but whenever Mom was around, he hardly ever said a thing. Even when I'd sat with him in his wood shop, doing my homework as he drilled and cut and sanded the wood he loved so much, we'd never spoken. If he hadn't taken Drew and me on fishing trips together when we were kids, I'm sure I would have grown up believing our dad was mute.

Mom insisted on walking beside me as I was wheeled out to Harper's car. Dad carried the plastic bags with my wet kerchief and my bodice. I couldn't have possibly managed to get that thing laced in my current condition.

"Harper is a nice man," Mom told me, her shoes tapping out a high-heeled rhythm as pointed as her words. "This is leap year."

The apparent non sequitur confused me. "What does leap year have to do with anything?" Beyond her right shoulder I could see my dad rolling his eyes.

"You know," she said.

"No, I don't know."

Dad leaned forward and spoke from the other side of Mom. "Your mother proposed to me thirty-two years ago, honey. It was a leap year."

"Dad! You're kidding."

"No, he's not." Mom sounded miffed. "You can do it, Margaret."

The aide pushing the wheelchair snickered. I ignored her. "Mother!" Good grief, I sounded like a fifteen-year-old. "Despite your antediluvian attitude about proper protocol, leap year or not, I have no intention of marrying the guy. I only met him a week ago."

"That's okay dear; I see the way he looks at you."

"You do not."

She pursed her lips.

Harper pulled up as we exited the building. Thank goodness the rain had stopped. He hopped out of his car and headed around the back of it.

"If you say a single word to him," I muttered out of the corner of my mouth, "I'm divorcing you."

She laughed that giggle of hers that I'd always hated—she was the one who sounded like a fifteen-year-old.

"Mrs. Winn. Mr. Winn." Harper sounded like a kid picking up his date on prom night. Why did I have teenagers on the brain all of a sudden? "Are you ready, Peggy?"

I thanked the aide who'd wheeled me this far. I couldn't get out of that wheelchair fast enough. Pointedly ignoring my mother's arm, I reached for Harper's hand. Warm. Comforting. Safe.

He reached across me to fasten my seatbelt. I clasped my hands on the strap of my purse and whispered, "Can we peel out of here? Fast?"

"You got it." He straightened, said a quick and extremely polite farewell to my parents in which he promised to take good care of me, and moved around to the driver's side. Mom stepped forward and tried to open my door. Harper had locked it. I was ever so grateful. I waved at her, smiled one of those smiles that didn't reach my eyes as she bellowed instructions, and sank back against the seat. That didn't work. The neck brace I wore wouldn't bend.

Harper didn't say a thing. I could have kissed him. No. I mean, I was very thankful. I turned the upper part of my body as inconspicuously as possible so I could inspect him as he drove. There had to be something wrong with him if my mother liked him that much. Or maybe she was just desperate to get me married.

He smiled. "I must have missed quite a conversation."

"Don't ask. Don't even think about asking."

"Your dad's a nice guy. I talked with him for a while in the waiting room."

"Mom let him get a word in?"

"Well," he admitted, "she was at the nurse's station."

"Poor Amy."

"Don't worry about Amy. She can hold her own." He eased into a left turn. "Once, when we were kids, my brother and I had been beleaguering her about something, I forget just what, and she pushed both of us off the dock. Got us in awful trouble."

"What's wrong with pushing somebody in a lake?"

"We were on the way to school at the time. And it was November."

"Brrr!"

"Yeah." His mouth twisted sideways in a grin. "She lured us down onto that dock, pointing at a really big fish with huge teeth."

"Let me guess. No fish? No teeth?"

"You got it. She ran like crazy, and we were too cold to

chase her, so we had to go home and change. We were late, but that was okay. We got her back."

"What did you do?"

"I held her down while my brother cut off one of her pigtails."

"You rat fink!"

"Nah. Her mom just cut the rest of her hair. It was kinda cute. She looked like a poodle."

"Did she ever get you back?"

He chuckled for a few seconds. "Oh, did she ever. She stayed home from school one day the next week. Said she was sick. Painted our bicycles pink. I think her mother was in on it."

"Cool mom." I didn't say anything about my own mom. I was beginning to be a little bit less angry with her, but the comparison between Amy's mom and my own hung in the air before my eyes. What would my mom have done under the same circumstances? She would have blamed me for it. Probably would have said I'd brought it on myself by playing with boys. And she would have left my hair lopsided to teach me a lesson. No. That wasn't fair. She would have cut my hair to one length so she wouldn't be embarrassed by how I looked.

I felt Harper's hand on my arm. "You okay?"

"Yeah. Yeah. Just a little sore. Tell me more."

"Take your mind off your hurts?"

"Something like that.

He told me more stories of the indomitable Amy, enough to fill the entire ride home. "My brother ended up marrying her." He turned onto Hickory Lane. "So now she's my sislaw."

"Huh?"

"That's what we call each other now that we're in-laws: sislaw and brolaw."

That explained her comment in the hospital. She knew her "brolaw" was going to give me a ride.

"Here you are. Home sweet home."

I looked up and saw Dirk at the front window. If Harper took me inside—as he showed every intention of doing: unfastening my seatbelt, picking up my purse, and helping me out of the car—Dirk would want an explanation, and I was in no mood to juggle two conversations at once. All I wanted to do was lie down.

I leaned on Harper's arm a bit harder than I would have thought was necessary.

"Do you have the key?"

"It's unlocked."

His eyes widened. I half expected a lecture, but he simply opened the door, which was suddenly filled with an irate Scotsman, waving his dagger and scared out of his wits.

"I thought ye might be deid!"

"Harper," I said, "I'm exhausted. The ride home from the hospital was harder than I thought it would be."

"Could ye no have sent a message?"

How on earth would I send a message to a ghost nobody else can see?

"I'll get you tucked in bed and call you later to check on you." He ushered me through the door and stopped. All the books I'd left lying open for Dirk's perusal covered the living room floor. It looked like a library had exploded. The afternoon sun slanted through the windows, illuminating various spiderwebs that cloaked the books in silvery glory.

"I couldna even stop the wee spinners."

"That's okay. Spiders eat bugs." I tried to shrug, but the movement hurt my neck. "An experiment," I said to Harper.

"About spiders?"

It was easier just to say yes.

"What do spiders have to do with books?"

I took a good look at my living room. Tornado damage. That's what it looked like. "Uh, it was just an idea, but it's not working very well."

"'Twas working verra well until ye were carried off in the carriage with the horrible red flashing lights."

"You couldn't have been bored. You must have read something while I was at the hospital."

"Aye."

Harper's eyebrows went up. "No, I was working. I don't usually read on the job."

This was a ridiculous conversation. As lopsided as I felt.

"Let me lie down on the couch. Oh God! Would you call Gilda and let her know I'm home, so she doesn't drive to the hospital after she closes the ScotShop?"

"I already contacted her. Karaline, too."

"Good. Karaline will bring dinner over later." I wouldn't even have to ask her. I knew she'd be here as soon as the Logg Cabin was closed for the day. She should be along any minute.

"I'll make you a cup of tea."

"No. I'm doing okay. I want to take a nap."

"Ye should take him up on his offer. Ye look as if ye could use a drop of tea, mayhap with a dollop o' whiskey in it."

I screwed up my face at the thought of it.

Harper reacted instantly. "What hurts?"

"Uh, nothing. Just a twinge in my neck." *And the thought of whiskey in my tea.* "I'll be okay once I sleep for a while."

He set my purse and the plastic bag on the table behind the front door. "You need a path to get to the couch. Do you mind if I pick up some of these books, or will that mess up your, uh, experiment?"

"Go ahead. I was on page one for all of them." As if that had anything to do with spiders.

He took the ones closest to the couch and removed the assorted utensils that held them propped open. He held out a handful of forks and spoons. "What do you want me to do with these?"

I studied him to see if he was being sarcastic, but all I

saw was polite inquiry. "You can put them in the sink. Thank you," I added as he moved that direction.

I heard him whistling "Tea for Two." Damn him. Why was I just standing here, helpless? I took a brief inventory. Oh. That was why. I felt like if I moved, I'd collapse.

Harper came back and piled the utensil-free books at the far end of the couch. Four more of the standing books, complete with spiderwebs, graced the middle of the room. One, I noticed, was the English history book Dirk had been reading when I'd left this morning. I raised my hand to my mouth and rubbed my upper lip. As quietly as possible, under cover of my hand I whispered, "Did the spiders spin webs on every book you read?"

"What did you say?" Harper picked up the books in a path between the couch and me.

"Nothing, just muttering to myself." *And to my wee ghostie.*

"Aye. I couldna bend down to see a book before there was a wee spinner there."

"Creepy," I breathed. It was a good thing I liked spiders. It looked like I'd be living with quite a few of them from now on.

Harper lifted the webbed books carefully and moved them one at a time to the little table beside the bay window. "Your bed awaits, madam. Would you like to change first?"

"No. Karaline will be by later. She can help me. For now, I just want to get prone." I held out my hand, and he supported me gently along the path he'd created. I sat carefully. He lifted my legs and helped me ease down onto a pillow he'd plumped into place.

Without my asking, he took the afghan from the back of the couch and spread it over me. Shorty jumped up and settled in beside me. "Are you sure you'll be all right? Where's your cell phone?"

"In my purse."

"May I get it out for you?"

That was nice of him to ask. "Yes." I considered asking

him to hang up my kerchief and bodice so they could dry, but decided not to. Karaline could take care of that.

He touched the side of my head gently, right beside the bandage. "This new haircut is going to look good." He paused a heartbeat and grinned. "Almost like Amy's poodle cut."

I winced. At least I didn't groan.

He brought me some water, which entailed moving a spider-bedecked book from one of the end tables and setting the glass within my reach. We argued briefly about locking the front door. I refused. I thanked him profusely for everything he'd done, and he finally left but with so many admonitions he sounded like my mother.

Dirk had been uncharacteristically silent. Now he stepped forward and knelt beside the couch. "Would ye tell me what happened?"

"The garbage truck hit me," I said.

"What would be a garbage truck? I saw it from the window when I heard the great noise, but didna ken what it was."

That's the way it went for the next half hour or so, as I not-so-patiently explained landfills and hospitals and X-rays and white-coated medical staff. After that, I fell asleep, and Dirk had to fend for himself again.

When I woke, the shawl lay spread across the afghan, tucked gently under my chin.

Karaline breezed in soon after that, thank goodness, and helped me into the downstairs bathroom. I stood in front of the mirror, leaning on the counter, and unbelted the arisaidh. It fell in a wooly heap around my feet as I untied the chemise. I stretched out the gathers and let it fall. My bruises were getting more spectacular by the hour. They'd gone from a light reddish purple in the hospital to a medium purple with a hint of lavender around the edges. It was a good thing yoga class was still on hold. I couldn't have crossed my legs if my life depended on it. I wondered how soon after a birth a yoga instructor could return to work. I supposed she'd call us and let us know.

"Just drop what you're wearing on the floor and I'll take care of it all." Karaline handed in my sleep shirt, my fuzzy slippers, and my terry cloth bathrobe.

"Thanks, K."

"I'm going to clear up all these books. Why on earth are they lying around all over the place, and what's with all the forks in the sink?"

"Long story. I'll tell you later."

A few minutes later, her voice was back. "Peggy?"

"Yeah?"

"Did you take that shawl into the bathroom with you?"

"No. It's on the back of the couch. Why?"

"It's not on the couch."

I adjusted the bathrobe, took one more look in the mirror, decided to cut off the rest of my hair when I could lift my arms without pain, and stepped into the living room. Most of the books had been scooped into piles around the edge of the room. Dirk stood beside the bay window holding the shawl. "Don't worry," I told her. "It'll show up."

She cocked her head at me. "I know it was there."

"Maybe it fell behind the couch."

Dirk headed that way. By the time Karaline leaned over the back, the shawl lay innocently on the floor. Dirk gave me a bow worthy of Buckingham Palace, which probably didn't even exist in the fourteenth century.

"Mystery solved. Let's eat. I brought enough Cabin food for an army."

"Fine with me."

I took a detour by the sink on my way to the table. The African violets were thriving. I wouldn't have to water them for a few more days. By then my arms should be less stiff.

Of course, Gilda, Sam, and Shoe all showed up within minutes of our sitting down. Karaline showed no surprise whatsoever. No wonder she'd brought so much food.

I was surprisingly hungry. For a few minutes we just fed our faces. I deflected questions about what had happened to me, and the talk turned to Shoe's experiences in jail. "Not too bad," he said. "The food was good."

Karaline snorted. "That's 'cause I fed you."

"You fed him?"

"I have a contract with the police department to provide meals for the prisoners." She pushed a bite of lasagna around on her plate. "Not that they have that many."

"Mac questioned me two or three times a day for the first couple of days," Shoe said, dragging the conversation back to himself. "Then I think he forgot about me."

"From everything I've heard, you had it pretty easy." I pointed my fork at him, even though I knew that wasn't polite. "Especially if you had Karaline's food. How was the bed? Comfortable?"

"Too hard."

Karaline reached over and poked his arm. "When I was there, you said it was too soft."

"Yeah. Whatever."

"I smuggled him some books," Gilda said.

Shoe guffawed. "Some smuggling. You just walked in and handed them to me." He reached for another piece of garlic toast.

Gilda looked hurt, and Sam patted her hand. No wonder she'd picked Sam instead of Shoe.

"That was nice of you, Gilda," Karaline said with a pointed look at Shoe. He was oblivious, shoveling in food as if his life depended on it. "Cleanup time," she added. "Sam and Gilda, clear the table. Shoe, you've eaten enough to fell a horse. You load the dishwasher. I'll put the food away. You"—she pointed at me—"head to the couch."

"I'll just sit here and keep you guys company."

She glared.

"No, Karaline, the thought of moving is more than I can handle. Just let me sit. Please," I added, and her face relaxed. I pushed the chair next to me away from the table so Dirk could sit down.

Karaline looked from me to the chair and back again. She threw her hands in the air and turned away. Dirk grinned. I leaned my elbows on the table and hid my face in my hands.

After the gang left, Karaline lingered at the front door. I noticed she hadn't picked up her purse. "What on earth is going on with you? You talk to walls. You push out chairs when there's no need to. Tell me. Now."

I should have known she wouldn't let me get away with it.

"Ye might as well tell her," Dirk commented drily from behind my right shoulder. "Otherbye she'll think ye daft."

"She'll think me daft if I do tell her," I muttered.

"Huh?"

"Never mind." I glanced back at Dirk. "You really think I should?"

"Peggy," she growled.

"Aye. Now ye must, I think."

I nodded and motioned my friend to the living room. I chose the wingback chair beside the bay window, and Karaline perched on one end of the couch.

Dirk, with the shawl under his arm, sat down on the other end and turned so he faced her.

"Remember that shawl I bought in Scotland?"

"Yeah. The hippie one. What about it?"

"It's a lot older than you think. It had something . . . She's never going to believe this."

"Tell her any the way. Give her a chance. Mayhap she will surprise ye."

Karaline raised both hands to her head, clutched her hair, and screeched. Then she smiled. "Tell me. Right now. Unless you want me to do that again."

I took a deep breath. "The shawl has a ghost attached to it. He's sitting right there beside you, on the couch."

Karaline studied me, much the same way Sam had back in the ScotShop. "A ghost?" She slid her hand over the seat beside her, but Dirk stood before she touched him. "You're telling me I'm sitting next to a ghost?"

Her incredulity pushed a button I didn't know I had. "Dirk," I said sweetly. "Would you drop the shawl on the floor and step away from it?"

She drummed her fingers on her leg.

"I wouldna throw my Peigi's shawl on the floor," he said, and laid the shawl gently on the cushion next to Karaline.

She was watching me, not him. I pointed to the shawl beside her hand.

This time, she screamed for real.

20

Revelations

"Would you like a glass of water?" I asked in as sugary a voice as I could muster. Served her right for doubting me.

"She could use a wee dram."

Maybe he was right. I took a closer look at her. My friend. Shaking as if she'd seen a . . . I couldn't help it. I burst out laughing.

That brought her around. "You have no right to laugh at me."

"Sorry, K, but you were shaking like . . . you'd . . . seen a . . . ghost." Her upper lip curled. "Sorry," I said, curbing the giggles. "It was funny, that's all."

"You think giving me a heart attack is humorous?"

She sat there, elegant as always, glanced down at the shawl, and shuddered.

"Do ye think she might see me if she held the shawl?"

My shawl? "You want to give her *my* shawl?"

"There is nae need to ribbetysnippet so. I thought mayhap she might believe ye better if she could see me."

"But you're . . ." I stopped and closed my mouth. He was *my* ghost, and I felt singularly possessive. Singularly childish as well, but I didn't have to admit that to anyone.

"Who are—" Karaline cut herself off. She knew *who* I was talking to. "Peg," she said sounding half angry and half plaintive, "would you please explain all this to me?"

"Tell her the tale." Dirk chuckled. "'Tis a good one." He leaned against the window frame and crossed his arms.

I looked from him, my ghost, to her, my friend. He was right. She needed to hear it all.

I tightened the belt on my bathrobe again. It had a tendency to loosen, especially when my chest was heaving with indignation. "Karaline, promise me you'll just listen while I explain this."

She nodded, but I doubted she'd be able to keep her promise.

"I found this shop in Pitlochry, one I'd never seen before and one that seems to have disappeared since I saw it."

"That makes no sense, Peg."

Ha! I was right. She couldn't keep her mouth shut. "You're right. None of this makes sense, but I did buy that shawl, and he"—I pointed—"he showed up when I put it on."

"He? Who—what—where is he?"

Dirk bowed at her more politely, less flamboyantly, than he had bowed to me a few hours ago.

"She can't see you. You might as well relax."

"'Tis the intent that means something."

"What the hell is going on?" Karaline was back to a screech.

"He just bowed to you, and I reminded him you couldn't see him, and he said it was the thought that counts."

"I didna say that."

"Hush."

"Why?" Karaline looked thoroughly bewildered.

No wonder. "Him," I told her. "Not you."

She raised a hand to the right side of her face, as if she

were hiding her mouth from Dirk, and whispered, "What does he look like?"

Dirk stood a little straighter and eased his shoulders back. No, men hadn't changed much. "He's tall, has long black hair, a heavy five o'clock shadow, and wears a belted plaid."

"What's a played? What would be a five o the clock shadow?"

"An old-fashioned kilt. The kind you have to lie down on the ground and roll around yourself. And it means you haven't shaved for a couple of days."

Karaline looked dubious. Dirk looked indignant.

"He was born in . . . oh gosh, I don't know when, but the last date he can remember is 1359."

"I was born in the year of our Lord 1329."

I calculated quickly. "You're the same age as me?" It wasn't grammatical, but I didn't take the time to worry about it.

"Thirteen . . . Did you say thirteen something?"

"Uh-huh. Fifty-nine. I think that must be when he died. And he just said he was born in 1329, which makes him thirty years old. Plus the six or seven hundred years between then and now." I looked over at Dirk. He certainly didn't look dead. Except for the fact that I could sort of see the outline of a window in back of him. Through him.

"Is he wearing one of those poet shirts, the kind that makes him look like his shoulders are this wide?" She held her arms out at an angle.

I looked at Dirk. I already knew the answer, because I'd already noticed the way he'd filled up that porta potty, but I thought it might be a good idea to check just the same. He placed his fists on his hips and swaggered, I swear it, back and forth in front of the window. "Yes," I said. "It's a homespun shirt with long sleeves, and they're sort of rolled up above his elb—" What was this, a Paris runway? "Stop parading, Dirk."

I hauled myself, not too gracefully, to my feet and stretched my back.

"I bet he looks like Braveheart."

"What would be this brave heart?"

"It was a movie about a Scottish hero." I ignored his question about what would be a movie and Karaline's comment, which she stifled when she realized I must be answering a question she hadn't heard. "He married his childhood sweetheart and the English killed her and he attacked somebody or other and the English beheaded him. I'll find the story in one of my history books so you can read it."

"Would ye be meaning William Wallace?"

"You knew him?"

"Nae. He was executed four and twenty years before I was born, but my father, just a boy, carried water to him before his final battle."

I sat down.

Karaline, oblivious to the fact that we had a living history lesson in front of us, touched the edge of the shawl with her index finger. "It sure does feel real. Why is it haunted, do you think?"

I shifted mental gears. "It was woven by his lady love, a woman named Peigi."

"Peggy? Did they have people named Peggy back then?"

"Aye," Dirk chimed in. "Peigi means 'pearl.'"

It sure would be easier if I didn't have to translate. "It's spelled P-e-i-g-i, and pronounced more like PAY-gee, but it's essentially the same name, short for Margaret."

"And it means 'pearl,'" he prompted as he walked across the room between the two of us. He ended up in front of the overstuffed chair, examining Karaline from a new angle.

"Yeah, yeah," I said, "it means 'pearl.'"

"He's stayed stuck to this shawl all that time just because of his love for her?" Karaline's eyes went sort of fuzzy.

I rolled mine. "Never knew you were a romantic, K."

She stiffened her back, lunged for the shawl, and pulled it close, clutching it to her chest. She looked wildly toward the window where he'd been the last time I had pointed, sure she'd see him. Her shoulders drooped. I waited a dramatic moment, cleared my throat, and pointed the other way, toward the big chair. Her eyes widened. "Oh my God, oh my God, oh my God, oh . . ."

"You can stop anytime you want to, Karaline."

Dirk smiled a smile of surpassing sweetness, clasped his hands behind his back, extended his right leg forward, and inclined his torso a few inches. Perfectly proper. Karaline was ecstatic for about half a second, until she fainted.

I never could have caught her in time if she'd keeled over onto her face, and Dirk would have been no help at all. Luckily, she slumped backward.

I picked up the shawl from the floor, where Karaline had dropped it. "Don't worry. She just fainted. It happens when there's not enough oxygen to the brain."

"Oxeegen?"

Now I have to explain chemistry and biology? "Remember how women used to wear corsets so tight, they couldn't get enough air and they used to faint a lot?"

"Korsets?"

I thought for a second as Karaline began to stir. "The seventeen hundreds. You wouldn't know about those." I was going to have to bone up on the history of fashion. "They wore very tight, uh, undergarments that laced around them to make their waists as small as possible. The result was that they looked dainty, but they couldn't catch a deep breath."

He looked at me as if he thought I'd gone positively nuts. "For the love of St. Michael, why?"

I could see it in his eyes: he was imagining his sensible Peigi, who must always have been swathed in a very comfortable chemise and arisaidh—probably with no undergarments at all, although he might not have known that—walking unencumbered, the way women ought to walk. I thought briefly of Scarlett O'Hara holding on to that bedpost yelling, "Tighter, tighter!" Stupid. Absolutely stupid. Of course, now women subjected themselves to stiletto heels and the resulting back problems when they reached their forties. I'd seen it in my own mother. Her heels had gotten a bit lower over the years, but she still wore the doggone things and complained about her back almost constantly.

Karaline's eyes fluttered open. "Oh my God. . . ."

"Don't start that again," I snapped, and Dirk gave me a withering look as he bent solicitously over her.

"You're real. You're really real." She rubbed her temples. "Absolutely real."

"Stop, Karaline. We've established that he is real."

"Does he have a name?"

"Dirk."

"Dirk." It sounded as soft as melted caramel.

Dirk glared pointedly at me and turned back to her with another flourish. "My name is Macbeath Donlevy Freusach Finlay Macearachar Macpheidiran of Clan Farquharson. My family call me Macbeath."

"Mock-beh-ath? Do you mean like—"

"He's never heard of Shakespeare," I interrupted. "William wasn't born for another two hundred years or so."

"William? Who would that be?"

"Shakespeare." I pointed toward the piles of books. "Didn't you start *The Merchant of Venice*?"

Karaline raised her hand like a fourth-grader. "What are you talking about?"

"I left all those books open for him to read. Harper closed some of them—so did you, for that matter."

"Why leave them open?"

"He can't turn the pages."

At Karaline's look of utter incredulity, Dirk spun on his heel, walked to the table in front of the bay window, and swept his arm—rather ostentatiously, I thought—over the length of the table. In one fluid motion he passed through the stacks of books, the jade plant, and the lamp. His plaid swirled as he turned back and spread his hands in mute appeal.

"How can you eat?" Leave it to Karaline to think of that.

"I canna," he said simply. "Then again, I dinna ever feel hungry, so 'tis not so difficult."

"Let me get this straight. You can't turn pages, you can't eat, and you're usually invisible?"

Dirk nodded.

I nodded.

Karaline nodded. "So, what good are you?"

I bristled, and Dirk looked at the floor.

She must have realized how catty that sounded. "What I meant was, why are you here?"

Dirk's head came up slowly. "I dinna know," he said. "I dinna . . ."

"It's not like he chose to come," I said, grabbing the shawl away from Karaline. "This is the reason he's here. He's following the shawl."

"I didna follow it for six hundred years. Other folk must have held it during that time. Why did I not awaken before this?"

"Maybe he did wake up before," Karaline said, "but he just doesn't remember those other times."

Dirk rolled his shoulders back and lifted his chin. "I have a verra good memory."

Karaline jumped to her feet. "No. Think about it. Maybe each time somebody owns the shawl, you get to wake up and enjoy living. . . ." Her voice trailed off. "It's not much like living if you can't eat," she added, "but maybe there's some sort of time warp or something and you can't remember all those other times."

"What would be a thyme wart?"

"It's like sci-fi," she said.

"Sigh what?"

"Karaline. Get a grip." She curled her lip at me. "We don't know how or why he's here. He just is." I gripped the shawl tighter. "Can you still see him?"

"Of course I can see him," she snapped.

"Ye dinna have the shawl."

I thought about it while they babbled back and forth. "Dirk," I said, interrupting their useless-as-far-as-I-could-see discussion, "would you mind if we performed an experiment? Remember what happens when I fold up the shawl and put it away?"

"Aye." Even that one word sounded dubious.

"Maybe something has changed, now that Karaline can see you without having the shawl in her hands. Maybe you won't disappear this time?"

Karaline nudged my arm. "What are you talking about?"

"He goes away when I fold up the shawl."

"Where does he go?"

"I have told ye I dinna like that feeling, that nothingness."

"Maybe you won't go away this time."

"Mayhap I will. Mayhap I willna be able to find my way back."

I sat down as his words sank in. Of course he'd come back. He had to. He couldn't just . . . just not be. "Don't be ridiculous." I sat there, kneading a corner of the shawl in my fist. "You've always shown up before."

Dirk inhaled deeply and took the shawl from my arms. I felt like a pogo stick as I bounced up again. Bounce is a relative term, considering the neck brace and all my bruises. "What are you doing?"

He folded the shawl carefully, laid it on the couch, and simply wasn't there. Karaline gasped and lunged for the shawl. I grabbed her arm. "Don't do that!"

"Why not? We've got to get him back."

"No, not so fast. I mean, yes, we need to bring him back, but the last time I did that, grabbing it up right away, it threw him off balance." Me, too. I had been as rattled by that experience as he had been. *Dinna do that*, he had told me. "He needs a minute between . . . between . . ." I groped for a word. "Between visits. To reset himself or something," I added lamely. I certainly didn't understand the mechanics of this situation.

Karaline tapped her foot. "How long?"

"I don't know," I wailed. "You think I'm an expert at this?"

She reached for the shawl, but I was faster. I grabbed it. Not wanting to jostle Dirk, though, I unfolded it gently and placed it around my shoulders.

Karaline gasped at the same time I saw the swish of his plaid next to the arm of the chair.

"He's baaack," she intoned.

"Aye," said Dirk, not catching the film reference. "That I am."

"You can still see him, K?"

"Of course I can."

I wondered about that. "You couldn't see him at first. Not until you held the shawl. Once you'd seen him the first time, though . . ."

"I didn't need the shawl anymore. Maybe it's like looking at one of those hidden-picture things, you know? Once you see the lion in the grass, you can't ever go back to thinking it's just a landscape anymore."

"Have ye seen a *lion*?"

"No, she hasn't. There are these . . . Good grief, why am I trying to explain this?"

Inspecting our ghostie with a practiced eye, Karaline said, "We could plant him different places around town and get him to report back to us. He could find out who killed Mason!"

"Ye dinna need to talk as if I am no right beside ye."

"There's only one problem with that." I said, and Dirk nodded solemnly. "Anywhere outside this house, he can't get more than about six feet away from whoever is wearing the shawl."

"Why not?"

"What do you mean *why not*? How would I know why not? I have a ghost in my house and a shawl that's almost seven hundred years old." My voice rose in pitch, speed, and volume. "First you couldn't see him and now you can; I'm in a neck brace because I ran into a garbage truck, for crying out loud, and you're asking me to explain the rules?"

She looked at me for a long moment until the echoes died away. I could see her lips moving. She was counting to ten. Or maybe twenty. "Don't bite my head off," was all she said.

"Look, you have to get up early to get the Logg Cabin going." I stood painfully and Karaline put out a hand to help. "I need a good night's sleep. My bruises are throbbing, and my brain is even worse."

"You're right about that." She rubbed the back of her neck and picked up her purse. "Maybe we'll think clearer in the morning."

Dirk followed us to the door.

"Come see me at the shop after you close the Cabin."

"You're working tomorrow? Are you sure you'll be fit?"

"Aye. I mean, yes."

She grinned. "He's getting to you, isn't he?" She leaned back and cocked her arm as if to poke him in the ribs but thought better of it and hugged me instead, way too hard. I groaned, and she let go. "Can you make it up those stairs by yourself?"

I took a quick inventory. All the aches were settling in for what seemed like the long haul. "I think so?"

She set her purse down yet again. "Stay," she said to Dirk. "I'll handle this," and ushered me slowly upstairs. "Hot shower?"

"Nope. Just bed. I don't think I could stand by myself."

As we turned into my bedroom, Karaline asked, in a voice a tad too nonchalant, "Where does Dirk sleep?"

"Good grief, K. It's not like that. He's a ghost."

She looked around, probably checking to be sure Dirk wasn't on our heels. "He's really hot, and those shoulders—"

"He's been dead for six hundred and fifty years, Karaline."

She ignored the steel in my voice. "Wouldn't you like to maybe—"

"No. I would not." I patted Shorty as he curled into a feline O beside me. "Now, go away and let me sleep."

It wasn't that easy to get rid of her. She fussed around for a while, bringing me a glass of water and handing me my journal. "Write," she said. "Not that I think you ought to, but I know you're going to anyway, so just do it, and then turn out the light and get some sleep." She moved the lamp closer to the edge of the bedside table.

"Good night, K." I couldn't wait for her to leave.

"Good night, P," she said, matching my tone. "Sleep tight."

I ignored the suggestiveness in those last two words and opened my journal with great deliberation. She giggled and walked out, leaving the bedroom door wide open.

I listened to her walk down the stairs. "Sleep well," I heard, just before the front door closed.

Soon, Dirk stepped in the room.

"Were you waiting up here the whole time?"

"Nae," he said with dignity. "She would ha' seen me. I watched her out the front window until she got in her car. I even waved to her." He looked like an imp. "Then I came . . . then I just *was* upstairs." His look turned serious "What she said, about using me to spy on people, might work."

I stroked Shorty as I thought about it. I needed to take Dirk to a James Bond movie. What would he think of all those gadgets? "You really want to spy on people?"

"There's a murderer"—all those rolled *r*'s again—"roaming the streets."

"You can't spy on anybody. Not unless I'm there, too. You have to be within six feet of me."

"Mayhap not. Not if I hold my Peigi's shawl."

The silence stretched out. He'd obviously been thinking about it to have answered so quickly. "You think it will work," I finally said, and it wasn't a question.

"I dinna need any sleep."

"Yeah, but the rest of us sleep at night, and even if you could get into people's houses, you wouldn't hear anything, except snores."

"The murder happened at night."

He had me there.

"I could, mayhap, look around."

"You can't open doors," I reminded him.

"Och, aye. That I canna." He heaved a sigh that set his plaid to shivering. "'Twas a good idea."

"While it lasted," I added.

He leaned forward, and for half an insane second I thought he was going to kiss me. Before I could react, he inhaled loudly. "Are ye wearing a scent?"

"You mean perfume?"

"Aye."

"Yes. I put some on this morning." I hadn't had a shower since the accident. I hoped he wasn't smelling anything awful. I turned my head as inconspicuously as possible, as far as the neck brace would allow me, and gave a trial sniff. You aren't supposed to be able to smell your own stink, though, are you? At least not until it gets really bad.

"For a wee moment, I thought I could smell something." He turned away from me. "Now, 'tis gone."

He sounded wistful, disappointed, discouraged. I almost wished he'd been able to smell, even if it was stinky. Anything to raise his mood. "Good night, Dirk," I said as gently as I could. He nodded and kept walking, taking the shawl with him.

21

Birthday Breakfast

Why did I ever choose the back bedroom, the one on the east side of the house? The light was way too bright, and it was way too early to consider getting up, despite what my alarm clock, the fiendish one, said to me. I pulled Shorty closer and snuggled the blankets more tightly around us, surprised that my neck didn't hurt quite as much as it had yesterday. Maybe the brace was helping.

I had a busy day ahead of me. I needed to catch up with all the store business that probably hadn't been handled yesterday. Gilda was a good manager. She knew the merchandise well and was great with the customers—when she wasn't having one of her migraines—but when she was under stress, she tended to forget about things. Like bank deposits. I usually took care of those. The bank was just a block out of my way when I came home in the evenings, but it was a three-block detour for Gilda. She'd probably left the money in the safe.

That thought reminded me of the other safe—the one hidden inside the wall. There had to be a connection between that safe and Mason's murder. I felt a chill run up my spine, and it had nothing to do with the weather.

I glanced idly at the Bird-of the-Month Audubon calendar hanging across the room. One of the squares was circled in red. Oh crap. The birthday party. How could I have forgotten it was my birthday? I had to show up. Karaline had put a lot of effort into making this the best surprise party I would ever have. I'd seen her to-do list once when she didn't know I was looking. It was about a mile and a half long. Naturally, I'd told my brother all about it.

"I'm going to cook a private birthday dinner, just for you and Drew," she'd told me, "Just the three of us old friends. Something simple. At the Logg Cabin." It was a place Drew could get into easily. His chair was fairly narrow, but he needed a decent turning radius of blank space inside a door so he could maneuver without asking for help.

Private? Just for the three of us? Simple? Yeah, right. She'd invited half the town at fifteen dollars a head to cover the cost of the meal and all the trimmings. The whole group would get there early and be waiting for us with most of the lights out and party streamers everywhere. We'd both act totally surprised, and everybody would clap us on the back, there would be hugs and kisses and mounds of food, cards and maybe some presents, although the invitation said *No Presents, Just Your Presence*.

Drew and I had always had our birthday parties together, even when we were school age. You'd think a brother would want only boys there, and a sister would want her girlfriends, but—maybe it was because we were twins—our birthday never seemed complete unless we were together. Even the year he spent in the hospital and the rehab place, I'd baked a carrot cake for the two of us, our favorite kind, and smuggled it into his room an hour before Mom and Dad were scheduled to show up. We stuffed ourselves with cake and the chocolate cream cheese frosting slathered on it, and Drew laughed and laughed and laughed, until he dissolved into tears over his useless legs. I cried with him. What else was there to do?

By the time Mom breezed in with her boring white cake, we were too full to eat any of it. She got so mad at us. She could at least have put chocolate icing on it, but Mom didn't like chocolate, and she certainly didn't like carrot cake.

I raised my hands over my head and pushed against the headboard, judging my returning strength. Not too shabby. I eased the blankets down a bit and raised the hem of my sleep shirt. The blackish-purple bruises looked awful, but who'd see them? Nobody, that's who. I pulled myself up with an inward yank. No! I would not let my nonexistent love life get me down. I had a birthday party to get ready for. And work first.

The floor was cold. The fuzzy Winn tartan rug I'd hooked had scooted under the bed again. I fished around for it with one foot while I threw on my bathrobe. I was going to have to put a leash on those slippers of mine. Bending over while wearing a neck brace is not a fun exercise. I reached for my phone. I always call Drew on even-numbered birthdays and he calls me on the odd ones. He answered on the first ring. "Happy b-day, sis!"

"Stop it! I get to say it first. I'm the one who called you."

He chuckled, and I could hear his super fancy coffee machine gurgling in the background. "Beat you to it this time."

"When did we start this? Do you remember?"

I listened to him pour his coffee. "I dunno," he said. "It just happened once we weren't living in the same house."

"Gotta run. I'm hungry, but Drew?"

"Yeah?"

"Can we get together and talk sometime? There's something going on at the ScotShop I want to tell you about, but not over the phone."

"Anytime. Have to drive to New York next week, but I'll be around until then."

"Thanks. In the meantime, we've got that b-day party tonight."

"Oh yeah, the big three-oh surprise. Think we should show up early?"

"Karaline would kill us. Seven thirty sharp."

"How about letting Tessa and me pick you up? I'll stop by at seven and we can talk."

"Great idea. Make it six thirty, though, if you can. There's a lot to talk about."

"Sure thing. See ya, sis."

I sat there for a few minutes, trying to get my head around turning thirty. I wasn't a millionaire yet. My love life was nonexistent thanks to Andrea. And Mason, too—he was just as responsible. I'd spent a couple of years browbeating my brother for having been silly enough to fall off that dinosaur skeleton—*Couldn't you have held on to a vertebra or something?*—but now I'd gone and backed out in front of a garbage truck and had the neck brace and bruises to prove it. What kind of messed-up thirty-year-old was I?

But on the other hand, I owned my own store. I was able to travel when I needed or wanted to. I had good friends. I'd gone through the experience of loving somebody, even if it hadn't turned out the way I'd hoped it would. On top of that, I'd survived the shock of discovering a corpse, I had a hidden safe full of mystery, and I had my very own ghost. What more could I ask?

There was a grapefruit with my name on it in the kitchen, and eggs ready to be scrambled and cooked. I dressed faster than usual, even considering the bruises.

Still a bit groggy, but considerably cheered, I made my way out of my bedroom and saw my ghost sitting on the top stair. I sat down beside him. "What's up?"

He raised his head and looked toward the ceiling. "Up where?"

"What I meant was, good morning and how are you?"

"Och, aye. I see. I am doing as well as one could hope."

I waited a second for him to go on, but he just sat there. "What do you mean by that?"

"I have spent a good deal of the night thinking about what your friend said."

"You mean Harper?" Why was I thinking of him this early in the morning?

Dirk clenched his right fist. I couldn't see the other one. He might have been clenching it, too. "I didna mean him."

"Oh. You meant Karaline."

"Aye, Mistress Caroline."

"What did she say?"

He stared at his hand for a moment and gradually unclenched his fist. "She asked me what I am doing here."

"Well, that's easy. You're . . . uh . . . well, you're um . . ." I stuttered to a stop.

"Aye. Ye canna say, either."

I took a deep breath. "Macbeath." He raised his head when I called him by his real name. "I would like to invite you to my thirtieth b-day party this evening at half past seven. Would you be kind enough to accompany me?"

"What would be a bee-day party?"

"You never had a b-day party?"

"I dinna ken. If I knew what one was, I might be able to answer ye."

I reached for the bannister and hauled myself to my feet. "Look, I don't know why you're here. All I know is that I'm glad you are. Today's my thirtieth birthday, and Karaline is putting on a surprise birthday party for me and my brother, and I'd like you to be there."

"What would that have to do with bees?"

I put my hands over my face and exhaled long and hard. "It's a contraction, Dirk. Just for the fun of it. That's what my brother and I call it. B-hyphen-day. Get it?"

"Och, aye." He didn't look convinced.

I started on down the stairs, and he trailed after me. "It's a surprise party. That means Drew and I aren't supposed to know about it, so we'll have to act astonished when we get there."

"If 'tis supposed to be a surprise, why do the two of ye know of it?"

I drummed my fingers on the island in the middle of the kitchen for a moment. "I, uh, read some of her mail."

"Ye what?"

"Don't get so self-righteous." I pulled a grapefruit out of the fridge. "It was just lying on her counter."

Dirk was awfully silent. I looked up at him. He was staring at the grapefruit like he thought it might bite him. "What would that be?"

"This?" I cut it in half. "It's called a grapefruit. Why?"

"I travelled to Edinburgh once."

"Yeah?" I ran my knife around the first little wedge.

"I saw a fruit verra much like that, only it was smaller and of a different color. It was called an or-ange." His voice was hushed as he said those two distinct syllables, and filled with awe. "Only the nobles could afford them."

I set the knife down. "Dirk, you've got to get used to the idea that a whole lot of things, like books and fruit like this, are pretty common around here. Around now. I eat grapefruit all the time, and I ain't rich."

He frowned. "And crimes? Murders? Are those common, too?"

"Of course not!" I picked the knife back up and went to work on the hapless grapefruit.

"Yet ye have a number of constables who appear to do only that work. They are not farmers or blacksmiths or coopers. Their only employment seems to be finding people who have done wrong. Am I correct?"

I scooped the loosened sections out into a bowl. "Well, when you put it that way, I guess the answer would have to be yes."

"I lived my entire thirty years and didna encounter a single instance of anyone killing another human being.

There might be brawls between men at the pub occasionally, but little more than that. Reoch Macdonald did bear false witness against his neighbor Tawse Macleod for supposedly taking a pig from Reoch's sty, but the village knew the truth of it and wouldna allow Reoch to speak so."

"You mean to tell me everybody in your village was perfect except the brawling men and this Ree-guy."

"Nae, nae. Just that we didna solve our problems by murdering anyone."

"So why did you tell me you knew all about fighting?"

"Och, aye, I did, but that was to settle clan quarrels."

"Oh, big difference."

"We didna go out to murder."

"Well, we don't, either." I slurped the rest of the juice out of the bowl. "Not usually."

"So I must get used to books and grape fruits often and killing occasionally?"

"You had a war just before you were born." Sorry as I am to admit it, I sounded a little nasty.

He sighed. "Aye. There were wars and clan fights." He sat down across from me. "Are ye saying there are none now?"

He had me there. I pushed away from the table. "I, uh, have to go brush my teeth." I was going to be hungry by ten, but my scrambled eggs would have to wait for another day when the Inquisition wasn't going on at my kitchen table. "We have to walk this morning," I told him. "I haven't gotten a rental car yet."

"Could we no use the wee carriage out front?"

"What are you talking about?"

"This morning, before ye awakened, a verra big truck of garbage stopped in front of this dwelling. Behind it, a wee car drove into the . . ."

"The driveway?"

"Och, is that what 'tis called? Aye. Weel, a man got out of the car, climbed into the truck of garbage, and left."

"You're kidding, right?"

"This has nothing to do with goats."

I had to think about that one. I was halfway to the front door before I got it.

Sure enough, just as he had said, a wee carriage, a chocolate brown Volvo, stood in my driveway. "You didn't tell me he put a bow on it."

"I supposed it was meant to be a surprise. Mayhap 'tis for your bee-day."

It was a surprise all right. I pulled an envelope from under the bright red bow adorning the hood and read the note aloud.

Dear Miss Winn,

I hope you will forgive my running into you. The accident helped me make a decision I've been agonizing over for some time. Please accept this gift as my way of thanking you for your part in this drama. It's an older car, but it is in prime condition and quite trustworthy. The keys, bill of sale, and the registration papers are in the glove compartment. You'll see that I've sold the car to you for one dollar.

Sincerely,
Martin Cameron
Former Owner
Cameron Garbage
Arkane, Vermont

p.s. I feel a great deal happier than I have in a very long time. That alone is worth far more than the price of a used car.

p.p.s. I don't expect to receive that dollar. Let's call us even?

I ran my hand over the hood.

"Yon Master Cameron sounds like a courtly gentleman. I wouldna expect him to carry refuse."

I smiled up at Dirk, feeling completely right with the world at the moment. "Gentlemen come in all sorts of packages. Let me grab my purse and we'll take it for its maiden voyage."

Dirk looked at me sideways but must have gathered the gist of what I was saying. "All ye need to do is open the door, if ye wouldna mind."

Harper stood outside the ScotShop. Dirk made a low, grumbling sound, but I kept walking. "H'lo, Harper. Is anything wrong?"

"Why do people always assume something's wrong when they see a police officer?"

"Maybe it's because you're always after the bad guys."

"Aye, now. I was right, was I not? Your constables have no other work to do."

"Do you ever do safety talks at schools?"

Harper seemed mildly surprised by the change in topic. "Yes. In fact, I'll be at the elementary school next week."

See? I wanted to say, but I think Dirk got the idea because he grumbled a bit more sotto voce.

"New car?"

I didn't think he needed the details. "New to me."

"Martin, huh?"

"You knew?"

He shrugged. "He called me to see if I thought you'd accept it."

I narrowed my eyes at him. "What did you tell him?"

"I told him that anything worth doing was worth trying."

I didn't have an answer for that.

That lovely smell of wood floors, rich wool, and ancient walls enveloped me in its welcome when I opened the door.

Even the jangle of the bell sounded less irritating than usual. "You might as well come on in." I looked at my watch. "Am I going to have to delay opening this morning?"

"No. You can open on time. I wanted to see how you were feeling and have another look at that storage area in back."

"I'm feeling fine and you're welcome to it. When Sam gets here, he can clear off the shelves if you need him to."

"That won't be necessary." He patted his pockets.

"Looking for something?"

"I must have left my measuring tape in the car. I'll be right back."

"I have one. It's twenty-five feet. Is that long enough?"

"Should be. Thanks."

I locked the door behind us and headed for the counter. He followed along, his footsteps in time with mine.

The lost-and-found basket was balanced precariously near the edge. I pulled it out of the way and located the tape measure. There was entirely too much junk under here. I handed the tape measure to Harper, motioned him toward the back room, and rifled though the basket. How long did I have to keep these things before I dumped them? A ring— not an expensive one, and I knew for a fact it had been here at least a year. I tossed it in the waste can. Then there was one of those super bouncy balls and four keys. One looked like a house key. A little one, like for a padlock. A longer gold one. There was a car key, too. Some poor tourist, probably. I hoped the owner was part of a married couple, so the wife might have had an extra key in her purse. A Swiss Army knife just like the one my dad had given me on my tenth birthday. Three cheap earrings, none of which matched. I tossed them, too.

I glanced around to see where Dirk was. The far side of the room, over by the front windows. Just as in my house, he seemed to be able to drift farther away from me here in the store. I wondered what he would think of the mishmash

of items in my lost-and-found basket. Did people in the
fourteenth century lose things so casually? Did they even
have such bunches of junk?

Harper poked his head through the staff door, and I lost
my train of thought.

"Come look at this." He stepped forward and held the
door wide open. I set down the basket slowly to give Dirk a
chance to catch up with me, but he popped up at my elbow.
He must have been closer than I'd thought. I paused in front
of Harper and motioned surreptitiously for Dirk to walk
through the door ahead of me. Weren't ghosts supposed to
be able to walk through walls?

I looked at my watch. It was the only excuse I could think
of to justify standing there. Dirk stepped around me and
into the back room. "Twenty minutes till we open," I said.
"Gilda should have been here by now."

I looked up at Harper's quizzical expression, patted my
watch, and followed my ghostie. Harper was going to think
I was an absolute flake.

He placed his hand lightly on the back of my waist and
steered me to the left and into the little bathroom/storage
room. My back stayed slightly warm where he had touched
it, even after he let go. I swallowed.

He handed me one end of the measuring tape. "Hold this
against the wall." I did. He reeled out the tape to the front
edge of the old wooden built-in shelves. "Six feet, two
inches," he said, and reeled it in.

"Yeah? So?"

"The shelves are twenty-four inches deep. When you add
that to the six-two, you have a room that is two inches over
eight feet front to back, right?

I nodded, wondering where this was heading.

He led the way out into the workroom and around the
corner of this eight-foot-two-inch room. He hooked the
metal tape measure onto that corner and gestured to me to
hold it in place. He reeled out the tape again, all the way to

the wall and marked the tape with two fingers. On the other side of that wall was the ugly brown wallpaper at the back of my shop.

"If you allow six inches or so for the framing," he said, "this wall ought to be close to eight and a half feet long, right?

I did the math and nodded.

He walked back to me, holding the yellow metal tape. It crinkled as it bent in his wake. "Look." Dirk leaned closer. Harper's fingers were on either side of the line that said 132 inches. Eleven feet. "Where," Harper asked, "did the extra two and a half feet go?"

Dirk shook his head. "The wall behind the wee safe was not that deep."

I thought back to the way the safe looked. "You're right."

"About what?"

It sure would be easier if other people could hear Dirk. "The safe wasn't that deep."

He nodded. "Eighteen inches front to back. Remember when I pushed that thin wire into the holes"—he looked at me askance—"the ones you didn't destroy when you pulled out the Sheetrock?"

Next to me, Dirk said, "Aye?"

"What about them?"

"The wire went in a good two feet before it hit something."

"So you knew there had to be a problem—"

"A discrepancy."

"A discrepancy between how thick the wall ought to be and how thick it actually is?"

"Right," he said.

"So the question is . . ."

". . . why is part of that false wall only wide enough to hide a safe . . ."

". . . while the other section of it is wide enough to hide . . ."

". . . something else?"

Dirk gave a groan. "Ye are doing it again."

I looked at him and raised my eyebrows.

"Sounding like the Sinclairs."

"Oh." I guess we did. Sort of like a Ping-Pong match, back and forth.

Harper followed the direction of my gaze, but all he saw was a wall. "Oh? Oh, what?"

"Nothing. I talk to myself sometimes." *And, of course, to my ghostie.*

"Care to let me in on your interior conversation?"

I spread my hands about eighteen inches apart, wide enough for the safe, front to back. Then I spread them wider. "You don't suppose there's, uh, a body hidden in there, do you?"

"A body? In where?" Gilda stood halfway in the room. How much had she heard?

"We were just throwing some ideas around. Nothing to worry about."

"Peggy was hypothesizing about what might be in the wall next to the safe." Harper must not have considered her a threat. Well, that wasn't such a hard call. I didn't consider her a threat, either. She looked perky this morning. No migraine, thank goodness. She was no good at all when she dragged around.

"Can we look?" She sounded hopeful. What had happened to the shrinking-violet persona? Sam wasn't around. She shouldn't feel a need to act helpless.

"Yesterday you were scared there might be a body," Harper said, "and today you want one?"

"Well"—Gilda sounded defensive—"Peggy said it would only be a skeleton by now, and that can't be very scary. We could rip out one more section of drywall and put up another bookcase in front of it."

"Now, wait a minute. You can't just go around destroying my walls."

"I thought you rented this place," Gilda pointed out, "so they're not your walls."

I had an unpleasant vision of me trying to explain to my landlord why I'd already damaged one section of the wall. Come to think of it, though, I didn't really know who my landlord was. I'd have to explain to the people at the property management firm that took care of collecting rent. I never seemed to deal with the same person twice there. They must have had an outrageous turnover rate. I wondered, not for the first time, who owned the building. "As long as I repair the wall and replace the wallpaper, I don't think there'll be a problem."

"You'll have to do that anyway where the safe is," Harper pointed out, like I didn't know that already.

"As long as ye have ruined one section, ye may as well discover what is hidden elsewhere in yon wall."

"Yeah, but I don't want to have to close the store, and I'd have to do that if we ripped down another section of the wall."

"That's not what I said." Harper furrowed his brow. "You have enough wallpaper in that extra roll to cover the section behind the bookcase."

"Aye. We would need some of that rock sheet as well."

"Sheetrock," I corrected.

"What about it?"

"Huh?" Harper and Gilda both sounded confused.

"I'll have to replace the Sheetrock, but I don't think there's enough wallpaper."

"There's enough to cover the safe."

"Harper, you're missing the point. We'd have to open up another several feet of the wall to find out if—"

"No, you're the one missing the point. We could take out the shelves in the bathroom back here and get into the wall that way. There wouldn't be any mess at all. At least not any that the tourists would ever see."

Hmmm. I'd have to think about that. The thought of

finding an old skeleton was . . . was downright ridiculous. "There's not going to be a skeleton in there, Gilda, and I refuse to spend the time taking apart a wall for nothing."

She looked a bit peeved at me, but before she could say anything, Sam's distinctive shave-and-a-haircut knock came from the front and she went to open the door. I looked a question at Harper. "It's up to you," he said.

Without Gilda there pushing me into doing it, the idea began to have some merit. "What are the chances?"

"Verra good."

"Not too great."

I looked at Harper. "Why do you say that?"

"Why else, I ask ye, would a wall be that wide except to hide a murdered body?"

"It may have been just an architectural anomaly." Harper sounded patronizing.

"You don't believe that," I said.

"I most certainly do, or I wouldna have said it!"

"Not you." I flapped my hand at Dirk.

"Who?" Harper sounded genuinely puzzled. I could see why. "What are you talking about?"

"I'm just surprised that you'd think something as obviously well planned and well hidden as that extra-wide wall could be a mistake."

Harper held up a hand. "That's not what I meant. Whoever built this obviously planned to hide the safe right from the start. So the wall was designed wide enough to be concealed by the little room in the back. When they went to put in the safe, they saw that they'd made the wall too deep, so they plugged up the area behind the safe with a few boards."

"Why would they have done that?" Dirk asked, quite reasonably I thought.

I waited for Harper to answer, but he just looked at me. Finally he asked, "Doesn't that sound reasonable?"

Shoot. He hadn't heard Dirk's question, of course. I slapped my forehead like in one of those V-8 commercials.

"Yeah, well, why bother to hide the extra room behind the safe? Presumably the only people who would know about it were the folks, or the person, who'd hidden the safe to begin with, and it wouldn't matter to them, or to him, whether there was extra space back there or not."

Harper thought about it for a minute.

"Mayhap there is something else hidden behind that second wall, behind the safe."

Rats. I was going to have to tear out the wall now, just to satisfy my own curiosity if nothing else.

"You're going to have to—"

"I know," I said. "You don't have to belabor the point." Gilda came back in with Sam in tow—I wondered what had taken the two of them so long to get back here. Maybe I didn't want to know.

There was nothing we could do while the shop was open. I'd have to get the whole crew in sometime, but it couldn't be tonight. The surprise party. Of course, I wasn't supposed to know about that. It was just going to be a quiet dinner, right? I might as well play along.

"I'm having dinner with Drew and Karaline tonight," I said. "Why don't we all"—and I swept my hand to indicate everyone—"gather here after dinner—say about nine—to tear down the wall?"

Gilda and Sam exchanged a quick glance. "Golly, Peggy. I just can't. Sam was going to, uh . . ."

"Take her to a movie," Sam added quickly.

She frowned at him. It wasn't a very good excuse. I could have suggested they see the movie another night, but I didn't want to push it too far. I'd proved I didn't know about the surprise party.

Harper scratched the back of his head. "I could stop by, and we could at least get the shelving torn out."

"No way!"

"Not on your life!" Sam sounded belligerent and Gilda sounded panicked.

"Okay," I said. "Why don't we do it tomorrow right after closing? That'll give us more time." Heads nodded. "In the meantime, we have a store to get open. Gilda, cash register; Sam, door."

They scurried off, and I looked up to see Harper staring at me. "What's wrong?"

"Nothing." He chuckled. "Just thinking about how much fun it would have been to tear down those shelves."

Was there a hint of some other meaning there? The comment was innocent enough. Before I could reply, Sam stuck his head in the door. "Customer wants to see you."

I said a quick good-bye to Harper and let him out the back door, where he muttered, "See you tomorrow night," and chuckled again.

I watched him walk all the way to the little courtyard, willing him to look back. Just before he turned to his left, he glanced my way and smiled.

In something of a daze, I turned to step back into the storeroom but stopped when I saw the long gash in the doorframe.

A worm of fear crawled up my spine. Dirk, sensing something was wrong, popped up beside me. I wished his feet would make some sort of sound, but I felt comforted to have him near.

I looked over my shoulder at the empty alleyway.

"Some ceorlisc feond has tried to break into the door foreby."

"Yeah, looks like that. Thank God for the new dead bolt lock." *Thank Harper for it.* "I haven't opened this door since . . ." I thought a moment. "Since the morning we discovered Mason's body."

"Mayhap ye should fetch the constable."

Dirk must have been worried indeed to want Harper back. "No." I ran my hand lightly over the gouged wood. "It's been here several days. See the dust caught in between the splinters? That doesn't happen overnight. I'll call him tonight before the party."

Sam called from the door. "Are you okay, Peg?"

"Sure, why?"

"Just checking. It's not every day somebody gets stitches in their head."

I relocked the wonderful dead bolt and went to deal with whatever the day brought.

22

Surprise!

At six o'clock, Gilda and Sam left together, and Gilda made a big point of telling me she'd see me tomorrow morning. I toyed with the idea of staying late, peeking to see how soon they'd come sneaking into the Logg Cabin, but decided that was juvenile. Anyway, I had to get showered and changed before Drew showed up at six thirty. I eased the shawl around my shoulders and left by the front door. The only excuse I could think of for opening the passenger door for Dirk was to bend and place my purse on the floor next to his very long legs, in case anyone was watching. Bending was a mistake, though. My head swam, and I grabbed the seat to steady myself. Amazing what being hit by a garbage truck can do to one's sense of equilibrium.

"Are ye a-swoon?"

"No, I'm dizzy."

"Is that nae what I said?" He studied me for a moment while I caught my breath. "Ye didna call the constable yet."

"When I get home." I closed his door, wishing I could tell Harper in person and see the concern on his face.

As I slid behind the wheel, Dirk said, "Did ye see some-one spying on us from the wee cabin of Logg?"

I glanced casually over my shoulder, hoping it would look like I was checking traffic behind me. A curtain twitched at the Logg Cabin. Uh-huh. "Karaline," I said, "or somebody, making sure I'm gone. They'll probably start showing up soon." I drove away without looking back again. "I wonder if she could see you, now that she's not at my house, I mean."

Dirk didn't answer. He folded and refolded the end of his plaid. That seemed a strange way for a man to while away the time, but mayhap—*maybe*—that was a fourteenth-century thing. He was silent for several blocks. Finally he took a deep breath—I could hear it even above the sound of the engine—and said, "Ye think I frighten people away when I walk near them in the wee shop."

It sounded almost like a question. "Yes," I said slowly, not knowing where this was leading.

"Mayhap I should stay awae this night. Your bee party is, I think, important to you."

"No, Dirk. It wouldn't be the same without you." I'd said that almost reflexively, not wanting to hurt his feelings, but once the words were out, I felt the deep truth of them. I truly wanted him to be there.

I could feel him studying my profile. "Aye," he finally said. "If ye wish, I will go with ye."

"Thanks."

"Could I ask a wee favor, though?"

I took a quick glance at him before turning into my drive-way. "Yes?"

"Would ye let me carry my Peigi's shawl?"

When Drew knocked on the front door, I ran to it, only halfway noting Dirk's look of approval as I passed by him. I put my finger over my lips before I opened the door. I didn't want to have one of those lopsided conversations. Karaline knew about Dirk, but I wasn't sure I wanted Drew in on the secret, although I couldn't for the life of me figure out why not. He was my brother, my twin. Why shouldn't I share Dirk with him?

Drew didn't even wait to wheel himself in before asking, "What's up, sis?"

"Come on in here," I motioned him into the living room, "and let's get settled. It's kind of a long story."

"I know. You mentioned as much when you called this morning."

I bent to pat Tessa's silky head and her angel-soft ears. She sported a bright green bow on her collar. Loved that dog. She was the best thing that ever happened to Drew.

Dirk leaned against the window frame in his usual place and seemed to be studying the wheelchair. Tessa pranced over to him and sat, looking up expectantly. Dirk crouched down, and Tessa reached out a tongue to lick his face. She stood up, backed away a bit, and shook her head, for all the world like someone trying to clear a foggy brain. I remembered that sense of fog in my own brain, that time in front of the police station when Dirk had tried to keep me from falling. She ran her tongue in and out of her mouth a few times, as if she were testing its workability.

"Tessa, here. What's wrong with you, girl?" She laid her head on Drew's lap, and he took a quick but thorough look at her teeth and in each one of her ears. She looked back across her doggie shoulder at Dirk, who stood once again beside the window.

I raised my eyebrows at Dirk, and he shrugged.

"What's she looking at?"

"Uh, maybe there's a squirrel on the tree outside the window." *Or a ghostie in front of the window.*

"She doesn't usually pay much attention to squirrels." He looked worried, and bent forward to run a hand under her neck and down her chest. "Wish I could tell what she was thinking."

What she's thinking is: *Why on earth did my tongue miss that guy over there?*

Drew settled back, and eventually Tessa turned around three times and curled into a doggie lump beside the left wheel, but I noticed that she seemed to be keeping an eye on Dirk.

I settled onto the couch. "I'm not sure how much you know about what's been happening."

"Mason's dead, Shoe was arrested and released for lack of evidence, and there's a safe in your back wall. Oh, and you wrecked your car." He looked downright smug, darn his hide.

"You know about the safe?"

He looked at me as if he thought I'd lost my mind, a look I remembered all too well from our childhood together. "Who are my two buddies?"

"Right. Sam and Shoe." I shifted mental gears. "Since I don't have to tell you all that, I'll tell you something that happened this morning."

"The fat wall, right?"

"Good grief, bro, what do you not know about my life?"

"Sam texted me just before lunch."

I thought back and decided I didn't need to fire Sam. Not this time. Texting while customers were in the store was absolutely forbidden, but we'd had a slow period for a while there. "Okay. Well, the question is, do you think Mason was murdered because of something that's in that wall? Either the safe or something else we don't know about yet?"

"Yes. There has to be a connection. But why did you invite me over so early if that's all you had to talk about?"

"Because I thought I was going to have to tell you the whole story, you twit."

"Don't grump at me. I haven't heard your side of it. You know Sam and Shoe both miss a lot."

Somewhat appeased, I relented and told him the whole story, leaving out only a few details, like Harper's shoulders and Dirk's presence. When I was through, Drew rolled his own shoulders, massive from three years of wheeling himself around, and twisted his torso from side to side. "That's quite a tale, sis. Tell me more about that piece of paper, though."

"The one they found in Mason's sporran?"

"Yeah."

"Well, I told you I can't remember the exact order of it. There was a number eighteen, and a four, and something about a thousand dentists, and a percentage of some sort. And it was wrinkly, like he'd balled it up; I think I forgot to mention that earlier."

"I need to see the list. If we could look at it together, we might be able to decipher it."

"Okay. I'll see Harper tomorrow night when he comes to help tear out the shelves. I can ask him to get me a copy of it."

"You can ask him at the p— Uh . . . never mind."

"What?"

"Nothing."

"Drew, what were you going to say?"

"Forget it." He looked at his watch. "We better leave if we want to get there right at seven thirty."

I opened the van door and held it while Dirk climbed in the backseat. Tessa always sat in front, where she could help Drew if he needed it. He fastened her into the doggie seatbelt as Tessa strained to look at Dirk. "Tessa, behave yourself. What's gotten into you?"

"Don't be hard on her; she's just looking around." *At a ghost.*

"It's like she's forgetting her training. That's not good."

"Mayhap she is excited about the party."

"That's right. Maybe so."

"No *maybe*. She's misbehaving!"

Oh crud. Here we go again. I made a quelling gesture at

Dirk. He gave me one of those *little mister innocent* looks. Tessa looked from me to Dirk to me again over the back of the seat.

"Down," Drew said, and her soft head disappeared.

Karaline must have been watching for us, because the door opened before we were halfway around the courtyard. "Welcome!" Drew reached over to straighten the bow on Tessa's collar, and Karaline took the chance to wave at Dirk, who gave her a courtly leg and a polite, "Good e'en, Mistress Caroline." Without missing a beat, she spread her arms, seeming to draw us in toward her embrace. Her bright orange caftan gave her arms the look of bat wings. Beneath it, there was a long expanse of legs encased in skintight leggings.

I returned her hug. She bent to hug Drew, quite expertly blocking me from entering the Logg Cabin until she was ready. I grinned at Drew over her shoulder and he crossed his eyes. "I hope you cooked a lot of food, Kari," he said. "Didn't have time for lunch. I could eat a small horse."

"No horses here. You'll have to settle for lasagna." Karaline's signature dish. I sure hoped the fifteen dollars from each guest would cover her expenses. I didn't have time to worry about it, though. The moment we stepped through the door, the place erupted.

Streamers, paper lanterns, and candles—electric because of K's strict adherence to OSHA rules and regulations. Somebody turned on one of those rotating mirrored balls. I thought they'd gone out of style shortly after I graduated from high school. Apparently not. I blinked. I absolutely refused to get a headache.

Speaking of headaches, Gilda, thankfully free of a migraine, threw her arms around me. "Were you surprised?"

I hate to lie, but what was I supposed to say? No? "Totally, Gilda. Thanks for not giving it away. I love a good surprise."

"Ye told me ye dinna like surprises." Why on earth was Dirk whispering?

"Oh, goodie." Gilda had a whole stockpile of those 1950s phrases.

Someone stuck a beer in my hand and gave one to Gilda. Sam reached around her and took it away. The two of them wandered off, and I idly watched Tessa dividing her attention between her master and her favorite ghost.

Everyone knew not to feed her, but I still kept a wary eye in case someone tried to slip her a treat. She'd supposedly learned not to take food from anyone except Drew, but the smells in here must have been driving her nuts. Drew as usual seemed to know what I was thinking. "I fed her just before we came. You can stop fussing." I denied it, but he just laughed.

It really was a fun party. People seemed to melt out of the way whenever Dirk passed near them, but nobody seemed to notice what they were doing. Thank goodness people hugged me gently. I still felt like my head was going to explode, or at least fall apart quietly. Luckily, the music in the background was soft and dreamy.

The next time I circled close to Drew, he picked up one of the half-dozen Nerf balls lined up beside a mountain of presents and threw one of them at Ethan, who threw it back. Tessa tensed, her instinct to spring for the ball fighting against her training. The training won. "Don't look now," Drew said, "but somebody else is here." Had he seen Dirk? No, not possible.

Behind me, I heard Dirk grumble low in his throat. Tessa whipped her head around and stared at him. I ignored the two of them and followed the line of Drew's sight.

Harper. I set down my garlic bread and swallowed quickly. He saw me. I know he did, but he looked calmly around the room, walked straight to Karaline, and returned her hug. K hugged everybody, but that didn't make me feel any better. The first thing she did after the hug was lead him over to where Drew sat. Karaline motioned to me rather impatiently, one of those gestures that said, *Get your duff in gear and join the party right here, right now.*

I got my duff in gear.

"Happy birthday." Harper shook Drew's hand and smiled at Tessa. Then the world stopped when he looked at me. I know there were people talking and music playing and food emitting the most delicious aromas, but my mind went fuzzy, just like Tessa's head.

Tessa nuzzled my leg, and I shook myself. "You okay, sis?" Drew's voice came through the sound of the music.

Harper held out his hand. "May I have this dance?"

Still in a bit of a fog, I let him draw me into the center of the room. It wasn't a dance floor exactly, but people moved out of our way, and a few couples even joined us. "Happy birthday," he whispered.

His warm breath on my ear almost did me in. "Th-thank you," I stuttered, feeling teenagerish again. I had an insane desire to rip off that stupid neck brace so he could brush his lips across my neck.

I could have stayed like that for a very, very long time, even with the neck brace, but Karaline clapped her hands and someone turned off the music. "Present time! You weren't supposed to bring any, but since you did, we need to find out what's in these boxes."

There were a lot of bottles of prune juice for the two of us, ancient beings that we now were, including two six-packs of the little cans. Dirk wondered what would be prune juice, but I decided the explanation would have to wait till later. What did they call constipation in the fourteenth century? Costive. That was it.

We each unwrapped an end of a cardboard carpet-roll tube and withdrew two canes. Drew demonstrated the proper use of his—poking at the middle of the guy who'd given us the gift. Most everything was a gag. When you're thirty and have your own place, you probably have all the stuff you're ever going to need. Thank goodness nobody brought us household goods. Just fun things that would most likely end up at Goodwill the next time we headed there. Somebody would need those canes someday, but not me.

As we got down to the bottom of the pile, Gilda handed me an enormous package wrapped in toilet paper, tied up with a string. "Thanks, Gilda." She giggled. Sam, beside her, laughed. I pulled on the string. It knotted. I pulled harder.

"Don't do that, sis. You'll just make it worse."

Drew reached for it, but I pulled it back. "It's mine. I can mess it up if I want to." I picked at the knot, wishing my fingernails were longer, wishing everybody weren't watching me and hollering suggestions.

A long arm reached in front of Gilda. Harper held a wicked-looking knife, somewhat longer than Dirk's *sgian-dubh*. The boisterous crowd fell instantly silent, except for one lone voice that called, "Hey, dude, bad knife." With one flick, Harper severed the string. He looked at me, not smiling, which seemed more devastating than a smile would have been. Those charcoal eyes of his were darker than I'd ever seen them.

"Gee, thanks, Harper," Gilda said, her voice squeakier than usual. "Open it, Peggy. Open it."

I should have known. A three-foot UVM teddy bear. My alma mater. Shorty would probably claim it for a cat perch.

The noise was back to its previous level, but Harper didn't say a word. I know, because I was watching him.

Then there were the cards. Funny, silly, crazy, and stupid. The ones to Drew were considerably more raucous than the ones addressed to me. Some were addressed to both of us together, and some were duplicates—two identical cards, one for each of us. We did have quite a few people who cared about us, and I could see that Drew felt it as much as I did. Through it all, Harper's eyes were on me.

We set down the last card, and Karaline erupted from the

kitchen with an enormous sheet of carrot cake with chocolate cream cheese frosting—she knew us both too well. It held sixty candles, thirty for each of us. We faced each other across the expanse of flames. "Hurry, before the sprinkler system goes off," Karaline shouted, and we blew like crazy.

Harper bent over my shoulder, and I saw Dirk's hand clamp on the handle of his dagger, but he did step out of the way. I wondered if contact with live people was as disconcerting to him as it was to us when we ran into him. "Do you need a ride home after this is over?"

Karaline shoved a plate of cake at me. A corner piece with lots of extra icing. "Eat hearty, and happy birthday to you both." She gave a second corner piece to Drew.

"Thanks, Kari. You know how to please my tum-tum."

"Thank you, K," I said. "You got it just right. I love the party." She grinned at me and looked pointedly at Harper. I waved her away, and she went back to serving cake. "I, uh, I was going to ride with Drew," I told Harper, "but I don't think he'd miss me." I tried to ignore the distinct grumble from my wee ghostie.

Karaline moved in front of me to hand Harper a plate. He reached for it but stiffened. I heard another distinct sound, the buzz of a silenced cell phone. He set the plate down and pulled the phone out of his pocket. "Harper. . . . Yeah. . . . No. . . . Sure, give me five." He pulled the phone away from his ear and looked at it. I could almost see him tensing to throw it across the room, but he simply put it back in the holder on his belt. "I hate to run out on you, but I have to go."

"Aye. Go far and stay long." The words were whispered but clear.

I wanted to kick Dirk, but all I did was nod to Harper.

"Some other time," he said. It wasn't a question. And he was gone.

The party dragged on for a while, but people gradually came around to wish us each a happy birthday and take their leave. Finally, only Sam, Shoe, and Gilda were left in the

kitchen, and Karaline, Drew, and I in the main dining area.
And Dirk. Tessa lay curled beside Drew's wheelchair, her
green bow lying limp beneath her throat.

Karaline picked up several wads of wrapping paper and
shoved them into a cardboard box. "I meant to keep up with
this while the two of you were opening presents, but it got
away from me." She grabbed some empty envelopes and
stuffed them on top of the wrapping paper.

"You did a wonderful job, K," I said. "Thank you for
going to all this trouble."

"Yeah, Kari. This was better than great. It was
mag-ni-fi-cent." He drew out the syllables, one at a time,
punching the air with each one. Tessa opened an eye and
watched him.

"For you two—anything." Karaline used those words
like they were for both of us, but she was looking only at
Drew. Wait a minute. I thought it was Shoe she was interested in. She and I were due for a long talk. When there
wasn't a ghost around to listen in.

"Dishes are all done. Ready for inspection," Shoe hollered from the kitchen, and Karaline turned away, winking
at Dirk as her face turned out of the line of Drew's sight. He
bowed one more time.

My brother had an unreadable expression as he watched
Karaline walk away. Hmmm. Maybe I needed to talk to
him, too. I pushed the three stacks of cards to one side. One
pile for the two of us, one with cards just for Drew, and one
with the cards for me. I placed the first two stacks into an
empty cardboard box, empty except for a six-pack of prune
juice. I didn't like to hang on to things, but Drew was something of a pack rat. He was welcome to them. I didn't want
a lot of doodads around.

A tiny spider crawled across Drew's stack. I picked up
one of my cards and transferred the spider into my cardboard
box, between my six-pack of prune juice and the teddy bear.
I'd take her home and release her in my yard.

I reached for another pile of junk to go in the recycle box, but one of the envelopes didn't bend. An ivory envelope, thick, the size of half a sheet of paper, with Drew's name written on it. "We missed one."

"Huh?"

"This card. You didn't open it."

He looked around, as if somehow the donor of the card might show up. It was just the two of us. Plus Dirk, but my brother didn't know that. He held out his hand. "Let's see what it is."

He examined it with more care than it probably deserved. It was thick. I was betting it was one of those cards that played a little tune when you opened it up. Probably the funeral march, I thought.

He drew out an ivory-toned booklet.

The front cover said *1982*, in a fancy font at least three inches tall. *Your Birth Year* it said underneath in smaller but equally flowery letters. I pulled a chair close to Drew's right side and watched as he thumbed through the pages. The first page, headed *In the News in 1982*, informed us that Israel had returned the Sinai Peninsula to Egypt, seven people died from poisoned Tylenol in Chicago, the first artificial heart was implanted in sixty-one-year-old Barney Clark, Princess Grace died in a car crash.

There was a list of the top ten tunes of 1982, only one of which I recognized.

Cats opened on Broadway.

Ivory Soap in a Sink-Side Pump, said the next page. Drew gave a disbelieving snort. "Pump soap is only as old as we are?"

"Looks that way," I said.

"What would be a pump sope?" What with me on one side of Drew and Tessa on the other, Dirk couldn't get close enough to see the illustration. He might not have understood it anyway.

"I love being able to pump a little dribble of soap out of a container," I said, mimicking the motion required. "It's much more sanitary than a bar of soap."

Drew laid one hand across the ad. "What was that about?"

"Nothing. Just babbling." *Just explaining modern conveniences to my ghost.* "It's been a long day."

"I think you're slaphappy," he said.

Low voices emanated from the kitchen. "Hey, look! The space shuttle Columbia is thirty years old now, too." He raised his hand and we high-fived. Dirk asked what we were doing, but I just shook my head. Again.

The voices got louder. I tucked the card into Drew's box. Karaline came back, followed by the other three. "Kitchen is put to bed. Time for the rest of us to follow suit," she said.

Tessa stood and looked from Drew to the door. Smart dog.

Hugs and thanks and bye-byes and yawns. Drew drove me home. I wished it had been Harper.

As I stepped out of his van carrying a box of prune juice, cards, and one small spider that had already filled in about half of a web between the six-pack and the bear, Drew said, "Did you remember to ask Harper about the paper with the dentists on it?"

A clear vision of Harper's head next to mine, his arm around my waist, his hand on the small of my back, made it a bit difficult for me to answer. I cleared my throat, but that did nothing to shake the music and the image out of my head. "No. I . . ." I shifted my new cane so it wasn't pressing directly on that bone that sticks out on my wrist. "No, I didn't. . . . I forgot."

Dirk stepped out. He didn't say anything. I hoped he hadn't been able to read my mind.

"What are we going to do with her, Tessa? This here lady's so old, her short-term memory is shot."

I stuck my tongue out at him and slammed the door.

23

Discovery

Morning came way too early, although I was happy to get out of that dream I'd had about a garbage truck looming over me. I rubbed my eyes and thought about poor Karaline. She always had to get up at three thirty to get the Logg Cabin ready to serve breakfast. Maybe this wasn't so bad after all. I stretched and felt more aches where my bruises were. Thirty years and one day old, and what did I have to show for it? I groaned and stumbled into the bathroom. Surely there was life after thirty. The face looking back at me from the mirror didn't seem to agree. I stuck my tongue out at her, but she took it in stride. She stuck hers out at me. I groaned again, this time at the silliness, and took a long hot shower.

Dirk didn't turn around when I walked into the kitchen. He kept studying the magnets on my fridge. I waved him out of the way and pulled out the pitcher of orange juice. Mason used to love orange juice. I shivered.

"What would be wrong? Are ye having a chill?" He

looked somewhat disapprovingly at my knee-length skirt and short-sleeved tee.

"I'm fine." *F-I-N-E.* "I'm doing okay," I amended. I was not neurotic—or insecure, either. At least, not too much. I plopped a pan on the stove, added water, butter, salt, and oatmeal.

"Ah," he said. "Porridge."

"We call it oatmeal, but that's okay. I guess it's the same thing."

"What would be this oh-cay you always speak of?"

"We have a lot of words you didn't have back then, I guess." I poured myself a big glass and just barely stopped myself in time. I'd been ready to offer him one.

"Would it mean all is well?"

I plugged in the toaster and popped in two slices. Nothing like carbs for breakfast. "Yeah, I guess you could say that." I pushed a chair out for him and moved the butter onto the table. "Store opens late today. I'm going to get some paperwork done before I have to go in." I stirred the oatmeal and covered the pan.

"Ye dinna usually show your legs at the wee shop."

"Huh? Oh. No, I'll change before I head out." I sat and took a big slug of OJ. "You really don't like to see women's legs?"

He straightened his back. "I dinna feel it is seemly." Before I could object, he went on, "But I do understand that times are verra different now." He wouldn't look me in the eye.

"What?" I couldn't be sure. There seemed to be more light passing through him this morning, and it almost looked like he was blushing.

"I could . . . could become . . . accustomed . . ." His voice petered out as I laughed at him.

"You love it," I cackled. "You love seeing all those legs," and this time I could see he really was blushing. How on earth could a ghost blush? It made no sense. Of course, nothing about this whole situation made any sense.

I pushed aside the box of cards and presents I'd set on the table last night. The spiderweb was still there, much more elaborate now. I pointed at it. "I think this is yours." Dirk grinned and held a hand out to the tiny spider. It stuck out one of its eight little legs and seemed to palpate the air at the end of Dirk's finger. "It sure looks like it can see you," I said.

"I canna tell for sure. The wee spinner may just be tasting the air."

I lifted the top card, collapsing the web, and the spider swung from one strand. "I hate to mess up your beautiful web, little lady, but you can't live in my kitchen." Outside, I let it drop onto one of the bushes beside the stoop. When I came back in, I threw the card in the box, and the whole stack slipped sideways. Half of them fell onto the floor. One of them said *1982* in large letters. "Damn it! This is Drew's card. I thought I'd put it in his box, not in mine."

I piled everything back in the box and moved it to the counter.

Dirk questioned me as I ate, and the questions eventually turned to the meaning of all those advertisements in the 1982 birthday card. "I didna want to question ye there, after I saw ye couldna answer me."

"That was a good idea, Dirk. Thanks." I helped as much as I could, pointing him to the little pump bottle of soap beside the sink, telling him about EPCOT Center, explaining that *Cats* was a musical that anthropomorphized felines.

"What would be a musical?"

And so it went. I finally gave up and shooed him away so I could go brush my teeth and get to my computer.

In the downstairs bathroom, I looked at the wallpaper, remembering how Mason had helped me put it up, and burst into tears. Why? Why? I didn't even like him anymore. Anyway, he was dead. Why was I crying?

I'd been a coward, not going to his funeral. I hadn't wanted to see Andrea, but that was no excuse. I should have gone, for his mother if for no other reason. The card I'd sent her hadn't been enough. If I'd gone to his funeral, it would have given me some closure. I would have seen Harper there. Maybe I could have sat with him.

I took a good long look at myself, frowned, and stuck out my tongue one more time.

After my teeth were scrubbed hard enough to wear off two layers of enamel, I exited to find Dirk, arms folded, leaning against the bannister. He didn't say a word about the crying, although I was sure he had heard me.

I motioned him to follow me and went back to my office. "Here." I moved a stack of folders off the narrow chair. "You can sit while I work on my spreadsheet."

He opened his mouth, but I kept talking. "It's like a ledger for keeping my accounts, but it's on a computer."

"Och, aye?"

The pile of envelopes that I knew contained my four months' worth of bank statements looked like it was about ready to fall over. Why hadn't I thrown out the junk mail as it came in instead of piling it up like that? Did I think it would disappear on its own? I would work on the spread-sheet first, then toss the junk, then reconcile the bank statements.

I pulled out my purse and rummaged in a pocket where I knew I'd placed receipts from the Scotland trip. I was so behind on all this. As I pulled out the handful of receipts, something fell, and Dirk bent automatically to pick it up for me. Our heads connected somehow, and I felt that woozy, cold, dizzy, out-of-body feeling again. No wonder Tessa had shaken her head when she'd tried to lick Dirk. I drew back quickly, and Dirk leapt to his feet. "Peigi," he cried, and his voice was filled with anguish.

"What's wrong? What happened?"

His eyes seemed out of focus. He put a hand to his head. "I smelt her. My Peigi. When our heads touched, I could feel her presence, and could smell the . . . smell her hair. It always smelled like the herbs she grew."

"It must have been a shampoo she made."

"Aye? Think ye so?" He cocked his head, as if he were listening to something beyond the reach of sound. "Aye. She would wash her hair and pour a kettle full of one of her brews over it." He rubbed his hand over his chin and along his jaw. "I smelt her. How could that be?"

"Just a trick of the memory," I suggested. "Have you been thinking about her a lot lately?"

"I think about her always. She is ever in my . . ." He dropped his eyes. "Except when I am with . . ."

He looked so stricken, I put my hand out without thinking and touched his arm. The dizziness was there but not as bad as before. I knew my hand was on his arm. I could see it there, but the feeling was more like I'd put my hand into a bowl of warm water or—no, into a flowing stream.

He looked at my hand. I withdrew it slowly. "I had known her all my life," he said.

I'm normally a compassionate person, but the raw pain in his eyes was more than I could take. I backed away from him. Spreadsheets and bank balances—and Dirk—were just going to have to wait for another time, maybe this evening. "Dirk, I need to go get changed. Will you be okay?"

"Och, aye. That I will."

"Do you want to come to the shop with me, or would you rather stay here?"

He pushed his hair back from his face. It looked as soft and silky as Tessa's ears. "I dinna know. I will think on it, aye?" He turned away from me and fled down the hall into the living room.

I looked at the desk. Jeesh, what a mess. I turned over the card that had fallen on the floor. Harper's business card. I sat back down and sent a quick text asking him to send me a scan of the wrinkled paper they'd found in Mason's sporran so I could show it to my brother. I didn't even flinch as I typed Mason's name.

Upstairs, I threw on a pair of black slacks and a burgundy blouse and added a Winn tartan scarf around my waist. I looked about as inviting as a cardboard box. A cardboard box in a neck brace.

I changed the slacks for long, soft, wide-legged culottes, and put on a peasant blouse. Now I looked pregnant. Pregnant in a neck brace.

Enough of this. I ripped the Velcro on the neck brace and tossed it toward my bed, narrowly missing Shorty, who stopped his grooming with an indignant yawp. I gingerly moved my neck from side to side, tilting it this way and that. A little stiff, but it would have to do. Good riddance to the stupid brace. I went back to my closet.

I ended up, three tries later, with my old standby, a long tartan skirt and an off-white blouse with the Winn scarf around my neck. Thank goodness our hours were extra short on Sundays.

Dirk waited for me by the front door. "I'll go wi' ye. 'Twill keep me from brooding."

"Okay. Let's go." I grabbed the shawl on my way out and remembered at the last second to lock the door behind me.

Mr. P waited beside my new car on the driver's side. "Good morning, Miss Peggy," he said in an old-fashioned, gentlemanly manner. "I'm glad to see you getting about so well after your accident."

I gestured to my covered-up bandage. "My head must be pretty hard. Took a few stitches, though."

"Oh? May I ask who did the honors of sewing you up?"

"Dr. Carrin."

Mr. P's face went through a funny contortion. I wondered if he had a cramp or something. Before I could ask if he was okay, he said, "May I invite you to dinner this evening?"

"Nae," Dirk said.

"I'd be very happy to have dinner with you, but it will have to be tomorrow. I've missed our monthly tradition."

Mrs. P had always kept the conversation going. Talking with *him* over soup and sandwiches was rather awkward.

I opened the passenger door for Dirk and went through the ridiculous charade, placing my purse ostentatiously on the floor as Dirk moved his feet out of the way. I closed the door and walked around the back of the car. Mr. P opened my door for me. I thanked him but didn't linger. I shouldn't have agreed. I needed to spend time with Karaline. If she had her eyes on my brother, I wanted to know about it.

"You'll need to stay home tomorrow night, Dirk. I'll leave some books out for you to read."

"I dinna want to stay inside again and wait for ye to be hit by another truck of garbage."

I slowed down as Hamelin's one and only traffic light turned yellow. "I'll be walking next door, not driving."

He muttered something, but I chose to ignore him. I put on my Scarlett O'Hara persona and decided I'd deal with it tomorrow.

Gilda didn't show up for work. Sam called half an hour later, spouting excuses for both of them. Gilda had another migraine, apparently, and Sam said he needed to stay there with her for a while. There was already a crowd of customers. An early morning tour bus had stopped and most of the tourists came to the ScotShop before heading for brunch at the Logg Cabin. Fine with me, but I was swamped. "Call Shoe," I told Sam with a sharpness I tried to disguise from the nearby customers. "See if he'll fill in for Gilda. I need him here twenty minutes ago." I hung up without waiting for an answer.

Two boys, supposedly attached to the tour bus but unsupervised by parents, headed straight for the Loch Ness Monster

statues. I was fairly sure something was going to get broken.
Before I could intervene, Dirk stalked that way and laid a hand
on each boy's shoulder. They both jumped, shivered, looked
wide-eyed at each other, and darted out the front door.

"Where are you boys going?" Their mother's voice was
sharp.

"We're hungry," came the reply drifting back as they ran
toward the Logg Cabin. In less than a minute, I saw Karaline
usher them out into the courtyard. I could almost read her
lips. *You can wait here until your parents are ready to eat.*
She handed each of them a biscuit.

"'Twas well done, Mistress Caroline." Dirk stood beside
me looking out the window.

"Thanks, Dirk. You just got hired as my bouncer."

"What would be a—"

"You're in charge of getting rid of the obnoxious ones,
bouncing them out of the store, so to speak."

"Och. I see."

A quiet voice behind me said, "Excuse me? Would you
happen to have a Forbes tartan tie?"

I led her to the *F* section of the tie display and pointed
out a bright blue-and-green plaid. "Oh no," she said. "That's
the wrong one altogether. The one I'm looking for is mostly
brown, with only a little bit of green."

I double-checked the label on the package. Forbes. Before
I could speak, Dirk stepped up beside me. "That would be
Forbes of Druinnor she's needing."

"Right." I was truly going to have to get more familiar
with all these subclans, septs, whatever. Of course, with Dirk
here, why should I even bother? I looked farther along the
display and picked up a light brown-and-green tartan tie with
a narrow white stripe. "Is this more what you had in mind?"

"Oh, lovely," she said. She leaned close to me and lowered
her voice. "My husband has emphysema, you see. I ordinarily
wouldn't leave him, but this was just an early day trip from
Boston, and he insisted I come. It's our anniversary, and I so

wanted to visit Hamelin again. We honeymooned here fifty-nine years ago."

"I'm sorry your husband couldn't come."

"My sister came with me instead. She's widowed now, you know." Her eyes clouded, as if she wondered whether she might soon be widowed herself. "Henry will love having this tie. Our dog ate the last one."

I didn't know what to say to that. I ushered her to the cash register and gift-wrapped the tie. Dirk moved out of the way as she and her sister left, chatting happily. I lowered my voice. "You are now not only my bouncer, you're also the resident tartan expert."

"I am surprised ye didna know the Forbes tartans, and ye with a shop with Scotland in the name."

The bell over the door tinkled, and Shoe walked in, causing quite a commotion among the white-haired senior citizens. He did look good in his kilt. There was a flurry of sales once the ladies discovered he worked here. "I just love your store," one of them gushed at him.

He didn't try to correct her. "Thank you. We aim to please," was all he said. I could have decked him, but that would have been bad for business.

Around three o'clock, Harper walked in. I was in the middle of another flurry of customers and glad about it, so I didn't want to stop to talk quite yet. He pointed at himself, at me, at the storeroom door, and raised his eyebrows. I love sign language. I nodded and rang up a rather healthy-sized purchase. Dress kilt and all the trimmings. If this kept up, I'd more than make up what I'd lost in sales those days the store was closed. After Mason was killed. I shook my head. No cloud of gloom today. I absolutely refused to think about that.

Eventually the customers trickled out, leaving enough people that I thought Shoe could take care of them without me. "I'll be in back," I told him. "Call if you need me."

Dirk preceded me through the door and strode to the desk, where Harper sat thumbing through the old paperback. Harper looked up, almost as if he were aware of Dirk, but turned immediately to me and stood. "Do you have a few minutes?"

"Yes, although I'll have to go back in there if Shoe needs help. What's up?"

He reached into his pocket and pulled out a piece of paper. "I brought you the note, the one we found in the sporran."

"Don't you need it as some sort of evidence?"

"This is only a copy." Instead of handing it to me, he spread it on the desk. The ragged edges of the small wrinkled paper had left a shadow around the printing, so we could tell the exact size of the original.

Dirk bent over it. I hadn't explained photocopying to him. *Please don't ask anything*, I urged him inside my head.

"You said you wanted to show it to your brother?"

"We're twins. We discuss everything."

"Everything?" Was there a shade of something else in that simple word? "It's good you're so close."

I moved a bit to my right so I wouldn't run into Dirk's head again, and leaned over the paper. "I still don't get it. It's just nonsense." I read it out loud, line by line, thinking that, if I heard it, it might make more sense.

L side 18 to wl
         ,000 dentists
L
4
         _& 10

_ _stars

         /100 %
   1 R
brother against brother
      ended just in time

It still made no sense at all.

"Something like this is too definite," Harper said, "too distinct to be nonsense. It has to mean something."

I pulled my cell out of the holder at my waist and called Drew. "Listen, I've got the paper."

"Paper?"

"The one with the dentists on it."

"Great," he said. "When can I get it?"

"Let's get together tonight." I looked up at Harper and raised my eyebrows. He nodded. My girl-talk with Karaline—and our little project of tearing apart a wall—would just have to wait.

"Harper's coming over, too. Want to meet at my place?"

"Tessa and I will bring dinner." Drew loved to cook. "You supply salad and a table."

"If you're doing the cooking, that's fine with me. Maybe around six?"

Harper nodded, and Drew agreed. "While you're there," I told Drew, "don't let me forget to give you your card."

"What card?"

"The 1982 one. I put it in my box by mistake."

"You stole my card?"

"See ya, bro."

Harper scratched his chin. "Did I miss something?"

"How so?"

"The 1982 card? What's that about?"

Sam opened the door. "Need you, please."

"Be right there." I folded up the copy Harper had made for me and started toward the door. "It was after you left. We found a card we'd missed. It had a whole bunch of ads and news stories from 1982, the year Drew and I were born. I'll show it to you tonight." A sort of warm tingly feeling started way down around my toes and headed upwards. Tonight. Dirk growled, like a German shepherd guarding a bone.

24

Card Game

In an insane parody of "Goldilocks and the Three Bears," I couldn't decide whether my grandmother's china would be too much or just right. My mother's mother. No, too fussy, too formal. I put it away and set out three of the mismatched plates from Goodwill that I usually used. I gathered them back up. They wouldn't do for company. Drew wasn't company, but Harper . . .

"Why have ye changed the trenchers twice?"

"Trenchers?"

He pointed to the three plates I held. "Aye. Can ye no make your decision?"

"It's just . . . I don't want to be too . . . These aren't the right ones. They're too casual."

"Nae? Then what would be the right ones?"

I thought about it for a minute and pulled the little stepstool over to the left of the pantry. The white plates with the blue lines around them would be perfect. I lifted half of them down from the upper cabinet.

Dirk inspected them. "Would ye say these are the best?"

"I think so. Well, best for this evening." I rubbed one plate affectionately. "They belonged to my Granny Winn, my father's mother."

"Why would ye have them put awae like that?" He motioned to the upper cabinet.

"I never use them." If one got broken, it would be another little piece of Granny gone—and I didn't want to lose any more of her.

Dirk stepped back and inspected the table. "They look bonny indeed."

Tessa barked from outside, and thoughts of Granny faded as I went to open the door. My twin's lap held a great big casserole dish sitting on layers of what looked like a beach towel. Bright red oven mitts perched on either side.

"Good dog, Tessa. You make a great doorbell. How'd you train her to do that?" I slipped on the oven mitts and lifted the casserole. "Damn, this smells good. Chicken?"

"Yeah. Chicken, wild rice, mushrooms, broccoli, cream, and a few other things." He gave Tessa the release command, and she bounded ahead of us into the kitchen. "Stick it in the oven so it'll stay hot, would you? Did you make a salad?"

"Yep."

He repositioned each leg. "Is Harper here?"

"Nope."

Right on cue, somebody knocked, and I scooted to the door, followed closely by Tessa. Harper's eyes did one of those quick once-overs that men always seem to think women won't notice. "Beautiful . . ."

I opened my mouth to thank him for the compliment, but he kept speaking. ". . . dog," he said, bending to pat Tessa. "I didn't get a chance to see her closely at the party. Anyway she was working, so I wouldn't have patted her then."

My brother rolled his chair up behind me. "Thanks. You'd be surprised how many people don't know service-dog etiquette, but she's not a real service dog. She's just a natural for helping me."

I closed the door and listened to their enthusiastic dog conversation for quite a while. I felt thoroughly miffed, but I wasn't about to admit it.

"The chicken should be ready," Drew finally said, and I went to the oven.

"Here, let me." Harper took the oven mitts away from me and bent over the stove. I looked at Drew. He grinned and gave me a thumbs-up.

Once the casserole dish sat on a couple of trivets, I pulled out the copy of the old note.

"Good idea," Harper said. "Let's take a quick look at this, and then our brains can marinate ideas while we're eating." I laid the paper beside Drew's plate.

Drew read it out loud, and Harper glanced over at me.

I shrugged. "Twins think alike."

Drew finished the list and settled back in his chair. "This line about the dentists has to be a clue of some sort." He patted Tessa absentmindedly and signaled for her to lie down.

I motioned to Harper to start serving the salad while I spooned casserole onto each plate. "I think that line about the brothers is significant, but what's with the part about ending in time?"

He ran one thumb along the blue line on the plate I handed him. "My grandmother had plates just like this. Sure did eat a lot at her house. Granny could cook like nobody's business."

Granny. He called his grandmother Granny. I gave Drew his plate. He looked from Harper to me and back again.

"Where's your card?" Harper asked. "The one you said you were going to show me."

"It's *my* card," Drew said. "The one she stole from me."

"I'm going to disown you someday, brother, and then you'll be sorry for plaguing me so much."

"Yeah, like I'm worried about that." He winked and shoveled in a forkful of chicken casserole.

We batted ideas around while we ate, but nothing much came of it. Afterward, Harper insisted on washing dishes, and I let him. Drew dried, and I put everything away. We made a good team.

I ducked into the living room and retrieved the card. While Harper looked through it, Drew and I studied the dentist paper. I pointed three lines up from the bottom. "R for Republican, maybe?"

Drew tapped the R. "Could be. Or maybe R for Red?"

Harper set down the card.

"Mayhap it means right."

I looked at Dirk. "Oh, how obvious!"

Drew and Harper looked at each other. "She does this sort of thing a lot lately," my brother explained.

"Listen, you guys. What if the R stands for right, and the L could be for left."

Harper nodded, and Drew scowled. "That still doesn't explain the dentists."

"Okay, so what? Let's go through it line by line and see what we can figure out."

We started at the top. "If we're right and the L stands for left, then the top line reads: Left side one-eight to *w-l*. Right?" Drew looked at us both for confirmation, and we nodded.

"Aye. 'Twould seem so."

"Then there's the dentist line," Harper said.

"Dentists, plural," I reminded him. "And that comma with three *O*s after it—"

"They're not *O*s," Drew said. "They're zeroes."

"Okay, so we've got at least a thousand dentists."

"What would be a dentist?"

Poor Dirk. I hadn't explained tooth care to him. "So, dentists, uh, people who work on teeth." Harper looked at me funny when I said that. I kept going. "Why would we need a thousand of them?"

We all three looked at each other. Nada. Phooey.

"There's a Left after that," Drew reminded us.

"Yeah. But what's four and ten?"

"You're nuts, sis. The four's on a separate line, and there's a little underline before *and*."

Harper held up a hand. "Maybe it's meant to be five-and-ten, like a dime-store ad."

"What would be a dyme's torrad?"

I held up my own hand. "So, let's fill in what we have." I took a separate piece of paper from the junk drawer and wrote:

Left side 18 to wl
___,000 dentists—We need a number here
Left
4—no idea what this means
5 & 10

I set down the pencil. "What about the stars? Any ideas?"

"No," Harper said, "but I'd be willing to bet there are either two letters or two numbers there." He pointed to the two lines before the word.

"'Tis a number," Dirk said. "Except for the left and right, and the ending lines, these are all numbers."

"What makes you so sure?"

"'Tis logical."

"Yeah, but how do we find out what they are?"

Drew poked my arm. "Sis? Are you in there, or have you been abducted by aliens?"

"It's just . . . I've been . . . There's a . . . You wouldn't . . ." I petered out and tried again. "Maybe they're all numbers. So many dentists, so many stars, and some sort of percentage."

They looked at me, bent over the paper, and both of them nodded at the same time. "Ivory soap." They said it together and high-fived in front of me.

"What? What are you talking about?"

"Don't you get it, sis?" When I just looked blank, he blew

a puff of air out. "Females," he muttered. "What are you going to do with them?"

Harper took pity on me, I guess. "Ninety-nine and forty-four one-hundredths percent pure," he intoned.

"Oh. Yeah." Stupid me, why hadn't I thought of that? I added another number to my list. "So we have some stars, but we don't know how many, and a 9944."

Harper put his index finger on the paper. "We have blank lines above and below the stars. Something must go in those spaces."

"Yeah, but why wouldn't they give us a clue?"

"Mayhap they have." Dirk reached across my shoulder and pointed to the number four and then ran his hand down to the one. "Four," he said, "blank line, blank line, one." He spread his hands.

"Oh, yeah!"

"Did you see something?"

"What is it?"

I had a brief vision of my high school algebra teacher talking about progressions, drumming them into our thick heads. "It's a negative progression," I said, with just a hint of disdain for the poor mortals who couldn't figure it out.

Drew looked like he thought I'd gone bananas, but Harper worried his lower lip with his front teeth. "Four," he said, "three, two, one."

"Bingo," I said, and started to fill in the numbers. I held up the completed form, mostly so Dirk could see it more easily. He read it out loud over my shoulder while Drew and Harper mumbled to themselves.

Left side 18 to wl
____,000 dentists—We need a number here
Left
4—no idea what this means
5 & 10
3

_ _ stars
2
99 and 44/100 %
1 Right
brother against brother
            ended just in time ? ? ?

"So, we're stuck on the first line, the dentists, the number of stars, and the last two lines. Plus, we still don't know what the numbers mean. Are they supposed to have words after them?"

Harper laid his hands flat on the table. I looked at him. His eyes had gone sort of fuzzy. Was he having an attack of some sort? He wasn't breathing.

Concerned, I touched his arm, and he let out his breath in a big whoosh. "It's the combination," he said.

Drew leaned forward. "Combination of what?"

"Do you remember," Harper said, "when I asked you if there was a paper with five numbers on it in the desk?"

"Oh," I said. "The combination to the safe." I looked at the paper, the one Harper had brought. "You said this was found in . . . in Mason's sporran."

"Yes, it was."

"Mason was trying to break into my safe?"

Drew waved his hand at me. "Hello? Sis? It's not your safe, remember?"

"Thanks for that reality check, brother. I know that. It's just that I can't imagine why Mason would want to break into the ScotShop. All he had to do was ask me, and I would have let him in."

"I thought you weren't talking to him."

"I wasn't, but this is different. He didn't have to go and get killed like that." My throat felt tight. I swallowed. It wasn't easy.

Harper broke the small silence. "We still need to know what those numbers are."

"We know the four and the three and so on," Drew said.

"No." Harper pointed back to the paper. "Those old combinations had five numbers. The four means to turn the dial four times . . ."

"To the left," I shouted. "See? There's an L right above the 4, so it must mean turn left four times."

Harper nodded. "That would follow the pattern, all right. Then it would be three to the right, two to the left . . ."

"And one to the right," I finished for him.

Drew pulled the paper toward him and hunched over it. "That means all these phrases are clues to what the numbers are for the combination?"

"Yeah," I said at the same time Harper said, "All we need are the answers to the clues."

I pulled the junk drawer paper toward me and filled in what else we'd learned.

Harper took my pencil from my hand and drew a line through the ninety-nine. "The combination lock only goes to one hundred."

"So, why couldn't we leave off the forty-four instead?" Even as Drew asked, I could almost hear him answering his own question. He took a breath. "The number is the percentage part. Has to be forty-four. You're right."

I took back my pencil and looked at what I'd written. "This first line doesn't follow the pattern."

Harper stood and paced to the door and back. "You said the building was built in 1915."

"Yeah. It says so in the stone over the front door."

"So all of these clues would relate to things that were going on back then."

Tessa whined to go outside. Drew wheeled himself toward the back door. Over his shoulder he called, "You mean Ivory soap is that old?"

Harper kept talking. "The only brother against brother I know of is the Civil War. Unless there was some sort of feud going on."

"There've been several old and very famous feuds in the

Northeast Kingdom," I said, referring to that area of north-eastern Vermont known for its unique and iconoclastic inhabitants.

"None from around here," Drew said. "It has to be the Civil War. The guy that wrote this might even have served in it."

"What would be a civil war? 'Twould seem to me that war is seldom civil."

"You're right," I said, "but the Civil War isn't a number. We need a number."

"Sixty-five," Drew called out as Tessa bounced past him, her business taken care of.

"Why sixty-five?" Harper and I both asked at the same time.

"Because 1865 was when the Civil War ended—just in time, like the paper says."

I erased the three question marks and added a sixty-five. I leaned back in my chair. "Now we need the number of dentists, the number of stars, and that first line."

Harper sat back down. He fiddled with Drew's birthday card for a moment, thumbing through it.

"Advertisements," he said. "Ivory soap's tagline was well known back then, and everyone knew about Woolworth's."

"What would be a wool worth?"

No time to explain. "Do you think there are any of those cards"—I pointed to the one Harper held—"for 1915? It would give us song names and advertisements, and news stories."

Drew whipped out his iPhone. "I'll let you know in a minute."

It took longer than a minute—considerably longer—but he finally let out a whoop and thrust his phone into my face. *Can 17,000 dentists be wrong?* An ad for Pro-phy-lac-tic Tooth Brush Company, complete with hyphens in the name. *Always sold in a yellow box.*

"Well," I said, "that's good to know," and filled in the number seventeen on the second line.

Try as he might, though, Drew couldn't find a single ad from 1915 with stars in it.

Harper pushed back his chair. "Let's go look."

I picked up both pieces of paper and watched as Dirk lifted my shawl from the back of the opposite chair. Fortunately, neither Harper nor my twin was looking that direction, so they wouldn't have seen it seemingly disappear.

Dirk slipped into Drew's van while Drew waited for the elevator thing to lift his wheelchair up and inside. I knew Dirk would be able to slip out the same way once we got to the shop.

Harper opened the door of his car for me. "This should be fun," he said as I reached for my seatbelt. Over Harper's shoulder I saw the curtains twitch upstairs in Mr. P's house. Nosy, lonely neighbor.

The one traffic light was green, so we made good time. I paused outside the front door and looked up. The 1915 above the front door was barely visible in the dim moonlight. The streetlights left puddles on the ground, but none of their light migrated upward. Harper followed my gaze. "Maybe there are clues inside," he said.

I unlocked the door and switched on a couple of lights. "I doubt it. This whole space has been renovated so many times. There was a hardware store here, and then a clothing store, before I took on the lease. Before that it was an insurance office, if I remember right. Wallace Insurance." I searched my childhood memories. I couldn't recall what had been here before Mr. Wallace. "I know it started as just a general office space for the manufacturing that was done in the other end of the building, but I don't know much else."

"Let's get some privacy here." Harper shut the blinds on the courtyard side of the store, and I pulled the curtains on the street side.

Drew knocked on the door and I let them in. We quartered the store, inspecting the walls, the ceiling, the woodwork. Nothing seemed out of the ordinary. "You know, I'm pretty sure I would have noticed, sometime during the past six years, if there had been anything unusual in here."

"You never can tell," Harper said. "Sometimes things are hidden in plain sight."

I thought back to one of my high school English classes. "Like 'The Purloined Letter.'"

"What would be—"

"You know, that story by Edgar Allan Poe, the creepy writer, about the letter that was framed and right out on the wall where everybody would see it, but nobody would notice it."

"Yes," Harper said. "I had English in high school. And college, too."

I waited until he turned away from me, looking back at the ceiling, and I made a *zip your mouth shut* gesture at Dirk. He was going to get me in a whole lot of trouble if I didn't watch out. I stepped back, intending to walk around a display of Scottish-themed bookends, and came face-to-wheelchair with my brother. He zipped his mouth, the way I had just done, spread his hands, and said, "You care to explain that?"

Harper looked back at us.

"No, I do not. It's my store, and I can do whatever I want in here." If Harper hadn't been watching, I would have stuck out my tongue.

I sidestepped Drew's chair and walked up next to Harper. "Do you want to take another look at the safe? Maybe we could try some of the numbers."

"It wouldn't do a bit of good. We don't have the first one, and without that, all the rest of the numbers are useless."

"We also don't have the one about the stars," Drew added.

"You mean we came here for nothing?"

"I should have brought my tools," Harper said. "We could have ripped out some of that shelving in the bathroom."

"Ye would ruin your gown," Dirk pointed out.

"I'm not dressed for it," I said. "Maybe another time."

Harper wandered back toward the bookcase. "Did you move anything before I got here last week?"

I thought back to that awful day. "No. I don't think so. We picked up the bookcase, of course."

"Of course. Anything else?"

"I don't think so." I looked around me and remembered Shoe with his hands full of broken pieces of pottery. "Wait. Yes. There were some things that got broken when the book-case fell, a couple of pottery bowls and such. Shoe and Gilda picked up the pieces before we lifted the bookcase."

He held my gaze for several seconds before shaking his head. "I know that. You already told me."

"There was something else, too." I tried to think, imagining Shoe in front of me. Mentally, I picked through the detritus in his cupped hands. "Part of a broken wooden bookend, a couple of keys, and my tape measure. I think that's about all there was."

"Your tape measure?" Drew sounded skeptical.

"Yeah. It's a twenty-five-footer. It must have fallen off the counter when the bookcase crashed over."

"I know," Harper said. "I used it to measure the bathroom walls." He looked at the forty-foot expanse of wall at the back of the ScotShop. "We're missing something here," he muttered, but he didn't seem to be talking to me.

We looked around a bit longer but without much enthu-siasm. When I locked the door behind us, I remembered that Dirk needed to ride in the van. "You left your casserole dish at my place, Drew. Why don't you swing by there on your way home?"

"Swing by there? It's out of my way, and you know it."

I did some quick thinking. "Hold on a minute, I forgot something." I dashed back into the ScotShop and picked up one of the largest Loch Ness Monsters. "I forgot I needed to do some repair work on this one." Drew and Harper both simply stared at me. "It has a hairline crack," I said and led the way to Harper's car. Naturally, I had to set it in the back seat, which gave Dirk the perfect chance to climb inside.

I paused, waiting to be sure my brother was up and safely in his van. I knew I shouldn't worry about him. But I did anyway.

Harper started the car. "Sorry I led you on such a wild-goose chase."

"Don't worry about it," I said. "We need to cover every angle until we get this figured out."

He stopped when the traffic light turned red. I looked around. Nothing was coming this time of night. "You could . . ." Then I remembered. Harper was a cop. With wide shoulders and beautiful eyes, but a cop nonetheless. Crud.

"I could what?"

"You could . . . uh . . . come back tomorrow. The shop is closed on Mondays. We can take the shelves out." I sat patiently until the light changed.

"Will do."

There didn't seem to be a lot more to say.

As he pulled into my driveway, Harper turned off the ignition and looked at me. "It's a real joy," he said, "to be able to be silent with someone and not feel awkward about it." Before I could say anything, he turned around and hauled Nessie out of the back seat. "I'll carry this in for you."

I looked at Dirk. As soon as Harper was out of the car, I motioned to my ghostie to crawl over into the front. He grumbled, but he did it. By the time Harper opened my door, Dirk was ready to slide out after me. What I do for my ghost, I thought.

Mr. P's voice floated across his front lawn. "Did you have a nice ride?"

I looked up at Harper and shrugged. "He watches out for me," I whispered. In a louder voice I called, "Yes. It's a beautiful night, Mr. P."

I didn't wait to listen for his reply, but hurried up the walk, with Harper and Dirk in my wake. At the top of the ramp, I slipped my key in the door and turned to Harper. He glanced sideways to where we could both see Mr. P peering over his porch railing. "I guess I'll say good night." He handed Nessie to me without letting go, leaned forward, and brushed his lips gently across my cheek. "See you tomorrow," he said, his words rich with possibility.

Beside me, Dirk fingered his blade.

I let myself in and turned to watch Harper as he got into his car, drove down the drive, and disappeared around the bend. Until Dirk cleared his throat, I wasn't aware that my left hand was holding my cheek and my lips were pressed on the soft mound at the base of my little finger. I dropped my hand and locked the front door. "Good night, Dirk. I'm turning in early. See you tomorrow." And I fled upstairs.

As I brushed my teeth, I studied the list. The first line still made no sense.

I rinsed my mouth out and carried the paper back to the little writing table under the windows. At the bottom I printed:

Left side 18 to wl ???
17—first number
Left 4 turns to 5
Right 3 turns to _ _ ??? (number of stars)
Left 2 turns to 44
Right 1 turn to 65

Two pieces still to go on this doggone puzzle. I turned out the light, but it took me a long time to go to sleep.

25

Betrayal

Still in my UVM T-shirt, I'd just finished breakfast when the front doorbell rang at seven. I looked at Dirk. He shook his head, walked into the living room, and peeked through the sheers at the bay window. His voice, when he spoke, sounded grim. "The constable."

Harper! "Tell him to wait," I said without thinking. "I'll throw some clothes on."

Dirk cleared his throat. He seemed to do that a lot around me.

"Oh, phooey. He can't hear you. Sorry, Dirk. I forgot." I raised my voice, "I'll be right there, Harper." I opened the coat closet and pulled out my bright pink raincoat. It was the closest thing to hand.

Harper carefully kept his eyes averted when I opened the door, although I did notice a quick twitch at the side of his mouth.

"I wasn't expecting anyone," I said. "The store's closed on Mondays, and I usually don't . . ." *Shut up, Winn. You're babbling.* "Oh, I forgot. We were going to take out those shelves. Come on in, and I'll run upstairs and throw on some clothes." Doggone it, I felt myself blushing. "I mean, I already have clothes on. I'll just throw on some different ones." Good grief. I gestured toward the couch. Why was I so unnerved? It had absolutely nothing to do with that little kiss last night. He was just being friendly, that was all. "Sit. Make yourself at home." I ran upstairs and was back, fully clothed in gray sweats, in fewer than five minutes, a scarf wound firmly around my head. Just so he wouldn't make comments about poodles.

He still stood just inside the front door where I'd left him.

"He hasna moved since ye left the room."

"Harper? What's wrong?"

He straightened his already ramrod straight back and indicated that I should sit. I crossed in front of him to my wingback chair. He crossed in front of me to stand next to the wood-burning stove, which was as cold as Harper's face looked. Dirk planted himself halfway between the two of us. I couldn't tell if Harper was angry or just uncomfortable. I'd already asked him what was wrong. I had no intention of asking again. I waited him out, fingering the bottom edge of my sweatshirt.

Finally, he cleared his throat, and said, "Would you care to explain why Mason deposited twenty-four hundred dollars in your business checking account?"

"Twenty—what? What are you talking about?"

"I'm talking about the weekly deposits of two hundred dollars to your checking account over the past three months. Don't tell me you weren't aware of them."

Those bank statements I'd never reconciled. Crudbuckets! "I wasn't," I said. It sounded awfully lame.

"How can anyone not know of twenty—"

"I can prove it. You just follow me." I stomped down the hallway to my home office and turned, rather dramatically I must admit, when I reached the desk. "There!" I pointed to the stacks of paper.

"That's supposed to prove something?"

Dirk pulled his dagger from the scabbard at his belt. "Dinna use such a tone with a lady."

I held up my hand, hoping Dirk would behave himself. "In this stack, or . . . or maybe it's in that one, there are unopened bank statements that I haven't looked at for at least three or four months." Dirk must have been sitting at my desk sometime in the recent past. There were delicate spiderwebs draped between the stacks, catching the morning light spilling through the window.

"Very convenient," Harper said.

"Do ye doubt her word?"

"Are you calling me a liar? If I'd opened them, if I'd seen those deposits, I would have known there was some kind of a mistake. I'd certainly enjoy having some extra money, but not like that." I crossed my arms over my chest. "I know where every cent of my money comes from, and it's certainly not from Mason Kilmarty."

I picked through the stacks and separated the bank statements. Six of them.

God, it was even worse than I'd thought. How had I let myself get so far behind? At least they were obviously unopened.

I whipped out my iPhone. "I want a picture of you with these so I can prove they were unopened when you took them."

"I'm not taking them." He sounded disgusted.

"Then why are you here?"

"I'm here"—he motioned around the room, narrowly missing a collision with Dirk, who stood with drawn knife just behind Harper's left shoulder. "I'm here," he repeated, "because you asked me to follow you back to this room. And I am fully aware that you could have been using the phone to call your bank each week. Or banking online. You wouldn't have had to look at these." He pushed the envelopes away from the edge of the desk, inadvertently destroying two spiderwebs in the process.

"You can't be serious. Surely you don't think I was mixed up in any of Mason's underhanded dealings."

He gritted his teeth. I could hear that grinding sound, and it felt like fingernails on a chalkboard. I shuddered.

"I'm just following the evidence," he said. "When there's murder, there's usually a money trail."

"You think I stole that money in cahoots with Mason?"

"I don't think anything, but I know one thing: Mason left a ledger showing twelve deposits in cash to an account he called *PW*. He deposited them in person. The teller identified him."

"He couldn't have. He didn't know my . . ." I remembered three or four months ago when I caught him rummaging through my purse.

"You just thought of something. What?"

"I . . . he might have taken some of my deposit slips."

"I intend to find out why you have that money."

"I'm not going to have it for long. As soon as I can get to the bank, I'm moving it out of my account."

"Just what were you planning to do with it?"

"I'll give it to his mother."

"It may not be hers, either."

"You think I don't know that? I'm the one who asked for a town audit. Why would I do that if I'm involved?"

"We had someone take a look at the town books. There's nothing wrong with them. That money came from somewhere else."

"And you think I had something to do with it? I'm innocent."

"A lot of crooks feign innocence."

"Crook! You're calling me a crook?" This was the same man who'd washed out my kerchief when I was in the hospital room? The same man who'd mixed up right and left? The same man who . . . who'd kissed my cheek so briefly last night? "How dare you? You're absolutely crazy! Get out of my house. Now."

"I wasn't . . ." His lips tightened, and he turned toward the door, just barely avoiding my outstretched arm.

"Shall I speed him along for ye?" Dirk raised that wicked-looking blade of his and lunged.

"No! Stop!"

Harper wheeled around and collided with Dirk, who jumped back as if he'd been burned. Harper staggered, stumbled, fell to one knee.

"Ohmigosh, are you hurt?" I ran to him, silently cursing Dirk's excess of testosterone and Harper's excess of . . . of copness.

Harper swung his head back and forth as if trying to free it of spiderwebs. Or ghost webs. "What just happened?"

"You fell," I said, conveniently neglecting to mention that he'd had a collision with my resident ghost.

He twisted his head around as if his neck had a crick in it. "You told me to get out, and then you told me to stop."

"No, I didn't." *I was telling my ghostie to stop.*

His eyes said *yes, you did,* but he didn't say it out loud. "Guess I'd better leave, then."

He looked too shaky even to stand, much less to walk. I placed my hand along the side of his jaw. He'd shaved, but even so, I could feel a texture there that made my fingers tingle. "Why don't you rest on the couch for a little bit first? I'll . . . I'll get you some water."

I helped him to his feet. He was a lot shakier than the man in Pitlochry had been. I thought back to that day in front of the display of chocolates. That man had walked into Dirk's arm, maybe even just his hand, and he had stumbled. But Harper had spun full-bodied into Dirk, head to head. No wonder he didn't feel well.

Once I got him settled on the couch, I threw the shawl over him without thinking. He clutched one edge of it as if he needed to hold on to something real and solid. Dirk towered over him, standing just to my left. The white line on the edge of the shawl shimmered between Harper's hands.

He shook his head one more time and looked up at me. "I could use that water, if you don't mind."

I walked, sedately, into the kitchen. "He couldn't see you," I hissed as quietly as I possibly could and still have it be a hiss. "He held on to the shawl and he still couldn't see you. Why not?"

"How should I know?"

"Oh, quit sounding so reasonable. Karaline could see you; I can see you; why can't he?"

I heard Harper's voice and shut my mouth. I had a jillion questions, all of them unanswerable. How the heck did I know how ghosts worked?

"What?" came the plaintive question again from the living room.

"Just wanted to know if you'd prefer ice in your water." If I didn't watch out, I'd be lying every other sentence.

"No thanks." He sounded awfully weak.

I put both hands on my hips and faced Dirk. "You quit running into people," I whispered between clenched teeth. "It's not nice."

Dirk placed his hands on his hips. "I didna intend to do it. And I dinna like the feel of it, otherbye."

"Other-by? What kind of word is that?" Without waiting for his answer, I filled a glass and left the kitchen.

After he drained half the water, Harper asked, "Is there a radio playing out there?"

"Uh, yeah, it's . . . it's a talk show I listen to sometimes. I turned it off." *Does having your own private ghost make lying easier, or am I simply becoming decadent?* I knelt beside the couch. "Are you feeling better?"

"I don't know what came over me."

It's called a ghost incident.

He raised himself onto one elbow. "I've never felt that dizzy before."

And I hope you never do again. I lifted the shawl out of his way. "I'm sure it was a one-time thing."

"I dinna intend to repeat it." Dirk managed to sound arrogant and apologetic at the same time. How did he do that? Come to think of it, there was very little apology in there.

Once Harper seemed to regain himself, I asked if he had come to arrest me.

"No. Of course not." He ran a hand through his hair, leaving it slightly disheveled. I tried not to stare. I was still very angry with him. There was no need to look at how his hair fell forward on his forehead. "I'm going through everything," he said. "Everything I can think of to try to learn who killed Mason. If this money's involved, I have to track it down."

"I honestly don't know why Mason would have put money in my account. We never combined our finances." Something niggled at the edge of my consciousness, but I couldn't bring it into focus. "I can't think of a single reason why, unless he felt guilty about cheating on me."

"Probably not," Harper said. "The deposits started three months ago. Every Monday. Mac—the chief, I mean—is the one who thought to check bank records."

I gaped at him. "Mac? He never does anything worthwhile except look at himself any time there's a shiny surface."

I could see him press his lips together as if zippering his mouth. Mac *was* the boss, after all. "The deposits went in every Monday."

I groaned. "Maybe the Andrea story started back then and I just never knew it."

"What would be an andree story?"

I did not even look at Dirk.

"I think you did the right thing, throwing him out."

"Yeah, I know I did. But I did not kill him, even if I wanted to for a while there."

"I never thought you did."

"Then why are you here?"

He sat a little straighter on the couch. "To give you a chance to explain what was going on."

"But I don't know what's going on!" I tried—unsuccessfully—not to whine.

"I believe you." He touched my shoulder, and a low sound emanated from Dirk. "I need to get back to the station. There are a few other leads to follow." He stood and put out a hand to help me to my feet. He didn't let go as he walked to the door.

I turned the handle and looked up expectantly.

He leaned closer and squeezed my hand. "Go balance your checkbook."

Crudbuckets! I gave him long enough to get into his car. Then I very deliberately kicked my front door.

"I dinna think that will help."

"Oh, hush! I have never been so humiliated in my life. How could that . . . that man think I could possibly be involved with thievery? How could he? How . . ."

Without thinking, I turned, nuzzling my face against Dirk's chest, and sobbed my heart out. For about five seconds. I jumped back. "How did I do that?"

"Why did ye no get dizzied?"

"Why didn't I walk right through you?"

We stared at each other. Dirk shifted his plaid and blinked a couple of times. "I dinna understand."

I reached out a shaking hand to lay it against his chest. It just kept going, and my hand felt that cold watery feeling again. "Something is going on here."

He reached an equally tentative hand toward my face, and I felt something rather like a cool breeze float from my temple to my chin. "I canna touch ye."

I put both hands over my face and growled as loudly as I could. "This is ridiculous! I've never been able to touch you, and now all of a sudden I can, and then I can't."

"Ye touched my arm once. Dinna ye remember?"

I sank into the wingback chair. "That's right. I did, but I

didn't really feel anything except . . . water, sort of. This time . . . you were . . . solid."

"Mayhap there is some rule that we simply dinna ken."

"Yeah," I said. "May-hap."

He stepped back, looking like he suspected sarcasm. Which was not too surprising under the circumstances. This was getting me nowhere. "I'm going in to the shop."

"Ye said the shop is closed today."

"That's a good reason to go. I won't have customers. I want another look at that safe." I hauled myself to my feet. "I'll be down in a few minutes."

"Ye canna move the bookcase by yourself."

Crudbuckets! Shoe had mentioned he'd be fishing today, and I knew Sam and Gilda were off on a jaunt of some sort, if she wasn't still sick. How long could migraines last? Who did that leave? Drew could help a little, but I needed muscles. I didn't want to let anyone else in on the secret, so that excluded Ethan and Mr. P and every other male in town. I deliberately did not even consider Harper. He wasn't available, anyway. And might not ever be again. Not that I would ever even think of asking him. Ever. Even though those shoulders of his would come in handy on a job like this. But I was absolutely not going to ask him. "You're right. I can't think of anybody." I started up the stairs.

"What about Mistress Caroline? Can she no help ye move it?"

"Karaline?" The Logg Cabin was closed on Mondays, too. "Thanks, Dirk. Be right back."

In my bathroom, I took off the scarf and probed the lump on my head. It was still tender, and I almost wanted to leave it open to the air, but I still felt uncomfortable going out in public with the left side of my head shaved. I eased my kerchief on and tied it loosely. Not that anybody would see me, but I felt a little better covered up.

26

Taking Your Measure

I could see Karaline by the front door when I turned the corner onto Main Street. I tooted the horn at her, just for a chance to try it out. She didn't recognize my car at first, of course, but when I waved out the window, she waved two-handed, one wave for each of us. I made a U-turn and pulled in right next to the shop. Mondays were always unbearably quiet in Hamelin. Everybody was closed. I saw two other cars, period. I didn't even consider looking to see whether Harper might be anywhere in sight. He wasn't.

Karaline opened Dirk's door.

"I thank ye."

"How's it going?"

Before he could spill anything about that man who'd come to my house this morning, the one I was never going to think of again, I said, "Come on inside, K. I have something I want to show you. Drew and I discovered it last night." I patted my pocket, the one where I'd shoved the papers, and purposefully put Harper out of my mind.

"What is it?"

"You'll see."

We paused while I opened the front door. Dirk, always intrigued with my display window, studied the mannequins.

Karaline laid her palm against the window. "They look kinda silly, don't they?" The same reaction I'd had a few days ago.

"Come on in." I made sure the sign said *Closed* and locked the door firmly. Karaline, without my even asking her, shut the blinds and curtains.

We went into the back room once the place was secure. I needed to explain what we'd learned about the code before we accessed the safe.

I spread out the paper, and Karaline read it over a couple of times. "See," I said, pointing to the lines at the top of the paper. "This is what it said on a piece of paper they found in Mason's sporran. We have no idea why he had it, but it looks like it's a code to the combination on the safe."

"Why would you think that?"

"Because Harper . . ." My voice faltered a bit. "Harper is something of an expert, and he says our safe has five numbers in the combination. These are the clues to show us what those numbers are and how many times you have to turn the dial before you stop on a number."

"So why don't we open it?"

I indicated the two blank lines beside stars. "We don't know what number goes here. And we can't figure out what the first line is supposed to mean.

She studied it for a moment. "It was written by two different people."

"Huh?"

"Yeah. See how the handwriting is different in this first line? And the pen has a wider stroke."

Now that she mentioned it . . .

She read it out loud. "Left side eighteen to wl." She looked at me and then at Dirk. "That's pretty obvious, don't you think?"

"Huh?" I was beginning to sound like an echo.

Dirk looked affronted. "Nae, 'tis not so obvious as all that."

"No, look," she said. "It tells where the safe is located. It's completely hidden, right? No way to tell where it is, right?"

I nodded, not sure where this was headed.

"So, the left side of the safe is eighteen feet from the wall."

"When you put it that way, I guess it *is* obvious." I braced my elbows on the table and leaned my forehead on my clenched hands. "I sure hate to admit how long we worried over that line."

"Think of all the time you would have saved if you'd asked me right off the bat."

"What . . . off the . . . ?" Dirk paused and straightened his plaid. "Would ye be referring to the base bawbat?"

"No, Dirk," I said. "*Off the bat* means right away."

He crossed his arms and gave me a disgusted look. "This language, as ye use it, doesna make a great deal of sense."

I seriously considered blasting him with *Whan that Aprille with his shoures soote*, but decided that might start an argument. "Guess not," I said.

Karaline had a sort of faraway look. When she came out of it, she asked, "If this was the combination the guy who killed Mason needed to get into the safe, why did he put it in Mason's sporran?"

"Mayhap Mason took it from him."

"But the guy didn't get the safe open. He didn't even find it, but I'd be willing to bet he hasn't given up. He still needs the clues. So why wouldn't he have taken it back after he killed Mason?"

"Maybe he lost it and Mason picked it up." I thought back to the number of times Mason had made fun of me for picking up stray bits of litter in the street. "Nah, forget that. Mason wouldn't have cared."

"So this is getting us nowhere." Karaline hunched over

the paper. With her height, she had to hunch quite a bit. "Blank blank stars. Hmm." She looked around the room. "It wouldn't be back here."

"What wouldna?"

"The clue. This is a nothing room. There's no character to it. Let's look out front."

"For what? What are you talking about?"

She spoke as if I were a three-year-old. "The clue has to be something that somebody could figure out easily, right? So let's see what's in the room out front that is part of the structure. Something that wouldn't have been changed from year to year."

"Oh! I see. You're saying it wouldn't be in, say, the wallpaper, because that could be changed, but it might be in the stone walls or overhead." I thought about it. "Overhead would make more sense, because that's where stars are."

"I'll grab the big ladder."

I stuffed the papers into my pocket for safekeeping. "I'll get a flashlight."

"I will go look at the ceiling, if one of ye would please to open the door."

We moved that ladder from one end of the shop to the other. We felt the surface up there to see if stars might somehow be embedded in the ceiling material. We shone the flashlight across every square foot, looking for something stuck on or in the ceiling. We tried it from different angles. Even the boarded-up hole, where the chimney pipe from an old potbellied stove used to go through the ceiling, yielded nothing.

Karaline stepped down from her turn on the ladder and rolled her shoulders back. I heard something creak. "We need to give up on this," she said. "Those stars, however many of them, are sure not here."

"Maybe we should call Drew. He might have an idea."

"What I would like to ken," Dirk said, "is why the person

who made the holes didna find the safe if the directions in that first line were so clear."

"Maybe he couldn't remember the number. If he'd lost the piece of paper."

"Good grief," Karaline said. "If he'd read it even once, he'd know that first line said eighteen. That's a pretty easy number to remember."

"Why don't we check?" I suggested. "Let's see if he was measuring eighteen feet." I stepped behind the checkout counter and rummaged for the measuring tape.

Karaline reached for the end of it. "I'll hold this against the wall, and you can measure to where the holes start."

"Did ye no want to move the bookcase first, so we can see just where the wee holes were?"

K and I looked at each other. *Men. Logical.* We laughed, and Dirk squinted at us. "What would be so funny?"

"Never mind, D," Karaline said and made as if to punch him in the arm, but he stepped quickly back out of range.

"I don't think you want to do that," I told her. Between us, Dirk and I explained some of the things that happened when ghosts and people made contact. He and I studiously avoided mentioning those few seconds I had cried in his arms.

We slid the bookcase away from the wall, far enough that we could crouch behind it. Karaline handed me the tape measure, but stopped short when a knock sounded on the front door.

Harper? I squelched the thought. I wasn't talking to him. I hadn't forgiven him. It had better not be him. Maybe it was.

"You'd think they could read the sign," Karaline said and headed toward the door.

I jumped in front of her. "I'll get it." She looked at me with one of those *what got into you?* looks. "It might be a customer. I'll let them know how happy I'll be to have them come back tomorrow." *And if it's Harper, I'll tell him where to get off.* The knock repeated, three light taps.

I pulled back the side of the little curtain and peeked, but I didn't see anyone. I opened the door a tiny bit and poked my head out.

No wonder I hadn't seen him. Harper stood well back from the door and off to one side, his neck craned skyward.

"Checking out aircraft in the vicinity?"

He kept looking up. "Nope."

"Then what are you looking at?"

"Come here and I'll show you."

Karaline reached a hand over my head and pulled the door back, almost knocking me off balance, but she grabbed me as I tottered. "You're really going to have to work on your stability, Peg." Before I could think of a good retort, she and Dirk joined Harper on the sidewalk. "What's up?"

He pointed overhead, to something above the door of the ScotShop. "I think I found our stars," he said.

I walked to his left side and peered upward. "What are you talking about?"

"Och, aye! The wee flags, like the ones in the history book."

I stared at Dirk. "Have you been studying American history?"

"Aye," he said rather smugly.

Harper, once again, looked at me funny. "Why would I need to do that?"

Karaline guffawed. "I see what you mean."

Dirk looked offended. Harper raised a hand, like a traffic cop. "Would someone like to clue me in?"

"I was, uh, just thinking about the flags up there on the sign, like you said."

"I didn't say anything about flags. All I did was point."

"Aye. I would be the one who mentioned the wee flags."

"I know that," I said to both of them at the same time. "We were just looking for stars inside, and here they were all the time out here, right in plain view."

"I wonder how many stars the American flag had in 1915," Karaline said.

"Forty-eight," Harper and I answered at the same time.

"But the number might be twenty-four," I added. "That's how many stars are on each flag up there."

Harper studied me. "How could you possibly know that?"

"My dad counted them when he installed the ScotShop sign."

Harper opened the door for us all, and I had to pause right beside him to give Dirk the room and the time to get inside. Harper must have misinterpreted. "Am I forgiven, then?" His breath made a faint stirring just above my left ear.

"I haven't decided yet." I stalked after Karaline, leaving him to lock the door.

"We figured out the first line, Harper." Karaline stood in front of the bookcase facing us, like a teacher before a white-board and raised her voice, although that wasn't really necessary. "It's eighteen feet from that wall"—she gestured to her right across the cash register—"to the edge of the safe."

"No," I said. "It's eighteen feet from *that* wall." I pointed the other way, indicating the opposite wall, the one closer to the street. I pulled the paper out of my pocket. "See?"

Karaline came up to my right side. Harper was on my left. Dirk stood in front of me and peered upside down at the code. "Look," Karaline said, pointing to the original list. "Left side eighteen to wall. That means you measure from the left side of the safe to the wall."

"Yeah," I said. "That's what it says."

"So, where's the problem?"

"Why dinna ye use the metal marker to show what ye mean?" Dirk pointed at the measuring tape in Karaline's hand.

She pulled out the end of the tape and thrust it at Harper. "Hold this up against that wall, will you?"

He shrugged and headed to his left, holding his end of the tape high so it would clear the various displays in the way. "Ready."

Karaline shoved the bookcase farther away from the wall—I didn't know she was that strong—and extended the

tape to the eighteen-foot mark. It fell about two inches short
of the leftmost drill hole. "See? The paper was wrong. No
wonder he couldn't find the safe." She pressed her index
finger to the wall and motioned Harper to come see. The
tape reeled in as he walked closer.

"You're right, Karaline." He frowned. "The code must
be wrong. I wonder why?"

She nodded. "Does this mean we can't trust the combination numbers, either?"

I thought back to the scene in the hospital room, when
Harper had held up my kerchief and told me there was blood
on the right side of it. Thank goodness I'd worn this thing.
I slipped it off my head, still tied, the way it had been at the
hospital. I lined Harper and Karaline up side by side in front
of the bookcase with their backs to the wall. "Show and tell
time," I said, and stood in front of them, facing them. I held
the kerchief in front of me as if it were still on my head.
"Please point to the left side of this kerchief."

Their hands shot out in unison, pointing to the side of
the kerchief I held in my right hand. "Bingo," I said. "Neither
one of you has good spatial orientation."

Needless to say, they looked at me as if I'd gone bonkers.
I took the tape measure from Karaline and gave the end to
Harper. "Would you please walk to *that* wall?"

Once he held it steady, I pulled it to the eighteen-foot
mark, which lined up exactly one inch inside the doorway
that had been cut out to allow access to the safe, a good three
feet away from the drilled holes. I held my finger there until
Harper joined us. "I rest my case."

"The murderer, then, would have been thinking like the
two of them"—Dirk pointed to Harper and Karaline—"while
the person who drew up the clues must have had good . . .
what did ye call it?"

"Spatial orientation," Karaline and I said at the same
time.

I was afraid Harper might object, but he just stood there,

staring at the measuring tape. He held out his hand and I gave it to him. "Have you measured anything else with this in the last week or so?"

I thought back. "No, I don't think so. Just when we measured the bathroom, and what we did tonight. And I measured the distance between the sheetrock nails."

"Did you open the tape any longer than eighteen feet tonight?"

I looked at Karaline. She looked at me. "Maybe an inch or so," she said. "Just enough so we could see the eighteen-foot mark clearly. Why?"

Harper turned and headed for the door. "Say a little prayer to the gods of forensic science," he called over his shoulder before he scooted out, closing the door behind him. I locked it and walked back to the bookcase, thinking.

"He didna even bide long enow to open the wee safe."

Karaline put a hand on my shoulder. "Did we miss something here?"

27

Open Sesame

"Looks like it's up to us," I said. "Are you ready for this?"
She grinned. "Like a cow at milking time."

"What does that mean?"

She put a hand dramatically to her forehead like a silent film actress. "I can tell you didn't grow up on a farm."

I just looked at her.

"It means let's go."

I led the way to the bookcase. It took only a moment to shift the bookcase and pull out the wall panel.

I pulled the combination paper out of my pocket.

"Here." She grabbed it out of my hand. "I'll read it and you do the turning."

I twirled the dial four or five times. "Ready."

Dirk leaned forward over my shoulder. "Aye."

"Don't bump into me," I said. "I don't want to pass out."

"I wouldna do that."

"Hush, you two." Karaline pointed a finger at us. "Now listen. Turn right to seventeen."

They watched me. I could have sworn they were holding their breath. Come to think of it, so was I. "Okay—seventeen."

"Now go four times around the dial to the left and stop on number five."

We counted together, each time the seventeen reached the top. I paused and moved the dial to five. "Now what?"

"Right three turns and stop on either twenty-four or forty-eight."

I rotated the dial three times. "Which do you think we should use?"

She studied the paper. "Don't see it makes much difference. We'll either be right or we'll be wrong."

What a brilliant observation.

"Twenty-four," Dirk said.

"Why?"

He tilted his head to one side. He looked like Dorothy's Scarecrow at the crossroads. "Why not?"

I stopped at twenty-four. "Okay. Now two turns to . . ."

"To forty-four."

"Done."

"One turn to sixty-five."

I dialed even more slowly until sixty-five stood at the top. "Now I open it?"

"I sure hope so."

Crud.

The second time we tried it with a forty-eight. I pushed the handle down, down, down. Click. I looked at Karaline, kneeling near my left shoulder, and at Dirk on my right. "I'm afraid to open it. What if there's nothing in there?"

Karaline snorted, one of her less-endearing sounds. "There was something in there that somebody thought was worth killing over."

On that sobering thought, I swung open the door and Karaline caught her breath. The scuffed metal floor of the safe held a stack of papers, bound together with a string, like bargain-basement Christmas wrapping.

We all let out whoops—half exaltation, half relief, half fear. I clapped my hands to the side of my head. "Ouch!"

"What's wrong?"

"I shouldn't have done that. I hit my boo-boo."

She giggled. Dirk rolled his eyes.

"It doesn't belong to us," Karaline whispered.

Propriety warred with curiosity.

Curiosity won.

I picked up the stack and pulled on the string. It knotted. "Crudbuckets. Why does that always happen? Would you go get me the scissors, Karaline? They're under the counter."

We unfolded the pieces of paper one by one, stacking them tidily. There were maybe fifty of them, certificates for thousands of stock market shares. "Somebody's really going to wish they had these." Karaline leaned against my arm. "Don't you wish it was you?"

I thumbed through the stack. "I'm not so sure. I've never heard of any of these companies. Do you know anything about Amalgamated Aluminum Excavation?"

She shook her head.

"American Standard Express, Buffalo Surety, Prince William Foods, the Pro-phy-lac-tic Tooth Brush Company. That one rings a bell." I told her about the ad that said seventeen thousand dentists couldn't be wrong.

"I guess they were wrong," she said. "You mean these are worthless?"

"Looks like it. There may be something in here, but so far, none of these companies seems to have survived."

"Think they went down in the 1929 stock market crash?"

"Economics is not my strong point, K."

"Why would ye—"

She interrupted Dirk's question and rubbed her knees. "Squatting is not my strong point." She slid to one side, leaned against a two-by-six, and stretched her legs out in front of her. "What are you going to do with them?"

"I don't know." I fiddled with the door. It swung gently on perfectly quiet hinges, even though it hadn't been opened in a hundred years. Amazing. "I don't even know who owns the building, and I guess that would be who owns the safe." I tied two pieces of the string together, rolled the useless stock certificates into a tube, and tied it tight. "I'll take them to the property management office. They certainly will know who the owner is."

"Don't you think we ought to turn these things over to Harper?"

She had a point. I thought for a moment. "I'll tell him about them next time I see him." I stood, brushing off my rear end, "It's just down the street. Wanna come along?"

"I will go with ye."

"I guessed as much." I smiled at him. It was nice to have a ghostie by my side.

Karaline stretched her long arms and said, "Aren't you forgetting something?"

"What?"

She hooked her left thumb over her shoulder, almost as if she were hitching a ride. "Don't tell me you didn't notice that."

"Oh. That."

That was a compartment in the upper left section of the safe. The lower left corner was discolored, the finish worn down to bare metal by the oils of a thousand fingerprints. "It's locked," I said. "What am I supposed to do about it?"

She pulled out her key chain and selected a small key. "Let's just give it a shot. There's always a million-to-one chance."

"Karaline, that's the most ridiculous idea I've ever heard. There's no way that padlock key of yours is going to open a hundred-year-old safe. What's it's for anyway, your bicycle?"

"You don't need to get huffy. It won't hurt to try." She

slid over until she was right in front of the safe. "Wish me luck."

I hate to admit it, but I did hold my breath again, silly as that seems. Of course, it didn't work, and I exhaled with more disappointment than I'd expected. "Crud," I said, the only word that seemed to fit. Dirk cleared his throat.

"You go on and take those certificates," she said. "I'm gonna sit here and cry."

I laughed and gave her shoulder a playful slap. "Come lock the door after me."

"Why? There's nothing left to steal."

There's still a murderer around. "Humor me." I picked up the certificates and headed down the street.

There was yet another new clerk behind the counter. She stilled her thumbs as I walked in and stuffed something into her back pocket. "What can I do for you?"

"You're Bethany, aren't you? I recognize you from the grocery store."

"Ye said ye would take me to that grosserie store, but ye havena."

"I got tired of ringing up all those cans and boxes all day. This is much more fun. There's hardly ever anything to do, so I can play lots of . . . I mean, get a lot of reading done. I'm going to go to junior college pretty soon." Her hand wandered toward her back pocket. It was probably buzzing.

"I'm sure they'll miss you here."

My sarcasm went unnoticed. "Did you come to pay rent?" She sounded confused. "It's not the end of the month."

"No. I need to speak with whoever handles the Pitcairn Building. Do you know who owns it?"

Her eyes glazed over a bit. I thought that meant she was thinking, but there was no way to prove it.

"Gosh, I don't know. You stay here and I'll go ask somebody."

Pulling out her cell phone as she turned away from me, she disappeared into the bowels of the building. Well, it wasn't all that gothic—she went through a door and popped back a few minutes later leading a man who introduced himself as Mr. Harrington. "I understand you're looking for the owner of the Pitcairn," he said in a voice more oil than air. "Perhaps I can help you."

"I dinna like this wee man." Dirk's hand hovered over the hilt of his dagger.

Neither did I. Nonchalantly, I moved the roll of certificates behind me. "Could you tell me who owns it? I'd like to contact the owner directly."

"Well, miss, I'm afraid that's privileged information. I'd be happy to pass on a message."

I'll just bet you would. "Fine. Would you tell him Peggy Winn found something he might be interested in."

"I'd be perfectly willing to give it to him myself." He held out his hand.

Dirk pulled his dagger halfway out of the sheath.

"That won't be necessary. Just let him know I stopped by."

Halfway back to the ScotShop, Dirk finally stopped muttering. I'd caught the word *constable* several times.

"Relax," I said. "I'm going to put these in my own safe, the one in the storage room. And I'll call Harper about it."

28

Death—1893

*S*tenhouse Pitcairn lay on his deathbed, alternating between desperate gasps for breath and an utter stillness that left Josiah in a quandary. Should he call for his cousin? Should he let his father die in relative peace?

"I've . . . left it . . . almost . . . too late," the elder Pitcairn stuttered. "Come, lean close."

Josiah did as his father asked, forcing himself not to draw back from the smell of the old man, the dying smell— of bad breath, vomit, a leakage of urine, and something indefinable that seemed to Josiah to be the dust stirred up by angel wings, although why angels would want to hover around this old reprobate was more than Josiah could imagine. Josiah's father had survived an early bout with the pox that had left his face and arms pitted. He had made it through the War Between the States with only one arm lost, more than could be said of many of their Hamelin neighbors.

"Closer." Father stopped, wheezed, coughed—a cough that seemed to originate in his toes, consuming all his *energy. But the old man rallied and spoke as quickly as he could. "Memorize these numbers, son. Seventeen, five, forty-eight, forty-four, sixty-five." He repeated them twice, then insisted that Josiah repeat the numbers in order. That was easy. Josiah's memory was well honed.*

"Why, Father?"

"Safe." Father waved a vague hand, and Josiah studied that corner of his father's bedroom. There was nothing but a short square table covered with a floor-length cloth embroidered in lilies of the valley. Josiah hadn't seen or even thought about that particular cloth since his early childhood. He recalled last having noticed it when his mother, long since deceased, had completed the final flower on the border and had told her young son and his cousin that when her time came, she was to be wrapped in this shroud and buried in it.

Josiah remembered his mother's funeral two years later, when he himself was ten. What had her shroud been? He only recalled her ghostly pale face in the candlelight as she lay, arms crossed in a parody of peacefulness, she and her stillborn child covered over with a white linen sheet.

Her death had not been peaceful. Josiah remembered all too well her screams as the babe would not be born. He had crept to the door, while young Barnaby, Josiah's orphaned cousin, slept through the chaos and while Father lay insensible from drink in the parlor. Even young as Josiah was, he felt keenly that his father had somehow abandoned his mother, but then again, the women with her had scurried about, chivvying the menfolk into getting out from underfoot. Perhaps it was no wonder that his father had sought oblivion. Young Josiah, listening at the door to the ghastly sounds from within, had heard snatches of words whose import he hadn't understood. Sideways, too big, blood, too much, losing her. The words still rang at times in his nightmares.

Now the old man's final oblivion seemed sure to descend within moments.

"*The safe,*" *his father whispered from the bed. Josiah crossed the room, removed the simple carved box centered on the table, and moved the cloth aside, revealing a sturdy gray safe, the front embellished in red and a blue so deep it was almost black. The shiny bright combination lock, he noticed, stood on the number 44.*

"*Four turns, three turns, two turns, one turn,*" *chanted his father, in a voice so low Josiah barely heard him.* "*Seventeen, four turns to the left, five, three turns to the ri—*" *He broke off, coughing, a deep mucus-laden sound that came close to raising Josiah's bile.*

"*I know, Father,*" *Josiah said. His ready mind had grasped the pattern, and he spoke the entire sequence for his father, so the old man could die in peace.*

Father's lips turned slightly up, although calling the movement a smile would have been too much. "*My desk,*" *he said, and went on haltingly to explain the trick to opening a secret drawer.* "*That's where the key is. You'll need it.*" *And he waved again in the direction of the safe.* "*Your cousin is not to know. Barnaby has been something of a disappointment.*"

Josiah kept his face strictly neutral, all the while thinking that his dying father had surpassed his usual tendency to understatement.

"*Call them in now,*" *Father wheezed.*

Josiah opened the door, and Barnaby plunged in as if he'd had his ear pressed tight against it. Josiah was sure, though, that Barnaby had heard nothing through the thick, solid oak.

The housekeeper, Mistress Stark, crept in after Reverend Meekins and the lawyer. As those men gathered beside Father, Josiah watched her move quietly to replace the lily-of-the-valley shroud. And stand in front of it.

"*My will,*" *Father gasped.*

"*Here.*" *The family lawyer held up a bound roll of paper.*

"Signed, sealed, and ready whenever . . ." He paused, unsure how to finish the unfortunate phrase. "Ready."

Stenhouse Pitcairn's final breath was something of an anticlimax. His breathing had settled into an uneven pace, with the space between breaths gradually lengthening while the minister quoted psalms and prayers. Father arched his back. One raspy gurgle. One deep, final exhalation.

Barnaby crossed his arms. "He didn't even say good-bye to me."

Mistress Stark spoke from where she stood in the corner. "Gentlemen, I've placed port in the parlor. Would you retire there while I prepare the body?"

Meekins, Barnaby, and the attorney left without a backward glance. Josiah patted his father's hand. "Do you need help lifting him, Mistress Stark?"

"Oh no. He's wasted away to practically a feather. I'll have him cleaned in no time and ready for the viewing. I'll need you then to carry him downstairs."

"Thank you," Josiah told the woman who had chivvied him with a rough affection ever since—and even before—his mother's death. "Call down when you need me."

After the funeral, after the reading of the will, Barnaby waited for the attorney and the other family members to leave. "A word with you, cousin."

Josiah turned slowly. "Yes, Barnaby?"

"Why did he not leave me this house? I have a large family to support, while you and Emelinda have only one son. You could make do with a smaller establishment." Barnaby's elaborate mustachio drooped a bit on one side, the end hairs trailing against his lip.

Josiah wondered if they tickled. "You know his office is here, brother. I am to run the business. Therefore, he left me the house and all its contents."

"Not quite all of them," Barnaby snarled. "You cannot cheat me out of my part of the inheritance."

Josiah kept his irritation in firm check. "You have been cheated of nothing. I was always the one interested in Father's business dealings, while you chose to go your own way—so long as Father supplied you with ample funds."

"Ample? You call that pittance ample?"

"What you had was more than enough for a man of moderate tastes. What you have received from the will may well support you for many years if you choose to live wisely. I ask that you remove the items of your inheritance before the end of the week." He paused, and tried one more time to include his cousin. "You have always had the option of working in the manufactory."

"Ha! Peasant work."

Josiah straightened his usual erect posture. "I learned the business by working there as a boy until I earned my position as a trusted assistant to Father."

"I am far too old to start that way. I choose to be your partner."

The portrait of his father above the desk had not moved—it must have been a flying insect Josiah saw from the corner of his eye—but Barnaby, facing the portrait, took a sudden step backward.

Josiah stayed where he was, beside his father's desk. "Never," he said. "Never."

Father stared down from the portrait, the eyes above his pockmarked face steady and his mouth firm, but with a secretive upturning on one side.

Josiah waited until Barnaby slammed the front door. He could hear his wife and her women friends beginning the necessary changes in the old house. Josiah had seen the relief on his wife's face when he'd told her Mistress Stark would stay as housekeeper.

He looked around the office. Why, he wondered, had Father not moved the safe down here? Light from three tall mullioned windows spread across the rolltop desk. Josiah adjusted his cravat and groped for his spectacles. Once they were firmly in place, he lifted his pocket watch to peer at the hands. He had enough time before he must leave for the manufactory.

Josiah locked the office door. Following his father's deathbed directions, he found with little difficulty the concealed drawer and extracted a small bronze key. He pulled a folded paper from a pocket in his trousers. He had written down the number sequence shortly after his father's death. It would not do to forget the combination, but he saw that he recalled the numbers perfectly. Fearing Barnaby's nosy ways, he placed the paper in the drawer and closed it until he heard the quiet snick.

Upstairs, he bolted the door of his father's bedroom and removed his mother's shroud. He caught himself. He had to stop thinking of it that way. He folded the . . . the cloth and bent to open the safe.

Rolls of papers, bound by various colors of ribbon, sat neatly stacked on the shelves within. He would look through them later. He used the key to unlock the small compartment inside the safe. First glancing over his shoulder, although he was certain the bolt was securely fastened, he withdrew a leather bag and carried it to the bed.

After unwrapping the contents, he sat in stunned silence for many long moments. One by one, he examined fifteen perfect jewels.

He was suddenly certain that whatever came his way he could handle. The company would thrive. Just the knowledge of this fortune at his fingertips gave Josiah a feeling of surety. If there should be another war, if there should be another outbreak of disease—whatever happened—the Pitcairn Company would last.

He fingered one of the smaller jewels, a brilliant sapphire. "Father," he muttered, "tell me, advise me, please. What am I to do with Barnaby?"

He placed the jewels back in the pouch, except for two of the smaller stones. Those two alone represented a fortune.

Should he now give these to Barnaby? Did blood ties count for more than honor? He rewrapped the two diamonds, added them to the bag, closed and locked the small compartment. He closed the safe and spun the dial. No. Barnaby had made his choices and would have to live with them.

One early spring morning some years later, Barnaby stormed past Mrs. Stark into Josiah's office without waiting to be announced.

"What is it, Barnaby?"

"I heard you were planning to build a new manufactory."

"Yes."

"I want to be the one to build it."

Josiah looked him over carefully. He tried to keep the incredulity from his voice but did not succeed. "You?"

"Yes. I have been quite successful in Arkane and some of the other towns close by."

"Doing what?"

"Building, of course. I have a steady, dependable crew."

"What do you pay them with?"

"You needn't sound so superior. I invested my money from the will in materials and wages, and now I make enough money from the projects I complete that I no longer have to grov . . . I no longer need your help."

Josiah studied his cousin, but Barnaby did not flinch from the gaze as he so often had in the past. "Give me a list of the buildings you've completed. I will talk with the owners and inspect them; if they are acceptable, I will consider your bid for the new manufactory job."

Barnaby did not thank him. He extracted an already-prepared list from his coat pocket.

Josiah investigated thoroughly. Barnaby's customers had nothing but praise for him and his work. Wondering what had become of the irresponsible little cousin he'd had to deal with for so many years, Josiah accepted his bid and ended up hiring him.

His own cash flow was somewhat depressed at that moment. He would have to sell one of the stones from the leather bag in order to pay the amounts he would owe his brother before completion. He also had by that time begun to wonder how much longer he would be on this earth. His son was well versed in the business now but did not yet know the contents of the safe. Josiah refilled his fountain pen and wrote out a code for the combination, using advertisements from his wife's latest magazines for several of the harder-to-remember numbers. The forty-eight stars in the U.S. flag, of course—that one would be easy for his son to remember. If he should die untimely, his son would carry on.

The new building that began to emerge under Barnaby's supervision was all that Josiah had hoped. A large front office, lit by windows on two sides, would hold enough room for his own desk, tables for various clerks, and a sales area, all to be warmed in the winter by a central potbellied stove. The back wall had not been constructed yet, but Josiah could easily imagine what it would look like.

Just beyond the wall, there would be a cavernous space for storage, with a smaller enclosed area behind a locking door, holding shelving for the higher-priced inventory materials. The room, as Barnaby described it, answered a need Josiah had not even seen.

Behind the storage room, work had begun first on the manufacturing section. It was far finer than Josiah could have wished.

Well pleased with the projected building, Josiah returned

*home and extracted the leather bag from the safe that still
rested in his father's—now his—bedroom. One, possibly
two jewels would be needed. As he pored over them, trying
to decide the best course, the door swung open and Barnaby
stepped inside. "Josiah, I need to talk—"*

*Josiah tried to cover the gems quickly, but they were too
spread out.*

"What? What is this?"

*"Nothing you need concern yourself with, Barnaby. I
need to sell one of these to get the money for the building
costs." He scooped up one of the emeralds and tossed a
blanket over the rest. "Let's go down to the office where we
can discuss this."*

*Barnaby agreed, but his gaze lingered for a moment on
the blanket. As he turned, he paused, and Josiah knew his
brother had seen the open safe.*

Again, Barnaby asked, "What is this?"

Josiah wished afterward *that he had not told Barnaby the
details of his father's financial arrangements. He often wondered if someone had been listening beneath the window, if
that was how someone had known. In the end, he gave Barnaby an emerald and a diamond in full payment for the entire
building. Three days later, the safe was gone, as was the
paper with the combination code. Despite extensive investi-
gation, no culprit was ever found, nor was the safe recovered.
Josiah died the following month. A key was found in his
waistcoat pocket. No one knew what it belonged to, but
Barnaby asked for it "as a keepsake."*

When Josiah's son *moved his newly inherited company into
the Pitcairn Building two months later, he found the back
wall of the office covered in an innocuous gray-patterned*

*wallpaper. He didn't like it but supposed his uncle had tried
to beautify the rather stark room. He moved the old rolltop
desk from his father's old office, installed his grandfather's
portrait on the back wall—the gray paper formed an unob-
trusive backdrop for the pockmarked old man—and went
to work.*

29

Dinner of Champions

I tried to call Harper about the stock certificates but got his voice mail. There wasn't any hurry about a worthless bunch of paper, but I was a bit ticked off with him for not calling me back. Not that I was planning on ever speaking to him again.

That evening, Dirk's glare meter was on high. He paced around the kitchen muttering imprecations—were they Gaelic or Middle English? I wasn't sure and didn't care. "Ye canna mean to go," he said.

"I certainly do. What do you think he's going to do, kidnap me? He's a lonely old man."

Dirk grunted a subterranean growl. "I *will* accompany you."

"Dirk," I said with a fair amount of exasperation, "I'm fed up with your overprotectiveness. I'll be fine. I prom—"

"Fed up? What would that mean?"

"Oh, for crying out loud, let up on the English lessons, will you? I don't need you hovering over me every single second. He's been my neighbor for *years*. When I moved in, he was next door. He was born here in Hamelin—in that house, in fact. He used to head the Board of Selectmen. He and his wife have always been dear people."

"Wife? I havena seen a woman there."

"She died last year. She used to invite me for dinner once a month; Mr. P's continuing the tradition." I closed my eyes so I couldn't see him pacing. "I'm going. You're staying. I'll be back well before nine o'clock."

I closed the front door more abruptly than perhaps I should have. I'd apologize later.

I paused at the top of Mr. P's front steps, took three deliberate breaths, crossed the somewhat saggy old porch, and knocked on the door. It swung open a bit. I heard a muffled sound that could have been a voice.

"Mr. P? Are you there?" My words echoed eerily. *Oh, good grief, Winn. This is not a gothic novel.*

A dim lamp in the entryway cast an uncertain glow, but I saw a shaft of light from the kitchen down the hall. When Mrs. P was alive, there always were bright lights throughout the house. Poor Mr. P—how had I ever missed seeing how sad he was? I called out again and heard an indistinct moan. Had he fallen? I raced down the hall, reaching for my cell. Crud! I'd left it at home.

I rounded the kitchen door and barely registered the movement to my right before a blow above my ear took me completely by surprise.

I woke with a throbbing pain in my head and a biting pain in my ankles. Not surprising, considering the sturdy twine that bound my feet. My hands were tied in front of me. That was good. I'd read horror stories of people whose arms had been yanked backward and bound in the most uncomfortable ways possible. *Peggy! Quit dithering and pay attention!*

Why would Mr. Pitcairn have hit me like that? What on earth had I gotten myself into? I had a brief vision of Dirk being very angry with me. *I'd give anything to have him here with me.* I squashed that thought before it could start me crying.

"She should be waking up soon. I didn't hit her that hard."

The voice wasn't one I recognized, although it seemed vaguely familiar. I kept my eyes shut.

"You didn't have to hit her." Mr. P's nasal words came from floor-level behind me. It took all my self-control not to wrench myself around to face him.

"You're wrong, Joe. I didn't want her screaming," the other man said. "Not that there's anyone close enough to hear." I didn't like that tone of smug self-satisfaction. "It was good of you to invite her over. The last time I checked, her back door was locked."

The tiny seed of worry in the pit of my stomach started growing leaves.

"What are you going to do to her?"

Whoever he was, he sounded downright cheerful when he said, "I'm not going to do a thing to her. When someone finds the bodies, they'll see it as a murder-suicide. *Her* murder. *Your* suicide, Joe. Too bad you had to kill such a sweet young thing." I took a quick peek, but all I could see were his legs. And a pistol held at his side. He waved it negligently.

"I always knew you were rotten, Barney. All the fancy schooling in the world couldn't change that."

"Yeah, I had the schooling, but you're the one with the fortune. After you sold the patents, you could have shared some of it with me."

"Just because our grandfathers were cousins? My great-grandfather was the one who amassed the fortune."

"And my great-grandfather was the one who built the building. You didn't know he built a secret into it, did you?"

"What are you talking about?" Mr. P sounded genuinely puzzled. I stayed as quiet as I could, hoping they'd forgotten about me.

"The first sons in my family have always known about the fortune hidden in the wall."

"What are you talking about? There's no fortune there. My father would have told me."

The first man let out a guffaw that echoed in the bleak kitchen. "He didn't know about it. The first Josiah, the one you're named for, had a fortune in jewels. My grandfather took the safe and the combination, but he couldn't get it open, so he built it into the wall, so nobody in the Pitcairn family would ever find it."

"That's nonsense!"

"No, Joe. It's not. You may own that great big building, and you may have sold off the patents for a lot of money, but there's been a treasure under your nose the whole time."

"I say again, you're talking nonsense. If your grandfather had the safe, why didn't he keep the jewels himself? From everything I've heard, he was not a generous man."

"No, he wasn't. I'll give you that. He was also not a very smart man. The combination was in code. He decided that, if he couldn't have the jewels, then your family never would either."

My left leg, the one I was lying on, was cramping. I took another peek between my lashes. This time I recognized the man who had hit me. I gasped without thinking and could have kicked myself when Dr. Carrin turned and glared at me.

"How much have you heard, Ms. Winn?"

"Enough to know the safe I found was stolen by your stupid great-grandfather, so it belongs to Mr. P." I rolled onto my back and bunched my knees up, trying to alleviate the cramp.

"Not if nobody knows about it, Ms. Winn. My father and grandfather managed that property for years, and a little company I own manages it now."

"You mean I'm paying rent to *you*?" I invested the word with as much scorn as I could manage, considering that I was lying on the floor and Dr. Carrin stood over me.

He actually laughed. "No. No, the money goes to your neighbor here, although my company takes a small percentage."

"A *large* percentage," Mr. P said.

Good for you; that's the spirit.

"You know, Joe, I could kick your brains out right now." Dr. Carrin sounded singularly calm. "But I won't."

Because it wouldn't look like a suicide.

When Mr. P spoke, he sounded equally calm. "Why are you doing this, Barney? What did I ever do to you?"

"You personally? Nothing. My great-grandfather, Barnaby Carrin, should have inherited half the fortune. Josiah cheated, made Barnaby build the factory, and never gave him anything for it. You owe me. And *you*"—he turned in my direction, and I saw Mr. P scoot closer toward our tormentor—"are going to give me back the paper I lost."

This was beginning to make sense. "The paper with the code on it? How did Mason end up with it?"

"Mason? He had it?" Barney scowled. "How could he have gotten it? I must have dropped it in the store, but I never gave him a chance to pick up anything."

"*You* killed Mason." I wasn't asking a question. Mr. P moved another inch or two.

"He deserved it, the cheating blackmailer."

"Blackmailer? What do you mean?"

"Two hundred dollars a week, for—"

But there was no time to waste. I lashed out with both legs aimed straight for the front of his knees. I heard a bone crack. He screamed—and the pistol exploded—as he fell backward over Mr. P. We both hauled ourselves on top of him as quickly as we could to pin down his arms.

Dirk and Harper charged into the kitchen, armed with dagger and gun.

"Took you long enough to get here," I said.

That night, just before turning in, I thanked Dirk for coming to my rescue. "Even though we'd already pinned him down, it was nice to know you were there . . . to protect me."

Curious, I asked, "Do you think women always need protection?"

"Nae," he said. "I dinna believe that, but I believe that it is my purpose to protect the ones I . . ." He lowered those ridiculously long eyelashes. ". . . the ones I love."

The only sound was the breeze through the open window. And my beating heart, but I didn't think he could hear that.

Eventually, I asked him how he'd gotten out of the house.

"The constable came looking for ye. When there was no answer to his knock, he tried the handle, and the door opened. He whinged a bit about leaving the door unlocked but stood back enough for me to slip through. I yelled at him to hurry as I rushed past, and something"—Dirk's face took on a puzzled expression—"made him turn and follow me to the neighboring house."

"Did he hear you?" That didn't seem possible.

"Nae. I think not. But he *heard* me, if ye ken what I mean."

That was good enough for me.

30

Gathering

The next morning, we tore down the wall and found the skeleton of the man whom Barnaby must have hired to help him carry away the safe.

We searched my lost-and-found basket for the compartment key, the one Dr. Barney Carrin had dropped. There would undoubtedly be legal wrangling over the leather bag of jewels for some time, but it looked as if my poor, sad, lonely neighbor would be a very rich man.

That evening, we gathered in the back room of the ScotShop—Karaline, Mr. P, Sam, Shoe, Harper, and myself. And Dirk. Gilda wasn't there. Once everyone was seated, I asked where Gilda was. Shoe and Sam looked at each other. "She, uh, had to be somewhere," Sam said.

I knew something was going on, but Sam obviously didn't want to talk about it, so I let it ride. I'd corner him later and get the story out of him.

"I don't quite understand what happened," Mr. P said. He looked even more forlorn than usual.

Shoe started to talk, but Karaline drowned him out. "I'll

tell what I know, and each of you add in your part as we go along."

After the story was told, we dissected it.

"Why," Sam asked, "would Mason put all that money in your bank account?"

"I can't imagine," I said, "but I could hazard a guess. I think he felt guilty about cheating on me. He used to give me roses, which I came to hate. I think he just added money to his misguided intentions."

"What I'd like to know," Karaline said, "is what Mason was blackmailing Dr. Carrin over?"

"He clammed up on us," Harper said. "We're looking into his background, but we may never know."

"So," I asked, "did Dr. Carrin kill him for the blackmailing or because Mason stumbled on his midnight search?"

"No way to know. Carrin tried to plead innocent, but we have a perfect fingerprint at the twenty-one-foot mark on the measuring tape. The first Barnaby Carrin was clever," Harper said. "That whole shelving system and the enclosed storage room masked the fact that he'd hidden a body—and the safe—in the wall."

"Didn't the body stink?" Shoe had been so quiet, I'd almost forgotten him.

Surprisingly, Mr. P answered. "The men in my family have a decided inability to smell anything. If the body stank, he wouldn't have known, and nobody working for him would ever have mentioned it."

Harper and Karaline both raised eyebrows at this.

"Anyway," Mr. P went on, "the manufacturing process used a lot of products I'm told were quite smelly, so maybe *nobody* noticed."

Harper walked me home. We didn't say a lot in words, but our hands spoke quite a conversation.

Without preamble, he said, "I have to leave."

"Leave?" I opened the front door and surreptitiously motioned to Dirk to precede me. As soon as he was inside, I set my purse on the living room floor and closed the door.

Fortunately, Harper couldn't hear Dirk's indignant yelp.

I stepped back out onto the front porch.

"Leaving Hamelin? For how long?"

"My dad is . . ." He gripped my hand more tightly. "I'm flying . . . overseas . . . tonight. I'll be gone a few weeks. Maybe longer." He cupped his right hand around the back of my neck. With a voice full of possibilities he said, "I'd rather stay here."

I nodded. I didn't trust my voice.

Hand in hand, we walked down the ramp to his waiting car.

I leaned against his chest for just a moment, and then I stepped away from him.

"I will be back." His voice was husky. He opened the door and slid behind the wheel. "After all," he said, "I really want to see how the poodle cut grows out."

Before I could kick the car, he was gone.

Author's Note

If you, dear reader, wonder why Dirk isn't always consistent with certain ghostly rules, I can only say, in Peggy's words to Karaline: "What do you mean *why not*? How would I know why not? I have a ghost in my house and a shawl that's almost seven hundred years old. First you couldn't see him and now you can; I'm in a neck brace because I ran into a garbage truck for crying out loud, and you're asking me to explain the rules?"